Praise for *We Set the Dark on Fire*

Also by Tehlor Kay Mejia:

We Unleash the Merciless Storm

TEHLOR KAY MEJIA

WE SET THE DARK ON FIRE

 KATHERINE TEGEN BOOKS

An Imprint of HarperCollins Publishers

Typography by Molly Fehr
20 21 22 23   PC/LSCH   10 9 8 7 6 5 4

First paperback edition, 2020

To A, who already moves mountains.
This is for you. Everything is for you.

"Until we are all free, we are none of us free."

—*Emma Lazarus*

In the beginning, there were two brother-gods: the God of Salt and the God of Sun.

On the inner island, the Sun God warmed the soil, shone down on the plentiful foliage, and browned the skin of his chosen children. On the outer island, the Salt God kept the water teeming with fish, the waves calm, and the beaches safe. For thousands of years, Medio existed in harmony and prosperity.

But then the Sun God fell in love.

Constancia was the daughter of Medio's king. She was strong, brave, and her brilliant mind rivaled the god's own. Each morning he shone brighter and brighter into her window, until one day he walked through in the form of a man, fell to one knee, and asked to be hers forever.

So Constancia became a goddess as well as a queen, and for a time, the divine walked the island in human form. Gods and rulers alike. But into the room that the Sun God shared with his bride, the Moon Goddess shone night after night, and soon she, too, fell in love.

One summer midnight, when the Sun God had walked alone into his moonlit garden, the Moon Goddess descended in the form of a beautiful woman. Her hair was tossed by darkness, her eyes glittered with stars, and her passionate love for the god-king swayed him. Constancia was his equal. His partner and his wife. But in the Moon Goddess he found his opposite, and he was intoxicated by her. For six days and six nights he sat still as a statue in the garden, trying to choose between them as the island waited in darkness.

Meanwhile, the Salt God tasted his brother's indecision, and seethed. For eternity, the tides of his sea had obeyed none but the Moon Goddess, but each time he glimpsed her face she would turn slowly away from him, shrinking in his eye until she showed him nothing at all.

When the Sun God had finally made his choice, his angry brother ascended from the sea as a man to hear his proclamation.

With Constancia on one arm and the Moon Goddess on the other, the Sun God announced that from that moment onward, the three of them would rule as one. Constancia, his equal, and the goddess, his opposite. The kingdom, he promised, would prosper beyond anything they had ever imagined, and for each of the six days of his isolation, there would be a celebration day to follow.

The Salt God quietly disappeared, but a few days after the Sun God's revelation, a storm lashed at the island. Houses were destroyed, and the villagers huddled in terror as the beaches and flatlands were destroyed. This was the Salt God's revenge against a brother who he felt had stolen what belonged to him. After days of rain and punishing waves, he appeared at his brother's house and issued his ultimatum:

He would wed the Moon Goddess himself, or he would destroy the island his brother loved, and all the people who resided there.

The Sun God met the challenge in his god form, shedding his human skin to battle his brother. The fight raged for a day and a night. Fire and waves. Destruction on top of destruction. But in the end, the Sun God was victorious, and the Salt God was banished from the island forever.

Knowing he was outmatched, the Salt God agreed to exile, but as he left he placed a curse on the outer island he had ruled. Anywhere the waves could reach. The fish turned up bloated and dead on the beaches. The ground was gorged with salt; nothing could grow.

Heartbroken by his brother's betrayal, the Sun God took to the home he shared with his wives, and for weeks rain fell like his tears onto Medio's ravaged soil. Soon it became clear that he could no longer remain at the site of all that had befallen him. With a heavy heart, the Sun God relinquished his human form permanently and returned to the celestial body that bore his name.

But before he did, the god-king gathered his people, the ones living inside the island. He called them chosen, and he demanded that as their last act of loyalty they build a wall to contain his brother's curse and protect the pure. In exchange for this devotion, he would give his chosen children a gift.

From that day forward, for each of the Sun God's faithful servants, there would be two wives to serve him as the Sun God's wives did him. At birth, the women of the island would be destined: One touched on her brow by Constancia for her wise and *discerning nature, her quick wit and loyalty. The other would be kissed on her brow by the Moon Goddess for her beauty and bravery, for her nurturing warmth and the passion that lurked beneath.*

They would be named Primera, for his first wife, and Segunda, for his second.

And so it was. . . .

—*Medio School for Girls Handbook,* Introduction

━┝━✳━┥━

DANIELA VARGAS WOKE AT THE first whisper of footsteps coming up the road.

By the time the sound of shattering glass in the courtyard alerted the campus to the presence of intruders, she was dressed and ready. For what? She wasn't sure. After a childhood of heavy-footed military police in close pursuit, she knew better than to mistake the luxury of her surroundings for safety.

She was only as safe as she was vigilant.

The shouting grew louder. There had been rumors of riots at the border for months, in the capital for weeks, but Dani hadn't thought they'd make it as far as the Medio School for Girls' gated sanctuary. The campus was private and insulated: white stone, lush greenery. A place where the country's brightest and most promising young women could train to become the wives Medio's future husbands deserved.

Dani had been here five years. Enough time to rise to the top of her class, to secure placement as Primera to the capital's most promising young politico. Graduation was only two days away, and then she would begin the life her parents had sacrificed family, home, and more to give her.

Assuming what was happening outside didn't get her arrested or killed first.

Another bottle shattered, closer this time, the smell of gasoline drifting in through the open window. Dani closed her eyes and muttered a half-forgotten prayer to the god in the air, to the goddess in the flames. *Keep calm*, she beseeched them.

No one around her would understand. Her parents' gods weren't in fashion this far inland—only the bearded visage of the Sun God, who ruled masculine ambitions and financial prosperity.

For a brief, unexpected moment, Dani wished her mama were here. It didn't take long to dismiss it as ridiculous. She was seventeen, a woman grown, two days from being a wife herself. Primeras didn't need comforting.

"Wake up!" came a voice from the courtyard. Drunk on booze or rebellion. Dangerous. *"Can't you see this is all a lie? Can't you see people are dying? Can't you see?"*

For the first time in her life, Dani awaited the arrival of the military police with something other than terror. She wanted them to come. To disperse the protest so she could go back to doing what they all did best—pretending Medio was prospering and peaceful. Pretending there was nothing but infertile ground and ocean beyond the looming border wall that kept their island nation divided in half.

Once they left, Dani could get back to pretending, too. That she belonged. That she wanted to be here as much as her parents wanted her to be.

Footsteps passed too close outside the window, and Dani ducked below the sill, leaning against the wall, listening to the pleading sounds of a home she didn't remember fleeing. Up and down the hall, the other fifth-year girls were likely still sleeping. Secure in the knowledge that they had no secrets to discover. Dani envied them.

The rioters didn't attempt to come inside. They screamed the names of family members they had lost in grief-soaked voices, chanting, pleading for the people hiding inside to *wake up* before it was too late.

Dani almost missed the snoring presence of her room-mate, Jasmín, who had graduated the year before. With an odd number of Primera students, Dani was given the option of a single room for her final year, and with all she had at stake, she had leapt at the chance. But at least with Jasmín here, Dani would have had someone to pretend for. Some reason to quell the fear that curled in her stomach. She banished the thought. Jasmín was miles away now, in a mansion inside Medio's most exclusive gated community.

She had succeeded. And Dani would, too. She just had to get through tonight.

By the time the police arrived—all authoritative boots and helmeted heads and rifle barrels—the school was locked down. The protesters had scattered in a hundred directions, the shouts increasing in volume as the officers gave chase through the tangle of trees.

Though she was glad for the peace, Dani couldn't bring herself to thank the goddess of law for the presence of the officers tonight. Most of the protesters had escaped, from the sounds of it, but a few were being captured and restrained, and Dani shivered at the thought of where they were headed.

The cells in Medio's only prison were all dank and hopeless, but the ones reserved for rebels and sympathizers were rumored to be windowless as well. Dark as the sap dripping down the citrus trees, day and night.

People who went into them rarely came out.

A rapping on the door interrupted the quiet, and Dani found relief in the way she dropped her prayers, her fear of discovery, everything that was out of place in this room. By the time she answered the door, she was who they expected her to be. Not a hair, or a thought, out of place.

"Everyone okay in here?" asked the resident, flanked on both sides by police. Her voice shook, and Dani wondered what she had to be afraid of.

"It's just me," Dani said. "And I'm fine."

The resident Ami, Dani remembered—only nodded. Of course Dani was fine. She was a Primera, after all, and Primeras didn't let their emotions take control. Not even when everything they held dear was at stake.

Especially not then.

"We need all students to report to the oratory," Ami said. "We're here to escort you." She was afraid but sure, Dani thought. The picture of a young woman who had never had anything to lose. Who had never entertained the thought that something truly bad might happen.

"Is everything alright?" Dani asked in a careful voice.

"Someone disabled the gate alarm from inside," she said. "The officers need to speak with all students and staff."

Dani nodded, not trusting her voice. *She* had done nothing wrong, she told herself. Unlike the people being arrested outside.

She repeated it in her head to keep calm: *I'm not a criminal. I'm not like them.*

"And please," said Ami as Dani adjusted her dress at the shoulders, the familiar motion calming her, "bring your identification papers."

Dani's eyes begged to widen, her fingers to tremble, her heart to hammer at her ribs. She refused them all, her face carved from stone as she'd been trained to hold it. No emotion. No weakness.

She kept her posture as carefully restrained as her face, approaching her desk, drawing out a battered folder that had crossed an entire nation with her. Its contents had cost her parents every cent they'd earned by the time she was four years old.

They had gotten her through thirteen years, these papers. She could only pray to the gods of fate and chance that they would get her through one more night.

In the hallway, the police took the lead, expressionless. The courtyard was deserted, but the officers drew their guns as they searched for intruders, shoulders tense. Ami held her hands in front of her face, as if the protesters were malicious, toxic. As if they had something she could catch.

Dani knew better. They were just broken.

The oratory doors were open, light spilling out into the darkness. Dani's deities didn't live in this room. Not anymore. Not the goddesses in the stars, nor the winking gods in the trunks of the trees. Here, the Sun God held court, bare-chested, muscled, and proud. Even his wives were missing from the largest paintings. He was mostly ornamental now, this fierce god-king at the center of so many of Medio's myths. The powerful used him as proof that they were chosen, but the only things people worshipped on the inner island were money and power.

Even still, the oratory looked hopeful inside—hundreds of tiny candle flames, standing against the night. In this corner of the world, if nowhere else, light was winning.

Dani was ushered inside by Ami, who left her to sit on a bench unnoticed. As police and maestras tried to create order among hundreds of scared, exhausted girls, she clutched her papers in her hands, refusing to allow her palms to perspire.

The Primera students sat mostly still, self-control as much a part of them at this point as their names. The fifth-years would be overseeing households by the end of the week, staffing enormous houses, managing social calendars. Supporting the husbands they'd spent a lifetime training to earn.

Across the room, the Segundas were utterly beside themselves. In various states of undress, they held hands and leaned against one another, expressing their fear and exhaustion unreservedly to anyone who would listen. Near the front of the oratory, one was actually sobbing.

Dani couldn't even remember the last time she'd let herself cry *alone*.

She could roll her eyes all she liked at the preening, fluttering Segundas, but things were the way they were supposed to be. The way they had always been. Opposites, coming together to make a perfect whole. And when Dani finally stood up and took her vows, she would be part of it at last, just like her parents had wanted.

Two more days, she told herself.

There were one hundred and ninety-six girls in this year's graduating class, and ninety-eight young men from prominent families waiting for them when they completed their studies.

Within these walls, they trained perfect wives. Primera and Segunda. The tried and true way to run a fully functioning home at the caliber required by the country's elite. Inner-islanders had flourished this way for thousands of years, long after faith had stopped driving the equation. No one was about to change the method now.

Looking around the ostentatious oratory, artistic renditions of Medio's origin story depicted across its walls, Dani tried to remember the last time she'd even heard the gods mentioned. They were everywhere at home, but what need did the inner-islanders have for gods? Faith, it so often seemed, was for the lacking.

Her musings had almost returned her heart to its normal rate when two maestras began to whisper, sunk low into a pew behind her. Dani listened closely. She'd been trained to be aware, resourceful, to find knowledge where she needed it, and to use it.

"Do you think it was one of ours?" asked one nervous voice.

"I hope not, but we'll know soon enough either way," said the second.

"What do you mean?"

"They had them bring their identification papers. I heard

there's a new method for verification. If there are any forgeries in the school, they'll find out tonight."

The conversation continued, but the blood pounding in
Dani's ears drowned out whatever came next. The battered
envelope crinkled beneath her grasping fingers. At her hairline, sweat began to bead.

If they really had a new verification system . . .

Dani stood as surreptitiously as she could, inching toward
the wall. With those few whispered words, everything had
changed. If she could just lean against this wall a moment,
maybe she could make her way toward the door without anyone seeing.

But what then? asked a practical voice in her head.

Down the hill into the capital? Blend in until she could
make it back to her parents? But going back would only
make them targets as well. The Medio School for Girls could
hardly fail to notice the disappearance of their star student
two days before graduation.

And even if they did, they'd certainly miss the small fortune the Garcia family was planning to pay for her. The
school would keep most of the money, of course, but the
wealthiest families paid the most generous sums, and Dani's
portion was meant for her parents. To buy them a small piece
of the life they had earned for her when they fled the only
home they'd ever known. When they left behind family and
friends and every ounce of certainty. They'd lived in fear of
discovery for years so Dani could have a chance to shine, but

daughters in prison weren't worth a cent, and dead ones were even worse.

For a moment, framed by the doorway of the oratory, Dani hated the protesters. Why tonight? When she was so close to getting everything she'd worked for, to giving her parents their due . . .

"Daniela Vargas?" came a gruff voice.

Her heart sank. She was out of time, and no closer to deciding what to do.

When she didn't come forward immediately, several of her classmates' heads swiveled in her direction. When had Daniela Vargas ever failed to respond to an order?

She took a single step toward the officer, who was twice her width and half again as tall.

The room was too bright, every sound too loud. The windowless cell that had haunted her childhood nightmares swam to life behind her eyelids whenever she blinked. Once her papers were proven false, they would assume *she* had let the protesters in. They would think she was here to spy, to help the rebels, when all she wanted was to keep her head down. Be a good Primera. Make her parents proud.

If she could have, she would have whispered to the goddess of duty, to ask her to show the way, but there was no time, and too many eyes were on her now.

Tears began to threaten. She could not let them fall.

She moved ever so slightly forward.

"Señorita?" the officer said, an edge in his voice that hadn't been there the first time. "This way, please."

There was noise in the room, of course there was—other names were being called, other girls interviewed. Segundas were complaining about the late hour, and the dark circles they'd have beneath their eyes come morning. But Dani felt as though she was the only one moving, the only one anyone could see. Her heartbeat was audible to everyone, wasn't it? Wasn't it?

The officer stepped forward, taking her elbow, steering her toward the classrooms in the back. But he stopped when her knees locked. She couldn't move. She couldn't breathe.

"Señorita?" came another voice, a kinder voice. "Are you feeling alright?"

Dani turned toward him, feeling like a fish washed up on the beach. He was in uniform, like the others, but he was slighter, younger, his eyes bright and curious.

"Who are you?" growled Dani's would-be captor.

"Medic," said the younger man, gesturing to the band around his left sleeve. White with a red cross. Dani's breath came easier for a moment, though she couldn't have said why.

"I need her in the back for questioning," said the officer, tugging on Dani's unresponsive arm. "We have half the list to get through still, and those girls in the front are giving me a headache."

Under normal circumstances, Dani would have smiled.

"I understand, sir," said the medic. "But my orders are to care for any student experiencing shock after the riot. These aren't common rabble, you know. *Their* fathers write angry letters when their precious daughters faint."

A staring contest ensued, and Dani swayed again for effect. If they took her to recover from shock, maybe she would get a second chance to run. "I don't feel so well," she said in the smallest voice she could fake. Primeras used whatever resources they had at hand.

One hand flew to her stomach, the other to her mouth.

The enormous officer stepped away in disgust. "Take her," he said, shoving Dani toward the medic. "But she better be back in this room in ten minutes."

"Yes, sir," said the boy, managing a clumsy salute as he shouldered Dani's weight.

He smelled like cinnamon and warm earth. A familiar smell. A comforting one.

"Right this way," he said with a smile, and Dani followed, a tiny flame of hope alive in her chest. Maybe it wasn't too late.

"Let's find somewhere you can relax," the medic said, mostly to himself, trying several doorknobs before settling on one.

"This is a—" Dani began, but he silenced her with a look, ushering her into a supply closet full of empty candle glasses and brooms. Goose bumps rippled up and down Dani's spine.

"Nice performance back there," said the boy, closing the door behind him. "Even I almost believed you." His face transformed in the dark of the closet. From stoic and soldierly, he was suddenly foxlike, all sharp angles and mischief.

"I don't know what you—" Dani began.

"Save it," he said. "We don't have much time."

And with that, he took Dani's papers, the hard-won key to her whole life, and tore them cleanly in half.

Analysis and logic are a Primera's greatest tools, irrationality her greatest enemy. There is no room for emotion in her decision-making.

—*Medio School for Girls Handbook,* 14th edition

THE MEDIC-WHO-WAS-NOT-A-MEDIC stood still, gauging Dani's reaction.

On the outside, she was frozen, but inside her, whole cities were being razed to the ground. Explosions were shaking the walls of her stomach. People were screaming in her throat.

"Let me explain," he said, looking almost sheepish.

"You . . . ," Dani spluttered. "I . . ."

"It's not what you think."

"It *better* not be," Dani replied, finally finding her voice. What had she learned every day in this place, if not how to handle herself in any circumstance? Dani pushed every feather of panic deep into herself and summoned all the authority she had. "Because you are clearly not military," she said. "Now, you have about ten seconds before I start screaming that there's an intruder here holding me against my will."

She expected an instant reaction, and she was disappointed. The boy's smirk only grew more pronounced. "Oh?" he asked. "And what will you do when they come?" He tapped his chin in mock thoughtfulness. "Sure, they won't be thrilled with me, but I'm sure they'll at least *investigate* my claims before hauling me off."

Dani felt her expression hardening. She let it. She did not scream.

"You know, the claims about the star Primera student with forged papers?" He brandished the shabby things at her, the tear down the center adding insult to injury. "The one who was about to be placed with a seriously decorated government family?" He shook his head sadly. "I don't imagine they'll be very happy with you at all."

"Who are you?" Dani asked through gritted teeth. "And why are you trying to ruin my life?"

"Relax," the boy said, rolling his eyes. "These things were useless the moment you walked through the oratory doors. The new verification system would have proven they were fakes in about a second." He paused, like he was waiting for her to ask. "It's a pen," he continued when she didn't. "On the special stationery the government issues ID papers with, it turns blue. On the peasant stuff, red. Pretty genius, really. So simple. It reacts to a fiber used in the printing process that—"

"Who *are* you?" Dani growled again, interrupting. She hardly cared about the particulars of paper fiber when she was one misstep from handcuffs and a prison transport.

"Right, of course." The boy placed the torn papers inside his jacket, sticking out a hand.

Dani looked at it like it was a venomous snake until he withdrew it.

"You can call me Sota," he said. "I'm a member of La Voz, and I'm here to deliver these." From the same pocket where he'd stuffed Dani's forged documents came a set of new ones, the paper gleaming blue-white even in the dark closet. She caught a glimpse of her name, printed neatly below Medio's official seal.

"Forget it," she said, crossing her arms. Her palms were sweating against the sleeves of her dress. She could feel her quickening pulse along every inch of her skin. "I'm not taking anything from you."

La Voz was a name you whispered. Public enemy number one on the right side of the border wall. They were responsible for the riots Dani had heard about since she could remember. The fires. The dead officers. The violence. Being caught talking to a known member was good for a prison sentence, even if all you did was ask for the time.

Most people knew to fear the name and everyone who claimed it, but even the rest knew not to accept favors from them.

"I thought you might say that," said Sota after a long pause. "But I ask you again: What happens when you leave this closet? Sure, you might get lost in the shuffle tonight, but I happen to know there's a checkpoint being set up at the entrance to the government complex as we speak." He stopped here, assessing the storm clouds rolling across Dani's expression. "If I'm not mistaken, that's where your future *husband* resides?"

Dani glared at him, but she said nothing.

"And," Sota continued, like they were chatting over baskets of fruit in the market and not discussing her inevitable demise, "should you, say, fail to produce your identification documents? That certainly wouldn't be good, would it? They use a special word for people who try to trick the government, Dani; it starts with a *T* and it rhymes with . . ."

"I know what it is," Dani spat. "What's your point?"

"Only that the choice between trusting me and going it alone isn't much of a choice at all. One of them involves taking these papers and going along on your merry way. The other involves a very small prison cell and the knowledge that everyone you know and love is in danger of joining you there."

Trained by her Primera instructors to analyze and see logic in even the most impossible situations, Dani called on every faculty she had been born with, as well as the ones she'd learned on this campus. There had to be another way out. One that didn't involve dying of exposure in the jungle while fleeing the police *or* accepting a favor from the least trustworthy group of cutthroats in Medio.

The seconds ticked away.

There was no other option.

"What's in it for you?" she asked.

"Why, Daniela, I'm offended."

"Come on," she said, impatient. "I know who La Voz is. You're a criminal, and you're not here to be my savior, so what do you want in exchange for those?"

Sota held out the papers, and much to Dani's disgust, she took them. "Unlike your friends out there, who are so eager to join the ranks of good little upper-class dolls," he said, gesturing to the closed closet door, "we're in the business of helping people. Freeing them. Ask yourself who's imprisoning those same people. Torturing them. Sending their children over the wall to starve. It's so easy to join up, so easy to forget the harm being done every day. Even when you've seen it firsthand."

Dani felt the beginnings of a flush creeping up her chest, and she was glad for the high neck of her Primera dress. It wasn't her fault people were starving and dying. She didn't have to feel guilty just because she'd gotten out. She was about to say as much when Sota continued.

"Think about the crimes your precious government condones, not just the ones they punish. Then you can talk to me about who the real criminals are. If we're not all free, none of us are free. You remember that."

There was fire in his eyes when he spoke, a song in his throat, nearly turning his words hypnotic. There was a small part of Dani that wanted to buy into his logic. But Primeras thought with their heads, not their hearts. This was what these "revolutionaries" did. They made everything emotional. They leaned on pretty words until violence sounded like freedom. Until the extreme seemed justified.

"Save it," she finally said, though her voice was rougher than she liked. "I just need to get out of here. I'm doing what I have to do to survive. I'm not signing up to set things on fire."

"Whatever you say." Sota smirked, already turning toward the door. "But you're already seeing things differently. Your face might hide your feelings, but you can't hide who you are. Not forever."

Dani opened her mouth to protest, but he didn't give her a chance.

"I marked you as interviewed on the student manifest," he said. "You're safe for tonight. Present these to the officer at tomorrow's checkpoint and you won't have any trouble."

The door opened, and the sounds of Dani's world came pouring back in as he disappeared into the crowd.

No one seemed to notice her walking out of the supply closet, and Dani drew the persona that had gotten her through five years in this place around her like a shawl. She was calm, collected, in control. Her restraint was her strength.

Students weren't permitted to leave until everyone had been questioned, and Dani sat alone at the end of a pew toward the back until they were dismissed, just as the moon had begun its slow descent in the sky.

Back in her room, she should have fallen into bed and slept like the dead, but instead she sat awake, gazing at her new papers in the dim light from a candle.

They were beautiful. A job like this would run someone thousands of notas in the back-alley places frequented by desperate outer islanders with everything to lose. And that's if they could find someone good enough to make them without a waiting list a year long.

Dani's parents had saved every penny until she was four years old to get identification for the three of them. The riots had been getting worse, modern-day politics reinforcing Medio's mythology until they formed an impenetrable hatred between the island's two sides.

She barely remembered the crossing. Her mama wrapping her in a long, woven cloth on her back even though she was much too old to be carried. Her father hushing them when the beams of the guards' lights passed too close. And then the climb. The darkness. The way her mama's feet slipped against the stone and her breath whistled through her teeth.

That was all.

They had left everything behind. A family, a history, and a home Dani barely remembered. She'd seen the ghosts of that life in her parents' faces sometimes, passing like shadows, and felt guilty because they'd given it all up for her.

Dani sniffed as she traced the clean lines of her name on the paper. The town they'd settled in when she was a child had been filled in as her birthplace. Polvo. She'd loved that little town. It was the first home she really remembered. She'd loved the kids, and the noise, and her run-down schoolhouse. Loved the trips with her mama into the small city nearby, where street vendors sold roasted corn on sticks and frozen fruit with chili powder in paper cups.

But when her parents had come up with the idea to enter her into Primera selection the year she turned twelve, what could Dani really say? They wanted the best for her, they'd said. Wanted her to rise so high that the place she was born could never be a danger to her again. In the face of all that, what did it matter that Dani had loved Polvo? Loved her best friend, Marisol, and the boys across the street who always had a scraggly puppy or two in tow. Loved the idea of growing up to make the little place they called home better, instead of fleeing forever and leaving it to gather dust.

In Polvo, no one had been confused about who their loyalty was to. Parents worked long hours in desperate conditions; they made sure you had enough to eat even when it meant going without; they scraped and scrounged every day to give you something more than they were allowed, and duty was all they asked for in return.

And what were Dani's little loves compared to that? A belly mostly full of food when others went hungry or worse. Shelter, and both of her parents alive, and the chance to be considered for the highest honor a young woman in Medio could dream of.

What could she possibly give them besides her best?

It didn't matter that Dani had dreamed of a little house and a couple of chickens and the chance to learn her mama's recipes. Of taking care of her parents as they got older. It didn't matter that she'd wanted Polvo, and the life she had been born for. Because in Medio, safety required power, and to get power you had to move closer to the sun.

She had done well, she thought, looking around the lavishly appointed room, its white stone, the hand-painted tiles lining the walls. Her closet full of modest dresses, each worth more than her father made in a week back home. The Medio School for Girls had provided it all, confident that Dani would more than make up for it when her new family paid her marriage fee.

Maybe the girls she went to school with didn't know what it meant to feel that fierce loyalty to their families. That duty. But she did, and to turn her back on it would mean to let go of the last little piece of Polvo she'd been allowed to keep.

So tonight, Dani let herself take comfort in her new papers, despite the source. To take comfort in knowing she was that much closer to what her parents wanted for her. Maybe Sota had been telling the truth. Maybe La Voz had helped her because they thought she was one of them. Maybe it had been an intervention by the goddess of luck at her lowest moment.

Whatever it had been, Dani didn't intend to waste this chance.

The graduation ceremony is the culmination of a Primera's training; a first glimpse of the future she has earned, and the heights to which she will rise.

—*Medio School for Girls Handbook*, 14th edition

⊹⊱✳⊰⊹

ON GRADUATION MORNING, THE SUN rose early just to shine in the windows of Medio's most celebrated young women on their special day.

Dani was up earlier, sitting at her desk, reading a letter whose creases had smoothed out with time and handling. The date was five years earlier—the handwriting, her mama's.

Dear Daniela, it began. *I write you this letter with all the hope a mother can feel, on the first day of the life you deserve. It will seem strange, after the way we've lived, but I know you, m'ija. You have a big heart, a strong mind, and you will find a way to make a life you love. No matter how different it is from the one you left.*

Her mama couldn't say everything, of course. Not in writing. To the students at the Medio School for Girls, Dani was just a girl from somewhere below the capital. Even the ones who knew she was lower class could never know that Dani's hometown—shameful enough for its proximity to the border wall—wasn't in fact the place she had been born.

Her dress for the ceremony was pressed and laid out on the bed, her door open to the sounds of girls preparing for the arrival of their families. Normally, Dani ignored them; she wasn't here to make friends. Still, on this, the last day of her school career, she watched them a little more closely. She was envious, she realized. Of the excitement. Of the glow in their cheeks.

Dani felt satisfaction, yes. The solid, warm feeling of a duty accomplished well. But there was no joy in this day for her. No family arrivals. No celebrations.

In one of her infrequent letters home, Dani had sent two graduation tickets to her own parents, but it had been a formality. Something for her mother to pass around at the well. Dani had, of course, been vetted by the Garcia family. They knew what her papers told them—that she had been born in Polvo, and had risen far above what they'd expected of her here. Not everyone at this level was upper-class legacy, but it certainly didn't get you anywhere to flaunt your unseemly poverty. Especially in front of the people who'd just paid a small fortune to marry you to their son.

Overcoming obstacles was good. Showing off the salt-curse in your blood was not.

When the return letter had come from her parents, it said as much, wishing her luck, telling her how proud they were. Dani hadn't seen them in person since she'd boarded the bus to the capital at twelve. They didn't speak of it, but she'd likely see them only once or twice more in her life.

The island was a mountain, and the higher you climbed, the better off you were.

For a politico's Primera, a trip to sea level, to the place where the wall separated Medio proper from the lawless outer island, was nothing short of inappropriate. As tensions rose at the border and the frequency of the riots increased, a whisper of "rebel" or "sympathizer"—however untrue—clung like the smell of smoke. To spend too much time below the capital was to risk your loyalties being called into question.

The tensions had moved far past mythology. Far past brother-gods and curses as old as the island itself. It was political now. Rights and riots and the prosperous versus the destitute. On one side, there was the might of a nation. On the other, desperation. Every clash was a violent one, every victory bloody and hollow with loss.

There was no going back.

But still, her heart squeezed uncomfortably in her chest at the idea of her mama. She would look older now, Dani realized, and for a moment she was right back in Polvo, tiny brown fingers digging for candy in an apron pocket, bare feet in the dirt. For a moment, a kind word or a kiss was all it took to make everything better.

The promise of family and the guiding hand of the past had been such innate parts of life in Polvo that sometimes Dani felt like all the Primera training in the world wasn't enough to fully banish them from her bones.

This is inappropriate, said the nagging voice of a maestra in the back of Dani's mind. *Primeras don't cling to nostalgia; they're above such weakness. A true Primera keeps her eyes on the future.*

When the hall emptied, Dani followed the crowd. She might not have had parents to show around, but she had a few goodbyes to say before tomorrow's departure. Her father had warned her not to get too close with any of the girls, reminding her that closeness led to trust, and trust could be broken.

But the best climbing tree on campus couldn't tell her secrets, and neither could the view from the top-floor library balcony. The light-as-air tortillas in the cafeteria wouldn't dream of betraying her. And that tile mosaic in the south courtyard, the one everyone passed by without looking? It always kept its mouth shut.

Dani visited them all, the places where she'd found sanctuary from her early homesickness, the places she'd neglected as she rose in the ranks and started wearing her Primera dresses like more than a costume. This school had been her home, much more than the distant place she'd come from. She didn't know if she'd miss it, but it had earned a goodbye, at least.

Feeling peaceful and full after eating her last school meal—pork swimming in garlicky tomatillo sauce, perfectly spiced red rice that stained your fingers oily red, and a small tower of those incredible tortillas—Dani wove her way through the visiting families and back to the dormitory. It was time to prepare for the most important night of her life.

But before she could make it across the east courtyard, a whispering knot of Segundas sashayed into her path. Dani prayed silently to the god of hurry that she'd escape their notice. Unfortunately, he wasn't on her side today.

"I think you've got some . . . is that *oil*, on your cheek? I don't know how they eat where you're from, but at this altitude we try to use a little decorum."

The cold, ringing voice could only belong to one person, and Dani steeled herself before stopping to face her.

Carmen Santos towered over the girls simpering beside her, dressed in swirling turquoise silk that set off her golden-brown skin. Her curls were so black they glinted in the late afternoon sun like the dark metal of a loaded pistol.

By comparison, Dani felt weak as a reed in the wind, her black dress hanging from narrow hips and negligible curves. Her child's cheeks. The close-cropped waves of her unruly hair. The skin that cooled olive where Carmen's glowed like the setting sun.

Primeras were not vain, Dani reminded herself. Their value came from deeper wells than physical beauty. "I'll take that under advisement," she said, anger rattling the bars of her restraint, though her face showed nothing. "Enjoy your afternoon."

"Guess they don't teach you to stand up for yourself out there, either," Carmen said. "Just goes to show, you can take the girl out of the salt, but you can't take the salt out of the girl."

The anger was rattling harder now, and Dani stopped, standing perfectly still as she weighed her options and the other girls smirked and giggled among themselves. Maybe it was the finality of it all that made her pause. She'd been tolerating Carmen's unsubtle digs since they'd met on the shuttle from the capital, five long years ago. It was the first and only time Dani—alone and scared, miles from home—had confided in anyone about her modest upbringing.

Twelve-year-old Carmen had been no less beautiful, but her wide eyes had been friendly then, and Dani had trusted her against her father's advice. How could a girl with a pretty face and an easy smile ever betray her?

She found out all too quickly, when Carmen settled in with the girls of her own station, and the fragile friendship they'd built up over the miles became collateral damage.

"Hey, Carmen," Dani said at last, letting just a hint of her true feelings through. Just this once. Carmen turned, hand on hip, and waited. "You might be right about the salt, but I guess growing up in silk and silver doesn't guarantee class. Thanks for the lesson."

When Carmen's eyes flashed, Dani knew she'd hit her mark. "Listen to me, you border brat. You wouldn't know class if it barreled through that village of yours and flattened your family hovel."

"Maybe not," Dani said. "But I know desperation better than most, and you reek of it."

Carmen gestured once, sharply, and the other jewels fled the crown, leaving the two of them alone. "I'd work on that temper of yours, Primera," she said, her voice lower now. Almost dangerous. "Not that you'd know, but *well-bred* men like their women to have a little charm."

Dani took a deep breath, praying to the god of voice that she could hold hers steady. "That's one of the perks of having actual value," she said. "You don't have to rely on frivolous things like charm."

Carmen laughed, and Dani carried the mocking sound all the way back to her room, where she used slow, controlled movements to open and close her drawers, putting on her Primera-issued graduation dress with an exaggerated precision that masked her frustration.

There was something about Carmen that got under Dani's skin. Partially, it was anger at her twelve-year-old self for acting on instinct rather than logic, but that wasn't all of it. It was the way people treated Carmen, too. Doted on her. Acted like she was so special because she was rich and beautiful and everything came easily.

It had been a hard adjustment, coming here from a house with a dirt floor, but Dani had made it. She'd grown used to the way the other girls acted, like they expected the world on a silver platter and they weren't planning on being disappointed.

But in Carmen, that entitlement was magnified somehow. She was the face of everything Dani would never have, would never be, and she hated her for it. For the way her world was unfolding like a flower, while Dani was just trying to make way.

"The graduation ceremony will begin in one hour!" came the resident's voice from the hallway, calling them to order for the last time. "Please finish your preparations and make your way to the oratory."

Dani did her best to shove thoughts of Carmen into the little box where she kept off-limits things. Fears. Irritations. Longings. Regrets. It was one of the earliest lessons of a Primera's training—learning to wall off the feelings that could interfere with your restraint. By the time Dani walked out of the dormitory doors, she was smooth and gleaming like lacquered wood.

It was time to be the flawless girl this institution had invested so much in. Time to earn the notas that would keep her parents fed and clothed for years, patch their roof, and buy her father new work boots with solid soles.

It was time, she thought sadly, to put that other future to rest. The one she'd seen bloom in a look between her parents. The one she might have had if she'd stayed at home, where joining yourself to someone was more than just a business arrangement. The upper class had always looked down on the lower for the way they married. Pitied them for the lack of the sun's blessing until the pity twisted into prejudice. One partner, for better or worse—they thought it uncivilized. A relic of a cursed past. But for most of her life, it had been all Dani knew.

Primera training had reduced the memory down to a quiet whisper in her bones, but tonight it would be silenced for good.

On the way to the oratory, she opened the box for just a moment and let her memories of Polvo flood in. The looming wall that hid the place she had truly been born. The salt-hard ground where nothing much would grow. The laughter of children and the dancing feet of adults not too tired from another day of survival to feel joy. The fires in barrels and the sweet wine she'd sneak sips of with her friends under a million stars. Her home.

Polvo was lost to her. And it was time to grow up.

The oratory blazed once more against the night. Little as she loved the idea of pledging herself to a stranger tonight, Dani thought, at least she could feel good about her reasons for doing so. It would never be happiness, but maybe, like her mama said, it could be enough.

"Primera students to the left, please! Segundas to the right!" Residents prowled the aisles, hushing, herding, restoring order.

Dani found her place on her own, settling in, offering half-hearted nods to the girls surrounding her. The peers she'd never allowed herself to know or befriend. How could she have? When the only time she'd tried . . . Well, the scene with Carmen today had been proof enough of that outcome.

Across the aisle, the Segundas were a riot of color and sound, swapping lip stains and fluffing one another's hair, tightening the ends of braids, trading woven bracelets for friendship and luck. The difference across the aisle was stark. But that was how it was supposed to be. Emotion clouded your judgment, and logic hampered your ability to feel. The Sun God had been wise, and thousands of years of prosperous Medians were proof of his blessing's worth.

Even Dani, with her false papers and dusty memories, the little gods that turned on her in key moments to stick out their tongues, couldn't argue with results.

She closed her eyes against the bustle of energy and noise, and under her breath she recited the pledge she'd be offering to Mateo Garcia. It was tradition, the first impression a husband got of his new Primera, and she wanted it to be flawless.

Around her, a hundred other Primeras prepared in their own ways. A *hundred* weddings would be taking place here tonight. A hundred hopeful pledges by Constancia's chosen ones, hiding the trembling of their hands. A hundred promises by daughters of the Moon Goddess, who had never looked more beautiful than they would tonight under the candlelight. A hundred family cloths, woven by mothers, wrapped around the shoulders of the three as they vowed to accept their blessing. To be partners. To be one.

It should have felt like flying, and for some of the girls it probably did. But the part of home Dani thought she'd exhaled outside the oratory was back with a vengeance. She didn't want to be here, she realized with a dull sense of horror. She wanted to go home.

You will find a way to make a life you love, said her mama's voice in her heart. *No matter how different it is from the one you left.*

As they had been meant to do all those years ago when Dani boarded the bus to the capital, her mama's words kept her in place now, her face impassive as her heart threatened to break into pieces.

"Ladies and gentleman of Medio," said Headmatron Huerta. "Welcome."

Her voice had always had a subduing effect on a crowd. Even the Segundas' feathers settled as all eyes turned toward the front. Dani kept her mama's words close, repeating them like a mantra when her restlessness threatened to get the best of her.

You will find a way to make a life you love.

"This ceremony is the crowning event of our academic year. The young women before you have worked tirelessly to reach this moment, and we could not be prouder to present them to you tonight."

As applause filled the room, a buzzing numbness began at the base of Dani's spine and spread. Despite her calming mantra, the room took on an odd, shimmering quality.

Was this her body, sitting straight-backed and sure in this pew?

"But I don't need to tell you how outstanding these girls are," Headmatron Huerta continued. "You've seen it for yourself during your interviews with them. When you weighed their accomplishments, their virtues, and chose them to become members of your families."

More applause. The latch on the forbidden corner of Dani's mind rattled dangerously. Everything inside it screamed to be let free. Nights with her parents, their simple but hearty food between them, laughter painting the night. Days with her friends, people who had known her since childhood, people who protected her secret and even shared it. People she could trust.

And someday, maybe, a love that arose on its own. A marriage that wasn't forced. Blessing or not, was she wrong to want that? Her Primera training rebelled against the thoughts, but Dani found for the first time that it wasn't enough to stop them.

"We have a lot of commitments to make here tonight,"

said the headmatron, drawing Dani back to the present. "So let's get right to it." She gestured beyond the rear door to a classroom space, where a hundred young husbands waited for the wives their fathers had bought them. "Without further ado . . ." Her voice brimmed with satisfaction as she removed the list from a compartment below the podium. Dani could almost see the gold coins spilling over in her mind's eye.

Some girls were worth more than others, some families willing to pay more for the best. But the real winner here was the Medio School for Girls, who sent a dowry to each girl's family and took a cut for themselves.

All this white stone and intricate tile-work didn't come cheap, after all.

"Will Juan Felipe Tejada Alvarez please come forward?"

The door behind the headmatron opened, and a boy strode forward with an abundance of confidence. The atmosphere among the graduates became electric just as Dani's nerves threatened to corrode her iron restraint. This was it.

Juan stood to the left of the podium, scanning the crowd eagerly. Traditionally the placements were kept a secret, to bring some drama into the night's events, but Dani knew there were few girls in these rows—on the Primera side, at least—without a very good idea where they would end up.

They weren't the most resourceful, intelligent young women in the country for nothing.

"The Alvarez family has chosen . . . ," said the headmatron, pausing for effect. "Primera Maria Luna Vega Sanchez!"

Dani clapped, relieved to feel sensation returning to her limbs. Maria stood, beaming and waving to her parents behind her before walking up the aisle toward her new husband, who had turned suddenly shy.

". . . And Segunda Sofia Rios Gomez!"

Predictably, several tearful Segundas clutched at the hem of Sofia's dress as she passed, shouting congratulations at her in high pitched voices that made Dani's head ache.

One of them was probably Carmen.

Not that Dani was thinking about her.

Maria and her new husband had been staring at each other, slightly awestruck, but when Sofia took the stage beside them, the dynamic changed. They seemed to settle into their roles in a way that transformed them into adults before the audience's eyes.

"Primera, please recite your pledge."

The room was silent as Maria promised to be Juan Alvarez's support. His perspective. His friend, and his partner in all things. His smile was stiff but seemed genuine, and he nodded solemnly when she'd finished, sealing the pledge with a handshake, as custom dictated.

Sofia went next, her voice low and confident as she promised to be the song his life had been missing, and to care for him until the end of their days.

"And now, the cloth," Headmatron Huerta said as Juan

turned to Sofia, unfolding a cloth in the Alvarez family colors of brown, red, and gold. He wrapped it around his own shoulders before extending it, bringing Primera and Segunda under its symbolic cover. For a moment they stood nearly forehead to forehead to forehead before they stepped apart.

When Dani thought Juan could look no more boyish and afraid, he spoke clearly of his commitment to provide for them, to protect them, to be steadfast and loyal until his dying day.

Next, the headmatron produced their marriage agreement, which they signed in turns before taking a bow and disappearing through a third door, leading out to the courtyard. Tonight, the husbands would return home alone. Tomorrow morning, their new wives would join them.

After the novelty of the first commitment, Dani let the names and slightly varied pledges slide through her mind without making much of an impression. Inside, she was still a nation at war with itself. On one side, the life she'd dreamed of and the uncertainty of the life before her. On the other, her family's hope and everything they'd left behind.

A lesser Primera would have shown it, would have trembled or gasped for breath or stood without meaning to. But Dani was not a lesser Primera. Her mask was all she had left.

Wearing it well, she waited for the name that would end the war, and after an hour or more, she heard it at last. Falling as destined by the alphabet—which was such an arbitrary way to choose to change someone's life completely, wasn't it?

"Would Alberto Mateo Luis Gonzalez Garcia please step forward?"

Dani's spine went straight as a sapling, and the tingling feeling returned as the room erupted in whispers. The Garcias were far and away the wealthiest, most decorated family present tonight. Every girl in Dani's class had coveted this placement. But only two girls in this room would walk away with the boy now stepping up to the podium, looking more like a man than any who had come before him.

He was handsome. Wide-shouldered and narrow-waisted, he stepped up looking self-assured, not bored or nervous. Like he was comfortable in front of a crowd.

The headmatron waited for the hissing to die down, and Dani thought of the elder Señor Garcia, Mateo's father. He was the chief military strategist to the president, and there were not so secret rumors that he was grooming his son for the presidency.

Mateo was everything her parents had wanted for her. Wealthy. Respected. With him, she would be above reproach. Polvo's salt-song lamented in her blood; a counterweight, a mourning cry.

"The Garcia family has chosen . . ."

Dani breathed in, making sure not to stand before it was official.

"Primera Daniela Noa Vargas."

Her legs held steady. Her papa's stories and the teasing laughter of her childhood friends and the vague memory of a night spent held against her mama's body, following a flash-light beam into a new world. Was this where it had all been taking her?

Outside, the school's top Primera took her place demurely beside the year's most promising bachelor. Inside, Dani was a storm without an eye. She looked up at him, trying to get a read on the boy aside from his pedigree. She, of all people, knew that where you were from and where you were going weren't always enough to tell a person's whole story.

But he didn't look back. A chilly sort of boredom emanated from the only Garcia son, like he got married every day. Like it was nothing. Dani felt her dread intensify. She needed a sign. A whisper from the gods in the candle flames or the starlit diosas outside to tell her she didn't need to run. That this was the right thing to do.

They stood together, Mateo staring unseeing at the contract before them, Dani with melting iron in her spine, looking for something to hold on to.

". . . And Segunda," the headmatron said, consulting the paper in front of her.

Dani didn't let herself close her eyes.

"Carmen Reina Lara Santos!"

✦

THE NUMBNESS DANI HAD FELT earlier was nothing compared to her shock when Carmen was called.

Where Dani's name had drawn whispers, too-polite claps, and eyes like daggers, Carmen's name caused hysteria. The girls surrounding her rushed in, embracing her, shrieking, even sobbing. The ones not lucky enough to sit so close whistled instead, applauding until the sound echoed from the walls and the headmatron was forced to call order.

Carmen rose from her admirers like a bird taking flight. Her smile was radiant, her dress an ostentatious bright gold.

Rather than cause panic, Carmen's presence had made Dani calm. This was the sign she had been looking for. On the night of her greatest uncertainty, the Moon Goddess had given her Carmen Santos.

She had trusted her instincts once before, Dani thought, the day she told Carmen who she was. It had been the worst decision of her young life, and if Carmen was here, it was as a reminder that Dani did as she was told. When she didn't, disaster struck.

There was no reason now to think of the future shaping itself before her, or to plan her escape. Carmen was taking her place on the other side of Mateo, completing the trifecta that would carry them through the rest of their lives together. She was dazzling. Perfect. Everything upper-class breeding and a lifetime of wealth and doting had bought her.

"Primera, please recite your pledge."

Carmen seemed to remember Dani's existence at that moment, and she turned her gaze across the podium with a smile that probably looked warm and welcoming to the audience. Friendly, even.

But Dani knew the truth. That every moment of her life would now be a fight. A competition. A battle for dominance. That Carmen would never stop looking for a way to intimidate and undermine her.

And if she paid close enough attention, if she discovered the secret Dani was hiding with those false papers in her desk drawer, Carmen would finally be able to ruin her. The way she'd inexplicably wanted to since their first day at the Medio School for Girls.

"Primera?" said the headmatron, a wrinkle of concern between her brows.

"Of course," Dani said, pushing her worries aside. "My apologies, señor."

Her apology was directed to Mateo, who acknowledged it with an impatient nod.

"Señor Garcia," she began. "As your Primera, I pledge to be a beacon of light when the darkness is closing. A sturdy boat in choppy seas. I will be your partner, your solid ground. I will honor and respect you as long as we both shall live."

Short and to the point, Dani had thought when she was writing it. It was only a formality anyway; everyone knew what was expected of a Primera without flowery language to belabor the point.

Mateo extended his hand, and she pressed her palm into his, hoping to convey with this gesture what she hoped for their life together: that they could make a life they loved, even if it was different from the one she had left. She was rewarded with a moment of eye contact, a brief softening of the hard lines around his eyes.

"Segunda?" said the headmatron.

Mateo dropped Dani's hand in an instant, turning with almost inappropriate eagerness toward his shiny new

Segunda, raking his eyes over her body in a greedy way that made Dani want to avert her gaze. Segundas were, of course, the child-bearers of the family, but Mateo wouldn't be sharing a bed with his Segunda until she reached childbearing age. Usually around twenty, but dependent on an examination by the family's physician.

Carmen responded with a smile, acknowledging his appreciation, but Dani noticed something tensed behind the Segunda's eyes. It almost made her feel sorry for Carmen.

Almost.

"Señor," she said, in a voice like the silk draping her curves. "In a world that will ask for much of you, I promise to be a respite, a joy. To nurture and to please you . . ." Several Segundas made whooping sounds, and Carmen winked at them.

Mateo allowed himself a grin.

Dani fought the urge to be sick.

". . . To fill your home with beauty and love as long as we live."

When Mateo mouthed *thank you* to her, Dani felt smaller than she ever had.

He pulled out the cloth next, woven of the Garcia family colors: blue, black, and silver. Powerful colors, and cold. The cloth his mama had woven was a marvel, much more intricate and sophisticated than the others Dani had seen tonight.

Dani thought she understood the symbolism as she

considered the real, glinting metal woven in among the silver threads. Though Mateo's eyes were a deep brown, it was as though you could see all his family's ruthless colors swirling behind them.

He settled the cloth over his shoulders before reaching out. Carmen and Dani moved closer, the strange electricity of bodies in proximity sparking between them. Dani's shoulders touched first Mateo's, then Carmen's, before the cloth was around them all.

She tried to lose herself in the colors. The clarity and purpose of the blue, the shadowy secrets of the black. Punctuating it all, the harsh, unyielding edge of the silver.

It's almost over, Dani thought, a jolt of panic racing through her veins. She had hoped to feel some camaraderie with her new husband before they stepped off the stage. Some indication that her mama had been right about her ability to build a life she loved.

But Mateo had barely looked at her. *Carmen Santos* of all people was standing beside them. This wasn't at all what she had been expecting.

"Ladies, thank you both so much," Mateo said, in a voice that sounded rehearsed. "In return, I promise to be a faithful, dedicated husband to you both. To provide for us all. It's my pleasure to formally welcome you both to the Garcia family. May we prosper."

The Garcia family motto.

"*May we prosper,*" Dani and Carmen replied together.

And then there was a pen in Dani's hand, gold and too heavy. There were more eligible bachelors waiting for their turn, and Dani grasped for her mama's words. For anything that would make this moment feel less like the death of something.

But nothing came. There was only Dani, and this cold, strange family that was nothing like her own, and the promise she'd made to take this better life and never look back.

Mateo signed, his handwriting made up of sharp, angular lines that pressed deep into the paper. Carmen was next, with an ostentatious flourish that said absolutely everything about her. They both looked at Dani, who moved precisely. Carefully. Like an expensive instrument unfolding.

And wasn't she?

The paper disappeared from beneath her hands the moment her name was signed. The headmatron was preparing to call the next name. Mateo was already pushing the door open, Carmen not far behind.

A dangerous feeling was welling up inside Dani, as if her duty and her desire were clawing at each other and the victor hadn't yet been decided. The cool air on her face whispered that it wasn't too late. That she could run into the trees and never look back. The darkness at the edges of the courtyard seemed full of ominous whispers. Her chest felt heavy, her movements too slow.

What would they say in Polvo if you returned empty-handed? a small, malicious voice asked as she stood poised at the edge of the darkness. *Perfect, brilliant Dani, off to save her family and do things the rest of them only dreamed of doing.*

Her heartbeat slowed. The urge to run dissipated, leaving a sad weight in its wake. No one in Polvo would ever understand if she returned. It wouldn't be the same as it was before. That version of her was dead. This was the only way forward.

And there were Carmen and Mateo, leaning toward each other beneath a glowing lantern. There was an instant intimacy and spark between them that Dani almost envied. Carmen was making a life she loved, or a life that loved her, at least. If this was Dani's life—if there was truly no going back—she had to do the same.

"Oh, *here* we go," said Carmen under her breath as Dani approached. "Mateo was just leaving."

"Yes, of course," said Dani, more to Mateo than to Carmen. "Well, señor, we'll see you . . . tomorrow, then."

But Mateo was bored again. Dani had been awkward and formal where Carmen was alluring, her posture flattering him even without words.

"Mhm," he said. "I suppose you will."

Carmen's smirk was poison.

"My madres will be here in the morning to retrieve you," Mateo said, nodding to Dani and kissing Carmen on the cheek. "Until then."

Once he left, Dani felt like she had just sold her most valuable possession for a handful of dried beans. She wanted to chase after him, force him to acknowledge the hard work she'd done to reach this moment, the life she'd never know because she'd chosen his.

But of course, that wasn't behavior befitting a Primera, so she just watched him walk away, ashamed of the burning sensation that started behind her eyes and traveled down her throat, leaving a red-hot ember in the center of her chest.

"Really?" asked Carmen. "Isn't *don't cry*, like, the only thing in the whole Primera handbook?"

Her laugh was humorless and mocking as usual, but tonight Dani was armorless. It went right through her, into that empty space where her sudden hope of running home had been, before she'd realized she had no home to run to.

"Get it together," Carmen said, a shimmer of gold departing the edge of Dani's blurred vision. "Your professionalism—or *lack thereof*—reflects on all of us now."

Once she was alone, Dani felt untethered. When was the last time she'd truly felt like she had a purpose beyond reaching this moment? Making her parents and Polvo proud?

Without warning, her memory conjured Sota and the oratory broom closet. He was an enemy, a member of the ruthless resistance group hell-bent on bringing to the forefront exactly what Dani had always fought to keep in the dark. But when he looked at her, there had been something in his eyes. Something that made her feel strange and, yes, purposeful. Scared, and a little proud.

She spent the whole walk back to her dormitory burying that dangerous thought. If she was lucky, she thought as she drifted off to sleep, she would never see Sota again.

But when had she ever been lucky?

Dani's view of her future was not improved by the predawn light. Her personal belongings fit in a single small carton, which she carried down to the school's driveway at sunup without ceremony. The pickups were staggered throughout the morning, to avoid crowding in the circular driveway, so when she arrived, she stood alone.

More than once, she patted the blue-white papers in the outer pocket of her leather satchel, just to make sure they were still there, though she'd checked and rechecked them a thousand times before stepping out into the hallway.

Sota had said there would be a checkpoint on the way into Medio's government complex. She had no choice but to trust him, even though the thought of it made her chest feel tight.

Just then, of course, Carmen arrived. Three of her minions pushed a rolling cart of dresses behind her, and she waved a hand to direct them, never lifting a finger herself.

Typical, Dani thought, not bothering to conceal her eye roll. She was at the far end of the driveway, and she hoped Carmen would have the good sense to stand at the other. But of course, Carmen beckoned her retinue closer, parking herself and her rolling closet right behind Dani.

"Good morning, Primera," she said without looking at Dani.

"Good morning, Carmen."

"You're not going to cry again, are you?" she asked, shattering any hope Dani had of civility. "I was out late, and my head is killing me."

The postgraduation Segunda party was legendary, even among Primeras. Dani's roommate, Jasmín, had been invited last year, and she had come back at sunrise actually *giggling*. Embarrassing, to say the least.

"Quiet today, huh?" Carmen asked, banishing her sycophants with a wave of her wrist. "Probably a better strategy than whatever you tried last night. It was hard to watch, I'll be honest."

"I see you're sticking with what works," Dani said without looking up.

"What's that?"

"Putting me down so you don't feel as insecure."

"Ha! Me? Insecure?" she asked. "I'm sorry, have you *seen* me?" But Dani saw her shoulders stiffen under the crisscrossing straps of orange silk.

"You know, I've heard you can be beautiful *and* still be a cruel, small-minded person with few qualities that endear you to others. But that may have just been a rumor."

Carmen's eyes narrowed in anger, but a nearly silent black

limousine crept up the drive just in time, preventing Dani from having to hear whatever came next. She picked up her carton and approached the door, leaving Carmen to wrestle with her wardrobe alone in her impractical outfit.

It was a small victory, getting the last word, but when it came to Carmen, Dani would take what she could get.

"Good morning, ladies," said Señora Garcia, stepping out of the car in a boxy black traveling dress. She had been the one to conduct Dani's placement interview, and her greeting was as warm as could be expected from one of the most powerful Primeras in the country.

Mama Garcia wasn't far behind, and Dani could immediately see why the Segunda had been taken with Carmen. They were practically copies of one another. Both dressed in head-to-toe silk, with long, cascading curls and expressions that said the world owed them a perpetual favor. They air-kissed on both cheeks, their smiles wide, as though they were close already.

Another one to watch out for, then, thought Dani as the driver loaded her meager belongings into the car and relieved Carmen of her cumbersome luggage. The four women settled into the back of the car, and Dani tried not to gawk. After five years at school, she was used to a certain level of luxury, but this car was the size of Dani's parents' living room.

"Mateo wishes he could have greeted you himself, of course," said the señora in a brisk, businesslike tone.

The car began to maneuver down the steep driveway, and

Carmen looked back as the Medio School for Girls disappeared into the trees behind them.

Dani did not.

"He has urgent business with his father and the president, but will be back this evening," explained Mama Garcia. "Until then, Señora Garcia and I will be introducing you to the house and grounds, and to your new lives as Garcia women."

Carmen nodded, and Dani followed suit.

"Now," said Señora Garcia. "I know you feel prepared, after your schooling, with your marriage contracts newly signed. But I assure you the real work has yet to begin." She dug down in her bag, retrieving folders. "Before Mateo returns, you'll need to have the house in order. He travels often for business, as most government officials do, and it will be your responsibility to present him with a well-maintained residence each time he returns. Tomorrow morning will be your first test, and we'd like you to be ready. Please turn to page seventeen of your household manuals."

She handed a folder to Dani, and one to Carmen. It was completely filled with what Dani assumed was Señora Garcia's tidy print.

"I'll give you a few moments to look it over," she said, folding her hands in her lap.

As they read section three in silence—about the supervision of housekeepers, and Mateo's preferences for everything from food to lighting to temperature—the tree-lined drive opened up into residential streets.

It was mostly widowed wives down here, the ones too old to be placed again when their husbands died. Some of them chose to remain together in old age, Primera and Segunda, already so used to living together that they decided not to part.

Looking at Carmen, her haughty expression unchanged by the mountain of work awaiting her when they arrived home, Dani couldn't imagine she'd make the same choice.

Item four, she read. *Señor Mateo requires a glass of room-temperature sangria be placed on the end table nearest his favorite chair up to, but no more than, twelve minutes before his arrival home.*

Was this going to be her marriage? Catering to the whims of a spoiled boy? Dani had pictured something slightly . . . grander. Then again, she reminded herself, this was only section three of the manual. Maybe the rest would be more satisfying.

Item seven: All of Mateo's personal correspondence must be placed on the northeast corner of the hall table. This task should not be entrusted to staff members but performed by the Primera of the house herself.

The tasks grew only more tedious and minute as the list wore on. In school, they had learned that a Primera would be her husband's equal, standing beside him, learning what he knew and sharing his power, but this handbook had her relegated to little more than an assistant. Scheduling social events, responding to invitations, placing Mateo's mail on the hallway table? This wasn't what she'd been trained for.

To dampen her rising irritation, Dani let her gaze drift out the window, where Medio's capital city was just coming into view.

She had spent so long in the quiet, sterile environment of the Medio School for Girls that she'd almost forgotten what the bustle of a city was like. Of course, the small city nearest Polvo was nothing compared to the capital, but Dani found herself nostalgic all the same.

The noise. The narrow alleyways between red-and-white stucco buildings. The overcrowded marketplaces, with their bulging baskets of produce and spices and fabrics in every color under the sun.

Street musicians gathered on every other corner, little girls in bright skirts spinning in front of them until they were breathless.

As the tightly sealed car maneuvered the hairpin turns, Dani inhaled deeply, like she could smell the grilling meat and open casks of sun-wine over the pervasive salt sea air. Everything in Medio moved upward, from the sea at the island's outer perimeter to the mountain in the center where the capital stood sentry, fed by the freshwater spring that made the lowlands' salt seem vulgar by comparison.

But even though the upper class might try to deny it, claim it was a curse by a vengeful god, this was an island. No matter how far up or in you went, you could always feel the beating heart of the sea.

The streets opened up again, less markets and food stands and more residential buildings. Between them, laundry hung like the flags of warring nations, and old ladies with wrinkled brown faces and flyaway white curls bickered through open windows over their imagined borders. A drumbeat started, audible even through the thick glass of the car's tinted windows. This was a place where you could trade limes for gold bracelets and old names for new ones. A place where you could disappear like smoke.

A place where you could stay and be anyone.

Dani looked between Carmen and Mama Garcia, then next to her at Mateo's stern-faced señora. Surely they weren't immune to the magic of this city?

"I assume you've already familiarized yourself with your list of duties?" Señora Garcia asked. "Given that you've taken to gaping out the window like an oversized fish."

Dani's face was as smooth and impassive as ever, her Primera mask in place. But maybe it would take more than a mask to impress one of the country's top Primeras.

"Yes, Señora," Dani said. "Of course."

"Then you won't mind telling me the protocol for the preparation of Mateo's bedchamber when he's been away from home overnight."

It was a trick question. Preparing the bedchamber was a Segunda's job. But it was on the list, and Dani was nothing if not thorough. She met the señora's eyes as she said:

"The bedding is to be washed and changed by the house-keepers under the supervision of the Segunda, who will then check it over thoroughly to ensure that the sheets are wrinkle free, his awards from the Medio School for Boys are polished, and his mirror is free of spots and dust."

Señora Garcia unpursed her lips for what seemed like the first time. "Well, it seems your reading comprehension and memory are up to snuff, at least."

Dani nodded deferentially, but inside she glowed. This might not be her dream, but she had learned the satisfaction of being exemplary. Because of the nature of their roles, Dani and the elder señora would spend little time alone together after this first week, but she would be the last of Dani's official teachers, and she found herself still eager to make a good impression.

Maybe it was the whisper of her own mama still stirring in her heart, Dani thought, that made her want to make this woman proud. But when she glanced up again, it was only to notice that Señora Agosta Garcia, with her stern face and her fastidious appearance, was as unlike Dani's mama as one woman could be from another.

As they left the city behind, Carmen studied her nails in that bored way of hers. Mama Garcia dozed beside her like a cat in a patch of sun. As for the señora, her eyes were a million miles away; she was probably thinking hard about the exact way Mateo liked his book spines dusted.

Item fourteen: Under no circumstances should the Primera, the

Segunda, or house staff be permitted inside Señor Mateo's private office.

This one caught Dani's attention. Maybe she wouldn't be the only one with a secret in the new Garcia household. But item fifteen was about the type of dessert Mateo liked if he was arriving home on a weeknight, and Dani sighed, a small and quiet thing, puncturing her breathless awe until it shrank in her chest.

The car began to climb, leaving the crowds behind, and this time it didn't dip down again. They were headed for the government complex, the exclusive, gated community where all of Medio's most influential and powerful people lived, like priceless jewels at the island's throat. As far from the sea and its salt-barren ground as you could get. As far as you could get from the desperation of people dependent on the tides and whims of those in power.

It had been a long time since they'd had anything to be thankful for out there. Since the Salt God denounced his brother's second marriage, according to some, but Dani wondered sometimes if that was just an excuse.

In the rear window, the sea was visible at last—a shimmering horizon line. From up here, you couldn't see that people were starving. Couldn't see the ancient wall with the armed sentries stationed along it. Couldn't see the mothers' hands reaching, begging for a scrap of something to give their children as armored trucks rolled through the gate with just enough food to keep most of their families alive and hungry.

From here, it was almost like quivering-chinned teens weren't probing for a place to sneak their younger siblings across, just hoping not to be gunned down or sent back. Like big men with knives and a little scraped-together power weren't taking more than their fair share, ganging up on the already downtrodden until they were forced to do something desperate and dangerous just to survive.

Suddenly, the false papers were heavy as stones in Dani's bag. She could try all she wanted to pretend she belonged in this car. In this life. But as long as she could see that horizon line, she would never forget where she had come from.

The gates of the government complex loomed ahead, and Dani found herself suspended between two worlds. The sea and the gate. The past and the future. But before she could deal with either of them, she would have to get through the checkpoint.

"Ay, I hate these things," said Mama Garcia as the intimidating iron gate became visible up ahead. "It's just a constant hassle for busy people. Who's really going to try to sneak in up here, huh? It's not like we don't know a criminal when we see one."

Her face was the picture of disdain, and inappropriate as it was, Dani fought the urge to laugh at the unbelievable irony.

Mama Garcia thought she should be able to tell. Like they all had scarlet marks on their foreheads to brand them. Like they were so decidedly *other* that even a glance at one would reveal them for what they truly were.

Ignoring the older Segunda's ranting, Señora Garcia instructed them all to take out their papers.

Dani swallowed once, hard, as the others dug through their shoulder bags. It was time to hope Sota had earned his cocky attitude.

Her life depended on it, after all.

A true Primera can turn her heart to steel, and her face to stone.
—*Medio School for Girls Handbook,* 14th edition

⊢⇝✳⇜⊣

AFTER A CHILDHOOD IN POLVO, beneath the shadow of the border wall, Dani thought she might never get used to the deference the police showed the wealthy.

Her papers securely in her lap, she watched as officers approached the glossy cars ahead with smiles, even laughter. A far cry from the scowling menaces who had made their way through Polvo once a week, scattering chickens, terrifying children and adults alike as they searched for stolen merchandise, punished families for "hoarding" food, and looked for people to send back over the wall.

Dani couldn't remember ever feeling as small as she had

on inspection days, and that had been their goal. To intimidate. To punish. Simply because she and her neighbors had been born with less.

But she wasn't the same person she'd been then, Dani reminded herself. She had spent five years in the company of the country's wealthiest daughters, learning their ways, becoming a Primera worthy of the Garcia family. That, along with her training, could be used to her advantage.

"Good morning, ladies," said a young officer when they reached the front of the line. Mama Garcia waited until the last possible moment to roll down the window, as if the air outside held something contagious. "We're so sorry for the interruption. With the influx of new faces around graduation time, we need to make sure we're not letting in anyone we shouldn't."

"Make it quick," said Señora Garcia, scarcely making eye contact with the officer.

Every girl Dani had ever been, from a scared child sneaking across the border to now, sat in awe of the way she dismissed him—and the way he let her.

"Of course, señora," he said. "If you could all just pass your papers to me, we'll have you out of here in no time."

The señora reached out, and Mama Garcia and Carmen handed their papers over, still looking bored. Maybe slightly irritated. But there was no fear.

And why should there be?

Dani hadn't moved. She needed to move.

"Come on, child," said Mama Garcia. "We don't have all day."

Of course, Dani thought. They wouldn't want Mateo's wine to be a degree over room temperature, now would they? "My apologies," she said instead, channeling the girl she'd learned to be in the classroom on the hill. The girl with iron in her bones, who would never let so much as a finger tremble.

You were trained for this, she told herself.

Once she handed the papers off, it was done. She would either be heading through that gate to the most exclusive community on the island, or down the road in handcuffs.

Every second was a year. Mama and Señora Garcia's papers came back in minutes, but all new residents were being double-checked. The air was growing thinner in the car. It had to be. Dani took slow, even breaths to keep anyone from noticing the lungfuls of remaining oxygen she wanted to gulp in. *Our restraint is our strength*, she told herself again and again.

Carmen's papers came back next. She didn't even look up as she took them.

The officer outside the car wrinkled his brow at Dani's ID. "It'll just be one more minute." Another officer joined the first, and together they held Dani's hummingbird heart in their hands. *If the papers didn't work . . .*

But there was no time for thoughts like that. Steel heart. Stone face. Dani shook herself mentally. She wasn't a little girl hiding in her mother's skirts when the scary men passed through the village. Not anymore.

In this moment, she was a girl who deserved deference, not the type of scowl usually reserved for dogs. How dare he.

Her voice was as steady as her hands when she rolled her window down and said in her most imperious voice: "Is there some kind of problem?"

The first officer's eyes went wide. "I'm sorry, señorita—" he began, but Dani interrupted.

"It's *señora*," she said. "Señora *Garcia*. And my husband is waiting very far up that hill for my safe arrival. We wouldn't want to make him impatient."

For anyone else, clenched fingers would have given it away. Trembling knees. Fear set deep in the eyes. But Dani was immune to it all. She was slick and smooth and impenetrable.

She was a Primera.

"Of course, señora, my sincere apologies, only we have a new verification system in place and . . ."

The glare Dani leveled him with cut him off midsentence. The irritation on her face was a tool, and it worked.

"But you all must be very busy?" the officer said, asking *her* for permission.

"We are," said Dani with a withering smile. "And if you consider my husband's position with the military, and the *rigorous* vetting process we've already been through, I'm sure you'll understand that this silly song and dance you're doing is really quite redundant."

The officer's face actually went red at this. "Of course, señora," he said, passing her papers back inside.

"We certainly appreciate you keeping us all safe," Dani said. "You can't be too careful these days."

"Yes, well," said the officer, waving at the car before turning toward the next. "Have a good day, ladies. And we're so sorry again for the inconvenience."

"About time!" said Mama Garcia. "*Somebody* had to put them in their place!" Dani settled back into her seat, resisting the urge to smirk.

Mama Garcia continued to fan herself with her oversized hat until the window was up and the car had been restored to its precise sixty-eight-degree temperature, but Señora Garcia gave Dani a small, approving nod.

The gate in front of them groaned loudly as two more officers pulled it open before them, the white stone drive almost blinding beneath the late-morning sun. The thrill of accomplishment made Dani feel giddy as the gate closed again behind them. Outside, there were still people under suspicion, but in here, she was safe.

Bold, she chanced a look at Carmen, expecting a look of irritation for the way Dani had impressed Mateo's madres. If this drive had been a competition, she'd just made herself the clear victor, and Carmen had never liked to be bested. Especially not by Dani.

She wasn't disappointed; Carmen *was* looking at her. But

her expression was far from envious. There was something sharp and appraising in it that Dani had never seen before.

In the face of that look, Dani realized: she enjoyed the power of being a Primera. The way it changed the posture of the people around her. The way it could make even an enemy admire her.

Outside the car, the complex proper was in full midmorning swing. House staff walked along the wide, tree-lined streets with harried expressions, while in the manicured grassy areas young Segundas played with children who would never know the feeling of hunger in their bellies.

Dani had expected this place to be sparse. Utilitarian. A place that would hold up to an attack from outside. The government of Medio was run from inside these walls, wasn't it? But while the complex might have been those things in practice, to the untrained eye it was nothing short of the most luxurious community Dani had ever seen.

Of course, she mused. The most influential people in the country lived and dined and socialized and raised their families within these walls. It wasn't as though the upper class of the upper class was going to live in windowless concrete bunkers.

"Here we are," said Mama Garcia, with the tone of someone unwrapping a rather impressive gift. All eyes swiveled toward the house as the car pulled into the circular drive.

Dani commanded her jaw not to drop. The house was an oasis of rose-colored stone rising from the expansive tropical garden that surrounded it. On its front alone, Dani counted twenty windows. Even Carmen had the good grace to look impressed.

"It's not quite as far up the hill as ours," Señora Garcia said. "But it's in a respectable up-and-coming neighborhood, and if Mateo continues on his current trajectory, you won't be living here for long."

"If Mateo continues on his current trajectory," echoed Mama Garcia, pulling open the door, "you'll be waving down at us and the rest of the island from your breakfast patio."

Señora Garcia actually smiled at this, her pride in her son the first crack Dani had seen in her perfect restraint. She cataloged it for safekeeping, this pride. Too much of anything could be a weakness. "Yes, well," the señora said. "We'll see, won't we?"

Dani had heard the whispers, of course, that Mateo was being groomed for the top job. But to hear it like this— intimately, in the very place where the office itself stood—felt like something different.

The presidency was the only governmental seat in Medio that was elected by the people. If Mateo ran, she would be a candidate's Primera, responsible for assessing the wives of his rivals for probing points, for showing the voting public that Mateo could be trusted.

But if he won, and she was allowed to assume the role her training had prepared her for, rather than just shuffling mail from one side of the house to the other, she would be the most powerful woman in Medio.

The tour of their "modest yet respectable" home took the rest of the morning. There were only two levels, but the floor plan was sprawling and open, with the same rose stone walls inside as out. The floors were tiled, each room a work of art.

It was a far cry from the dirt floor Dani had grown up on, she thought, remembering the fanned feet of her corn-husk dolls kicking up tiny clouds of dust in the summer months. The single bed the three of them had shared. When she'd moved into the dormitory at school, everything had felt temporary; she had still thought of that little slant-walled house as *home*. How long would it take to start thinking of this enormous place that way?

"And that's the house!" said Mama Garcia when they had finished at last, gathered back in the entryway.

"It's beautiful," Dani murmured, giving herself permission to be awestruck. She couldn't pretend it was anything less than magical.

Mama Garcia's eyes softened. "It's a good life," she said, tousling her hair absentmindedly. "Though it would be better if those miscreants across the wall were locked up in jail where they belong for carrying on like this and we could get rid of all these damn checkpoints. My hair is unacceptable after all that humidity."

There it is, Dani thought. It had been inevitable.

Señora Garcia grumbled her agreement, and Dani forced herself not to speak. It had taken only one morning for the ghosts of her past to invade her future.

"Well," said Carmen lightly, and Dani's chest tightened further still. Whatever Princess Carmen had to say on the subject, Dani was sure she didn't want to hear it. "I suppose they'll keep *carrying on* until they're not hungry anymore."

It was masterful, the way she did it. A statement that neither confirmed nor denied her sympathy. But the skin around her eyes was tight, a mirror of the way Dani's own face would have looked—had she been at liberty to express the tension now buzzing within her.

But what did Carmen care about the outer islanders? She'd made it her personal mission to make sure everyone knew just how deficient Dani's upbringing had been, and now this?

"I suppose," said Mama Garcia, to a statement that would have been incendiary if Carmen had been in rags at the border. "But I've been plenty hungry and I've never felt the need to disrupt the peace of an entire nation, for Sun's sake."

"Mateo will be home this evening," said Señora Garcia, skillfully changing the distasteful subject. "I expect the size and scope of the house won't prevent you from remembering your duties."

Dani was suddenly exhausted. They had toured the kitchens, the dining hall, three living rooms, a collection of studies, a library, and acres of gardens. Even without the unwanted foray into political commentary, she'd never imagined walking around a single house could make you so tired.

"Please make yourselves at home," Señora Garcia

continued, more tension in her face after Mama Garcia and Carmen's exchange. "It's been a long day, and there's still much for you both to accomplish before Mateo's homecoming. Once the house has been prepared, we've instructed Roberta to have dinner sent to your rooms. She's one of the girls from our kitchen, and she'll be assisting you until Daniela hires appropriate house staff of your own." Dani nodded her understanding. "Well, you have plenty of reading to do before morning," she said by way of dismissal, eyeing the thick folders in their hands.

"We're glad to have you both here," said Mama Garcia warmly, smiling at them in turn, her earlier distaste for the downtrodden already forgotten. "Daniela for the order and stability you will bring to our son's home, and Carmen for the warmth and beauty that will be your contribution."

"It's quite a job," said the señora with a self-mocking smile. "And Garcia men don't rise to great heights because they are docile or easy to manage. But, Dani, your background"—Dani cringed inwardly at the mention—"could very well have been a detriment. You managed to make it a strength. We know you're capable of rising to the top, despite any adversity. You and Mateo have that in common. Carmen . . ." She gave Carmen a once-over. "You've proven to have an attention to detail and an aesthetic sensibility that will keep him happy at home."

"And your children will be *lovely.*" Mama Garcia beamed. "We just want you girls to know we didn't make these choices lightly," she said. "We know you'll do your best to live up to our *very high* expectations."

Señora Garcia looked them each in the eye before turning away. "See that you don't disappoint us," she said on her way out. "The Garcia family isn't fond of failure."

And then, with a wave, Mama Garcia followed her Primera out the front door, leaving Dani alone with Carmen for the first time since they'd shared a seat on that fateful bus ride so many years ago.

Carmen flipped her hair in typical fashion, but for once, she looked determined instead of bored.

For a strange moment, Dani felt that same dangerous kinship flare to life again. Like she was looking once more at twelve-year-old Carmen, her straight shoulders and her careful braid, her eyes fixed on an unknowable horizon.

Carmen met her eyes, and all the air seemed to hang still. A constellation of possibility.

"I hope you read faster than you pick up on upper-class mannerisms," Carmen said at last, breaking their eye contact and the moment. "I'm not carrying you through this just because you've never lived in a house with a floor before."

Dani's posture stayed straight, of course, her face impassive, but everything inside her seemed to fold in on itself at Carmen's words. Would she never learn that there was nothing but misery waiting for her behind those eyes?

"I'm perfectly capable of reading a list," Dani said, too tired to fight back.

"Good," Carmen said, turning on her heel. "I'll start in the west wing and you start in the east. If we do this right, we should never have to see each other."

"Spoken like someone who can't see past her own *irrational* feelings," Dani said. Carmen, for once, didn't engage, and Dani wished she hadn't said anything at all.

Retreating for a moment to her new rooms, Dani took a rare unobserved moment to let herself slump back onto her bed. The relaxation was short-lived. Something crinkled beneath her, and without sitting up, she pulled a piece of paper from beneath her head.

Welcome home, Primera, it read, its edges worn and smudged. A single letter was all the signature he needed.

S.

Dani was no longer exhausted; she felt electric. He had been here. The fox-faced boy who had been both torment and savior.

Suddenly this room, which only an hour ago had seemed awe-inspiring, seemed like too much. Gaudy and over the top. With this smudged, honest sheet of paper in her hands, Dani felt the ache of Polvo stronger than ever in her chest. But not only Polvo. Stirring with Sota's handwriting was another whisper. A quieter one. Of the place across the wall where she had been born. A place that made Polvo seem like a paradise. A place her parents had risked everything to leave behind.

What right did the Garcias have to live like this when so many others went without?

What right did Dani have?

She was shaken from her thoughts by the faint trembling of the note in her hand. Was it an earthquake? A breeze from an open window? But no. For the first time since she was thirteen years old, Dani's body was visibly acting without her permission. She was angry, and her fingers had betrayed it.

She was angry with Carmen, for nearly luring her in again; with the Garcias, for having so much and appreciating it so little; with Sota, for soiling what should have been a satisfying if not joyful moment.

And yes, even with her parents, who had been so sure this life was better than the one they had fought so hard to earn.

Just as it had on graduation night—had it only been yesterday?—Dani felt her legs buzz with the urge to run. To take what was left of her self-respect back home, consequences be damned.

But what would that really change? This house would still be here. There would still be suffering out there. The world would still be the same. Just as unfair. Just as maddening.

"Señora?" came a voice from the hallway. "Will you be supervising the arrangement of señor's newspapers?"

Dani wanted to snap that Roberta probably knew the newspaper protocol better than she did, but she swallowed the words. She'd have a new staff to supervise after this week, after all, and she'd need the practice.

The trembling in her fingers had stopped as soon as it started. Dani checked that the room was secure and slid the note beneath the plump mattress. "Of course," she said when she'd answered the door, her voice reflective as metal. "Please, follow me."

Unfortunately, the questions followed, too.

Family harmony is based on four successful working relationships: the Primera with her husband, the Segunda with her husband, the Primera with the Segunda, and—perhaps most importantly—the three of them together.

—*Medio School for Girls Handbook*, 14th edition

⊢⇝✳⇜⊣

THE NEXT MORNING, DESPITE SLEEPING fitfully, Dani was up at the first lightening of the horizon. Section two of the pleasing-Mateo-Garcia handbook had stated explicitly that she join her husband for breakfast at sunrise.

If he bothered to show up this time.

Dani and Carmen had waited until the moon began its descent in the sky the night before—separately, of course—but Mateo had either not come home at all, or he'd returned long after Dani had given up and gone to bed.

This morning, however, she had left all revolutionary thoughts and sentiments beneath her mattress with Sota's note. She was determined to make a better impression on her new husband than she had on the night of their commitment ceremony.

On the terrace, the table was set for two, each place setting far more elaborate than anything Dani had seen at school. She sat, putting her napkin in her lap, trying not to judge the silver-edged plates or the heft of the cutlery. *Those aren't Primera thoughts*, she told herself sternly.

Her inner scolding was mercifully interrupted by the door to the terrace, swinging inward to reveal her husband bearing a small velvet box.

She had been braced for the cold boredom he'd shown on graduation night, but what she got was somehow stranger. When he turned, his face was mild, friendly, with no trace of the shadows she'd seen in his eyes.

"Daniela!" he said, approaching her, shaking her hand firmly. "I'm so glad we'll finally get a chance to chat. What an overwhelming night it was when we first met."

Dani knew it was an act, even his words seemed scripted and stiff. Even so, there was no helping it. That smile was contagious.

She smiled back.

"Not one of the calmer nights of my life," she said, though in the grand scheme of things it had hardly been the *most* overwhelming.

"I hope you'll allow me to make it up to you," Mateo replied, in a tone that made no secret of the fact that he expected her to, but he waited for her response all the same.

"Of course, señor."

He extended the box, its delicate hinges hiding something that surely wasn't appropriate for a Primera. Jewelry and trinkets were Segunda gifts. But there was no doubt that this box contained something . . . decorative.

Dani gave him a cautious look of thanks tempered with mild reproach. How would it appear to others if she started her life as a Primera sporting inappropriate baubles from her husband? How would Carmen react?

"Just open it, Daniela," Mateo said, reading her expression perfectly.

She obeyed. The lid gave way soundlessly, revealing the wide, round face of a silver wristwatch. The glass gleamed in the light of the early morning sun, the dull luster of the metal unmarred by any improper ornament.

It was beautiful. The perfect gift. Dani could feel the sparkle in her eyes, and she allowed it. He had chosen well; what was the harm in letting him know?

"May I?" Mateo removed the watch from its cushion and fastened it on Dani's wrist without so much as brushing her skin. "I hope it will go at least a small way toward apologizing for my rudeness the other night," he said. "As well as setting the tone for how things will be between us in the future."

"No apology necessary, señor," Dani replied. Though had he really offered one? Did he have his own handbook somewhere, with interactions scripted fifty years ago? She forced her eyes from the watch to his face. Rapt attention. No hint of distraction. "No matter how common the practice, marrying a stranger is an adjustment for anyone."

"Well said," Mateo replied, that smile lighting up his face again. Rehearsed, but effective. "Shall we eat?"

Dani settled into her chair, continuing to watch him as he opened his newspaper and she a book on Median philosophy she'd taken from the library the night before. A Primera didn't languish; she continued to expand her knowledge. If she could prove herself intelligent and useful, perhaps she would earn a role with a little more gravity.

In companionable silence, they waited for their breakfast to be brought in.

Mateo's face appeared wide open, even accessible, and Dani wanted to believe this was her real husband, the man she'd be sharing her life with. But the way he'd spoken lingered in the back of her mind. This was no eager young husband on his first morning with a new bride. This was a politician. A skilled actor delivering the performance of the year for an audience of one.

The only question was, what was hiding beneath it?

"Ah, here's breakfast," he said when the door to the kitchen creaked slightly behind him.

Carmen pushed onto the terrace bearing a heavy tray, and the intoxicating smell that accompanied it almost made Dani forget to be irritated by her arrival. Page twelve of the household manual: on weekday mornings, breakfast was served by the Segunda. On weekends the family dined together.

"Good morning, señor," Carmen purred, before turning to Dani, who flinched. Carmen wouldn't dare speak down to her in front of Mateo, would she?

"Daniela."

That was all. Dani relaxed her shoulders a fraction of an inch.

Carmen set the tray down, her body moving more sinuously than normal, the sway of her hips and the dip of her shoulders exaggerated in her white dress. Atop her loose curls was a crown of flowers from the garden in full, fragrant bloom.

Apparently, Mateo wasn't the only one performing this morning.

As Carmen took much longer than necessary arranging the dishes and utensils, Dani watched Mateo. His perfect husband mask was slipping, and beneath it was a predatory gleam, like the one Dani had seen on graduation night. One that said he didn't care about propriety or the rules. One that said he intended to take what he wanted by any means necessary.

For the first time, it occurred to Dani to feel lucky that Primeras were prized only for their mental faculties—or, in Dani's case, their ability to supervise a woman arranging newspapers. But used to their full potential or not, they were free of the burden of physical interaction. The fact had merely existed before, like the weather, or the nose on her face. But the choppy waters of that sea weren't part of her world, and at this moment, she was thankful.

Carmen turned around, the light breeze teasing her curls, a single flower petal drifting to the ground at her feet. The shadow melted off Mateo's face just in time. Little as Dani liked Carmen, she couldn't help a strange, protective flare from heating her chest.

"Enjoy your meal," Carmen said, before disappearing through the kitchen door.

"Shall we?" asked Mateo, back to his boyish charm. How many masks did he have?

"Of course," Dani said, turning to the table in front of them.

If anything could distract Dani from Mateo's motivations and Carmen's perplexing effect on her, it was food.

The hardest part of Primera training for Dani had been learning not to react to the smell or taste of it. To a Primera, food was a necessity, to be eaten at an even pace until one was fueled for the coming hours. Groaning, shoulder-slumping, finger-licking, and the like were heavily frowned upon by the Medio School for Girls maestras, which Dani had discovered to her disappointment on her first day, and most days of her first month there.

In Polvo, Dani and her mama had often eaten tortillas and salt alone for two meals of the day, saving the protein for when her father got home, overworked and hungry. The spread that had been laid out on her first morning of Primera training would have been the stuff of dreams, if her mind had even known to conjure them.

And the food in front of her now made even those meals look drab and uninteresting.

Small ceramic bowls littered the tray, each more seductive than the last. Tiny white beans in tangy green sauce, larger brown ones stained orange and red, slightly mashed with oil. A plate of cut fruit in a rainbow of colors, drizzled with citrusy yogurt sauce and honey, dusted with coarse chili powder. Dani's mouth began to water before she even reached the slab of crumbling white cheese, the dishes of chunky salsas and smooth sauces with tiny seeds that would sting a grown man's tongue.

Shoulders back, said the maestra's voice. *Ladylike bites, with generous pauses for conversation. Or at least breathing.*

"We eat simply during the week," Mateo said, spooning beans and cheese onto his plate like they were nothing, reaching for a steaming basket of blue-corn tortillas beside the tray. "On the weekends we'll all breakfast together, and that's when the real magic happens." He winked, but Dani hadn't recovered from the word *simply*.

The strange anger from the night before was back, though this time she caught it before her spoon started to shake, taking an unobtrusive but deep breath to bring her back to the moment.

"This will do just fine," she said, loudly enough to drown out the girl she'd been at eleven. Before Primera training. Before the bus to the capital. A girl who had thought a half-rotten mango an unspeakable luxury.

She dipped a tortilla into the steaming red beans, added a few flakes of cheese, and took her first bite in the name of that little girl, who in the back of Dani's mind was still wondering how anyone could be so out of touch.

"So, señor," Dani began, the sight of the newspaper spurring her into action. "I'd love to dig right in and understand what you do. Your work, the causes you champion, your interests politically. No detail is too small." She smiled, trying to seem interested rather than scolding. But she hadn't come here to make sure his sangria was the right temperature, and she wanted him to know it.

At first, Mateo seemed amused, but when she didn't break eye contact the shadow was back, the lines in his face deepening. "Why don't you make sure you can handle the correspondence and the staff schedules first," he said, his voice cold again. He'd dropped the script, and Dani's heart sank. This was the true Mateo after all. "I don't want someone representing me socially who can't accomplish a list of simple tasks. I'm sure you understand."

Dani felt the flash of heat in her cheeks that would become a flush if she let it. She had been trained at an institute for elite wives; how could he possibly think so little of her skills?

His eyebrows were still raised, like he was waiting for her response.

"I thought I'd finished the last of my tests in school," she said, her voice even and mild. "But of course, your wish is my command."

"I'll thank you to watch your tone," he said, his own face flushing now though his tone had gone colder still. "No one likes a mouthy woman."

Dani was stunned into silence. He was a high-society husband. A representative of his community, his government, and his family. And here he was insulting her during their first real meeting as husband and wife.

"Now, if you'll excuse me," he said, standing and pushing back his chair. "I've lost my appetite. See you at dinner, Primera."

Dani stood as well, reflexively, but he didn't offer her a hand to shake, and when he'd left the room she realized: he'd called her *Primera*. Apparently, her *mouth* had cost her her name.

Back in her office, she found comfort in the stack of applications Roberta had delivered while she was at breakfast. Gardeners, cooks, servers, maids. A house this size required a large staff, and if Mateo wouldn't allow her to be his partner or his equal, here was something she knew she could do well. Hopefully something that would keep her clear of him and Carmen for as much time as possible.

By sundown, she'd paused only to pick at lunch, and she had a full list of interviews scheduled that would carry her through at least three days. She placed the requests in her outgoing correspondence box and went to bed without dinner, daring Mateo to reprimand her.

As she'd hoped, the interviews kept her busy for the better part of the week. Housekeepers on day one, gardeners on day two, cooks on day three. She conducted them in various rooms of the house, both to familiarize herself with the layout and to make herself more difficult for Carmen and Mateo to find. At breakfasts and dinners, he was courteous but cold, and Dani found herself almost relieved that he'd dropped the act from the first morning.

At least when he acted like himself she knew what she was up against.

Next week there would be parties, dinners, fund-raisers, the beginning of her life as a high-society Primera. Next week there would be opportunities to show him what he was missing by relegating her to the sidelines.

By the end of the week, the house was fully staffed, the schedules written up for the month, and the correspondence basket was empty. Dani tried to find some joy in her menial tasks, tried not to think of her schoolgirl fantasies of touring the government offices and impressing the politicos with her knowledge and intellect.

Above all, she tried not to chafe under the weight of her new upper-class mantle, to forget Sota's note, smudged with the dirt and dust of her homeland, and to let the weight of gold pens and silver forks against her fingers and silk pillowcases against her cheek at night be only what they were, and nothing more.

Everything would have been peaceful but for Carmen, who seemed to have changed her strategy. She no longer lashed out with petty insults when she passed Dani in the house's halls, which at first had been welcome. But then Dani had realized: Carmen had replaced mocking and scorn with appraisal. Eyes that picked Dani apart and reassembled her, searching for all the shadows lurking between her bones.

She was subtle about it. Almost frighteningly so. Even Dani took a few days to notice. Segundas weren't trained in the art of reading a situation, only in anticipating emotional responses, so this skill of Carmen's was both unexpected and unsettling. Dani felt as if she were being constantly evaluated, but had no idea why, or what for.

The logical reason was that Carmen was looking for a gap in Dani's armor. At school, it had been enough to insult her low upbringing and her poverty. The other girls had been all too eager to join in. But here, her upbringing hardly mattered. She was a Garcia now, no matter who she had been before.

If Carmen hated her enough, she'd need some new material, and if she was determined enough, there was no telling what she'd find. With Mateo already underestimating her,

Dani couldn't run the risk of Carmen undermining her. It looked like she was going to have to do some appraising of her own.

At first, she took to avoiding Carmen during the day, seeing her only at dinner, when Mateo's presence forced her to orbit around him instead. Dani figured she'd bide her time, let Carmen think she had the upper hand. Figure out what to do with a rival she trusted even less than her condescending husband with his cold, still eyes.

When Dani had been in the house a full week, Señora Garcia appeared at breakfast, changing places with the departing Mateo. Dani was almost glad of the distraction. At least she wouldn't be forced to endure Carmen's strange vigilance with Mateo's mother at her side.

"How are you holding up?" she asked when they were alone, her face unsmiling but not unkind.

"Just fine, señora," said Dani, her expression neutral, her dutiful daughter-in-law manners on full display. "The house is beautiful, Mateo is more than generous, and I feel well-prepared for my duties here."

The older woman nodded approvingly, stirring her café with a tiny silver spoon. Her skin was a deep brown, slightly darker than Dani's own, her hair close-cropped and curly. It was the only thing the señora had in common with her mama, that hair, not that Dani ever could have said as much. It was far too nostalgic a sentiment for a Primera.

Something of it must have shown on her face, however, because when she looked back up, Señora Garcia's hawklike eyes were on her.

"We stick together in this family," she said, rather abruptly. "If there's ever anything troubling you . . ."

Dani nodded, not sure whether the words were an offer or a warning.

"Within reason, of course," she finished, pursing her lips.

"Of course, señora," said Dani. "Thank you." But inwardly, she laughed as the woman across from her sipped without loosening her lips.

Tell Señora Garcia what was troubling her? Had anything ever been so ludicrous?

Well, since you asked, she imagined saying. *There's this awful secret I have . . .*

"So," she said, cutting into Dani's imagination just in time. "Are you looking forward to the dinner party tonight?"

Dani seized on this appropriate conversation topic eagerly. "Yes, very much," she said. "I've enjoyed the quiet to get used to the house and the job, but I'm thrilled to meet Mateo's colleagues and friends, and begin actually applying what I learned in school . . ." She hoped the dig was subtle enough, but Señora Garcia quirked an eyebrow.

"You'll need to make them your friends, too," said Señora Garcia. "Well, as much as anyone is anyone's friend up here. It's a viper's nest, child, I'll not deny it. See that you have the strongest venom. Society has no use for a weak woman who clings to her husband's coattails."

For a moment, Dani wanted to break down, confide in the señora about Mateo's strange reticence to allow her a foothold in his life. But this was not Dani's sweet, mild mama, and something told her this woman wouldn't appreciate the confidence, no matter what she had said.

"Sound advice, señora," she said instead, sipping at her own iced water with mint and lemon as the morning grew more humid around them. "But I assure you, I've never been accused of clinging to anyone's anything."

The other woman offered a wry smile. "Why do you think I chose you?"

Dani sat up a little straighter at the compliment. The sun warmed her face, the glass was cool in her hand, and Dani closed her eyes for a brief moment, enjoying the feeling that nothing was in immediate danger of falling apart.

But then she opened them.

At first, she saw only a gardener, probably one of the many she'd hired herself just a few days before. He had climbed a ladder and was trimming a flowering vine that had wound around the ornate railing of the breakfast patio. It struck Dani as strange that he would choose to trim it right then, while she was entertaining, and she was halfway out of her chair to tell him so when he turned his face toward the light.

The angular features, the thick, arching brows, the fox's narrow smile. Eyes like obsidian, reflecting the sun. There was no mistaking him. But there was also no mistaking the emotion that welled up in her chest at the sight of him. The loosening of the bonds she'd tied up all her revolutionary sentiments with.

Suddenly, her fork felt too heavy in her hand again, her dress too impossibly soft against the back of her neck.

"Something wrong, Daniela?" asked Señora Garcia, who had her back to the railing.

"Nothing!" Dani said, just a little too hastily. "I'm . . . dizzy . . . from the sun, is all."

Over her shoulder, the gardener-who-was-not-a-gardener had the audacity to smirk.

"I think I'll head inside," Dani continued, standing and edging toward the door. "Big night tonight, as you know."

Señora Garcia pursed her lips again. Not a good sign. "If you're going to make it in this family, Daniela," she said, "you're going to have to develop a hardier constitution."

"Of course," said Dani, still backing away apologetically. Every twelve-hour day she'd spent racing up and down the dirt roads of Polvo played behind her eyes, mocking her choice of lies. A Vargas? Dizzy from the sun? The sand itself would get dizzy first. "Let me see you to the door, please."

"I'm more than capable of seeing myself out," said her mother-in-law with another searching look. "And you really don't look well. See that you get some rest before the party tonight; it's your first chance to show him who you can be."

"The most venomous viper in the pit." Dani flashed a weak smile, torn between terror at Sota's appearance and curiosity at the señora's words. How much did she know about the way Mateo was treating his new Primera? But there was no time. "You can count on me," she said, moving them both toward the door.

Señora Garcia gave her a once-over. "It's not me who needs to count on you," she said, then disappeared into the house.

Alone on the patio, Dani whirled around to face the intruder, but there was no one there. Just a neatly trimmed vine where chaos had been impending moments before.

She tried to look with only her eyes, to make sure she was truly alone. With Carmen watching her every move, she couldn't afford to be chasing shadows on the second-floor terrace. When she was satisfied that no one could see her, she crept closer to the balcony rail, scanning the lawn below, taking in the waxy leaves crowding the edges as they threatened to encroach on the civil gardens.

Dani had hired a dozen gardeners this week, but the only person in blue coveralls was sitting casually on the east gazebo stairs as if he had an appointment, and Dani was sure his application hadn't been in her stack.

I could go inside, Dani thought. *Just hide in my room and hope he goes away.*

At the thought, her heart sank in unmistakable disappointment. She could almost hear Sota's letter and all her previously contained thoughts rattling in the still morning.

His posture hadn't shifted an inch. This was a boy who was willing to wait.

Telling herself it was only to prevent what he might say if she left him alone, Dani took a deep, calming breath and descended the stairs to the lower lawn to meet him.

Though family is the center of a happy life, a Primera's friendships can take her far. Choose your social circle wisely, and maintain mutual usefulness for optimal social opportunity.

—*Medio School for Girls Handbook,* 14th edition

"FOLLOW ME," DANI HISSED AS she passed the gazebo. She didn't stop. "At a *distance*."

Her eyes scanned the grounds, the windows of the house open to the morning sun. There were a hundred places someone could be hiding. A hundred vantage points. Curious kitchen girls, downtrodden maids with a grudge against their employers.

Carmen . . .

Dani kept walking, focusing on her feet. She tried to act as though she were just out for an after-breakfast walk, no clear destination, just some exercise to aid in digestion. But it was hard to tune out the dangers: talking to a gardener in private would raise enough eyebrows, but talking to a card-carrying member of La Voz inside the government complex was good for a pair of handcuffs and a list of questions Dani could never answer. Not with the truth.

Not if she wanted to live.

Since the riots began, just before Dani was born, subterfuge had been the most powerful weapon of groups like La Voz, who no longer had anything to lose. They had been devastating in the early years, planning targeted attacks, delivering lists of demands, showing up two steps ahead of the military wherever they turned.

It had been war, until Medio got wise. Under the leadership of Mateo's father, who had risen quickly to the rank of military strategist, they'd stopped focusing so much energy on the border itself and started rooting out sympathizers to the cause. The hint of a whisper that you were working with the rebels was good for a one-way trip to a solitary cell. Families were dragged in and questioned. Even the innocent were forever tainted with suspicion. Soon enough, the informants all but dried up. No one wanted to take the risk.

The government had effectively removed La Voz's eyes and ears—the main source of their power. They never quite recovered, though they never stopped recruiting, either. In the border towns, they were almost as feared as the military themselves.

Now they had come to Dani's door. To collect on a favor she never should have accepted in the first place. And the worst part was, she wasn't entirely sure she was unhappy about it.

Behind her, she felt rather than saw Sota trailing her, like the darkness just outside a candle's protective circle. But whose darkness was it? His or her own?

Finally, on the south side of the house, she saw a small, sandy path leading into the trees. It was all the privacy she was going to get for now. Sinking into the part of the curious new Primera out for a walk, Dani peered into the leaves. The key to being in control of yourself, her maestras had taught her, wasn't in ridding oneself of emotion but in concealing emotion. To conceal a particularly strong emotion, you sometimes needed to layer another on top of it. Intentional expression was always preferable to unintentional.

She stepped onto the path, moving into the shadows, listening for any footstep heavier than a spider or a swallow.

None came. Not until Sota, his gardener's boots impossibly light on the path behind her, made his presence known.

The sound of a babbling creek was near enough; Dani could only hope it would mask their conversation. It was here, in the safest place she could find on short notice, that she turned to face him at last, determined not to let him know she was anything but furious.

Her anger was an intentional one, layered over her curiosity until nothing showed but fire. She prayed to the gods in the leaves around her that it would be enough.

"What in the salt and sea are you *doing* here?" she asked, resisting the urge to pinch his arm like her mama had done to her when she'd been naughty as a child. "Do you even *know* how much danger we're both in right now?"

"Relax," said Sota, yawning. "They won't see us. Nice digs, by the way."

"What are you doing here?" Dani repeated, refusing to let him placate her with his easy demeanor. "And I swear to every god I know it better be good."

"Feisty today, are we?" he asked, mischief dancing around his narrow mouth. "I have to admit I was hoping for a warmer welcome."

This time, Dani didn't have a clever retort. She just stood there, her mouth opening and closing without sound.

"Tough room . . . ," Sota muttered. "Look, you seem to be a straight-to-business girl, so I guess I'll come right out with it. I need a favor."

"No," Dani said. "Is there anything else?"

He actually laughed. "Hold on there," he said. "I wasn't finished yet. And if you'll notice, it wasn't technically a question."

"It didn't have to be," said Dani, adrenaline making her bold. "I never agreed to do anything for you."

"Ah, but you took my gift," he replied. "Some might say that you owe me one."

"Some might," Dani bit back. "But I don't."

Sota's eyes weren't smiling now. "I'm sorry, but it's not exactly up to you. Not if you don't want to give up all this." He encompassed Dani's entire life in one sweeping gesture.

She said nothing.

"Good, quiet. That'll make this easier. You're going to a dinner party tonight. It's very exclusive, as I'm sure you know, and I have reason to believe one of the little birds we've been speaking to is going to sing a very interesting song there. One we'd rather she didn't sing."

Dani stayed silent. He seemed determined to say his piece, but she wouldn't give him the satisfaction of admitting that she was curious about what he had to say.

"She's a new Primera, like yourself. Been married just a year. Her parents are hosting the party. It'll be the first time she's been in the same room as her parents since we got in contact, and we believe she'll attempt to come clean about our . . . relationship, to either her señora or her mama. Our intel says she's close with both."

"So you want me to, what, kill her?" Dani asked, her mouth getting the best of her in a way it hadn't since before her training. With Sota, she felt like that little girl from Polvo again. The one who could beat all the boys in races and leave her fingertips longest on a hot stone.

"*Observe* her," Sota said with an eye roll. "Listen in on any conversations she has with her señora or mama, especially in private. Then remember the details and be ready to pass them along at a time of our choosing."

Dani was silent again, but Sota was the more patient one. *He* didn't have a house full of people who would skewer him for speaking to her waiting just up the hill.

He looked into her eyes, not in the searching way Carmen was so fond of, but in a way that reminded her of still water or colored glass. This was a staring contest she couldn't win.

"I can't," she finally said, though the twinge of disappointment was back. "You don't understand. If anyone finds out I'm helping you . . ."

"It'll be the end of life as you know it," said Sota, not looking away. "It'll be arrest. Prison. Interrogation. It'll be the endangerment of your family and friends back home. Of people across the border you don't even remember."

"I don't need *you* to tell me that," Dani said. "I'm the one with something to lose here."

For a second that might have been a trick of the light, Sota's eyes looked almost sad. "Then I guess you'd better not fail."

"And if I refuse?" Dani asked, though she already knew the answer.

"It would just be a shame if everyone in that house found out how you got through the checkpoint," he said, like he resented being forced to spell it out. "Or how you got into school. Or how your parents got you across the border to that adorable little town in the first place."

"Blackmail," Dani said, spitting the word on the ground at their feet. "After all that inspiring talk about the Median government being the real criminals, this is your big play? Intimidate me? Blackmail me with a gift you gave me and the fear of a situation I can't control?" She couldn't help it; she had expected more. *Wanted* more, even. But this was just intimidation. Manipulation. The same kind perpetrated by all boys who thought they were stronger than girls.

Sota only shrugged. "Regrettable. But here we are."

"Let me tell you something," said Dani, stepping closer without noticing, suddenly not caring who heard or saw. "I grew up just inside that wall, in a place full of other people just like me. Scared people. Beaten people. The kids up here got ghost stories, myths, and legends, a lady with long hair searching the waves for lost children."

For his part, Sota stood, listening without impatience as she picked up steam. Around them, the bugs had gone quiet. The only sound was the water, carrying all their words away.

"Do you know what I heard instead? I heard about men with big boots and helmets who would come in the night, step on your garden and steal your food, and make your parents disappear. I heard about a dark room with no windows where they'd take you if you didn't behave. Where they'd ask you questions until you forgot what the sun felt like on your skin." Dani drew a shuddering breath. "I heard about a wall so tall and so wide that if you woke up on the wrong side of it you'd never find your way home again."

Sota nodded, just once, like he knew where she was going next.

"You know what the difference was between the scary stories they told my husband, and the ones they told me?" Dani asked, jerking her head up the lawn toward the massive rose house, filled with people who would never know her fears.

"Yours were true," Sota said.

"They were true," Dani agreed. "The night my best friend's papa was taken, her mama sent her to my house and she screamed and cried all night in my bed. The day my neighbor was dragged out after having lunch with his family, beaten and cuffed and taken away, never to be seen again. They weren't just stories. It was my life. The life I escaped. And now you want to come here and make those bad dreams real again, just to get what you want."

"Yes," said Sota simply, and Dani couldn't tell if she hated him more or less for the admission.

"You're not the good guys," she said, swatting at a mosquito buzzing curiously around her head. "I just want you to know that. I don't have a choice here. You don't get to pretend you're freeing me. You're a bully and a monster. Just like them."

"Understood."

"Who's the girl?" Dani asked, anger keeping her hands still for the moment.

"Jasmín Flores," he said. "She's a—" But Dani cut him off.

"I know who she is," she said, her chest tightening. "She

was my roommate," she continued, softer now, like she was talking to herself. "Until she graduated last year and became a Flores. Jasmín Reyes."

Sota's eyes narrowed, like he was surprised by this news.

"You didn't know?" she asked in a hollow voice. "Maybe you should find better intel."

"What do you think I'm doing here?" said Sota, cracking half a smile.

"She was my friend," Dani said, ignoring his joke. "How can I spy on her?"

"She was your friend?" Sota asked, going cold as quick as he'd smiled. "You must have a pretty low bar for friendship. What does she know about you? And I mean the *real* you? What does anyone? This world has made it so you can *never* have a friend, Dani; doesn't that bother you? Don't you hate them for it?"

"It doesn't *matter*!" Dani said, finally breaking, just a hairline crack. "It doesn't matter if I like them or I don't. If I want this life or I don't. This is what I have. This is how I survive."

Sota was quiet for a minute. "I understand that better than you think."

"So let me go," Dani said, using the unprecedented emotion in her voice, looking right into his eyes. "Walk away. Find someone else."

But he was already shaking his head. "You can do this," he said. "That training of yours . . . The way you slip into a lie like it's a whole new person. You're a hundred shades of a girl. You hold those shadows and bring them to life when you need them, and they're flawless. Look how far you've risen, how many people you've fooled."

Dani let him continue, but the heat that had flared to life in her chest went cold.

"And then those teachers at that school," he began, like solstice had come early and brought him everything he asked for. "They took all your history, your raw talent for deception, and they handed you the kind of training that gave you perfect control and restraint, taught you to ruthlessly value yourself and your potential above all. The way you can turn your face to stone. Use an expression like a weapon. The way you *see* everything around you . . . Dani." He shook his head, disbelieving. "They couldn't have made you a better spy if they'd been trying to."

By the time he stopped for breath, his eyes shining, Dani was all ice.

"Are you finished?" she asked, enunciating every word with perfect precision.

"I—"

"Good," Dani said. "Because you have a lot of nerve." She took a step toward him, the frost in her veins remaking her. "You think you can come in here and tell *me* what I am? What I know? What I can do? You think after a few weeks of voyeurism you're better equipped to judge my potential than I am?"

"I—" he began again, but Dani took another step forward.

"I'm talking now," she said, and he closed his mouth. "I don't *need* you to tell me how impressive I am, or how well-suited to your task. I'm well aware of my own skills. You think you can see something in me first? Give a purpose-starved girl a compliment and turn her to putty in your hands? Think again. I *know* I'd be good at what you're asking. But you said it yourself: I value myself and my potential above all. So what you've failed to tell me, besides some run-of-the-mill attempt at blackmail, is why I'd want to risk my life for you."

The ice had melted. Electricity buzzed through Dani's veins. Was this the grown-up version of the take-no-nonsense girl she'd been in Polvo? Someone who spoke her mind and never let anyone tell her what to do?

Sota was still silent, looking slightly dazed by her outburst.

"You can talk now," she said, raising an eyebrow.

"I'm . . . trying," he said with a self-deprecating smile. It took a moment for him to look up again, but when he did his face was more open. Honest. "Look, you're right. And I'm sorry. It was an insult to think I could bully you or flatter you, so I'll just tell you the truth. The reason you should help me is that people are suffering." He spread his hands helplessly in front of him. "They're starving. They're sick. They're dying just because of where they were born. And that's what we do. We try to stop that. Sometimes we don't succeed, but sometimes we do. And we need your help."

"Speaking to a girl like an equal," Dani said. "Was that really so hard?"

He smiled. She didn't smile back.

"So, if I do it, it'll be to help all those people. The sick, dying, starving ones. But if I don't do it, you'll still blackmail me?"

Sota shrugged, though this time he at least had the grace to look apologetic. "That's basically the deal, yes."

"I'm not saying I agree with you, or that you're half the savior you seem to think you are. But it looks like I don't have much of a choice."

"Thank you," he said.

"Don't thank me yet," she answered.

When he turned to leave, he saluted her.

It took Dani a moment to turn to stone this time. *A hundred shades of a girl*, he'd called her, and though she hadn't appreciated the delivery, he'd been right. Dani slid into her lies like a second skin. It was part of survival. She had no doubt she could do what he was asking her to do. The only question was, what would she be setting in motion when she did?

She thought about it as she wandered up the path, only shaken from her reverie by a rustling in the leaves to her right. From the bushes emerged Carmen, the smirk on her face and the sticks in her hair telling Dani she had just seen way too much.

While the Segunda's life revolves around the home, the Primera's domain is public. Social functions must become her second home, and her command of social graces may be the deciding factor in her husband's success.

—*Medio School for Girls Handbook,* 14th edition

⊹⊱✳︎⊰⊹

"ARE YOU FOLLOWING ME?" DANI asked, pulling disdain on over her fear, drawing the shadow's threads tight around her. "I know they don't trust Segundas with anything too interesting, but I'm sure you can come up with *something* better than this."

Carmen's smirk only widened. "Nice try, Primera," she said. "But you're not gonna convince me you're just out for a stroll. Not when I just saw your handsome companion leaving before you."

It was proof of everything she'd just told Sota that Dani kept her face impassive. She waited, hearing her maestra's voice: *Silence is a weapon; don't let anyone disarm you before you're ready.*

"He didn't look very happy," Carmen continued. "Though I can't say I blame him. I imagine there are more interesting girls than you to emerge from the bushes with. Maybe he just liked the scent of the salt on your skin." She smirked at her own insult, but she had just given Dani the key to her next lie.

The shadow wasn't a hard one to slip into. A besotted Primera with an innocent yet unrequited crush on the gardener. Leave it to a Segunda to reduce espionage to something as mundane as kissing among the leaves. Dani would have yawned if the situation weren't so dire.

She bit her lip, casting her eyes down. "Please don't tell anyone," she said. "I know you hate me, but I couldn't stand the embarrassment."

"Sun and skies, what did you do to him?" Carmen asked, the upper-class curse transitioning to laughter. "Did you recite the tenants of Primera restraint? Because I could have told you boys don't like that."

A tiny heat threatened to bloom in her cheeks, and Dani fed it, letting herself flush beneath her amber complexion. The blushing virgin. Whatever it took.

"It was nothing," she said to Carmen's shoes. Like it was an admission and not a denial. "Not that I didn't . . . well . . .

oh, why am I telling you this anyway? You'll just laugh."

"More than likely," said Carmen, already chuckling again. "But do it anyway; I'm bored of caterpillar hunting." She held out a golden-brown finger, and Dani noticed a green-and-violet caterpillar inching across it for the first time. It was just like the ones she'd pulled off the scrub trees in Polvo, and she was momentarily caught off guard. "Plus, I need something to do while I pick all this junk out of my hair. Here, hold him."

Dani was shocked into stillness as Carmen extended her hand, surprised when she reached out her own to meet it. The snuffling insect made its many-footed way across Carmen's index finger, pausing at the point where it made a bridge to Dani's hand.

For a moment, despite the uncertain nature of her situation, Dani's biggest worry was that the caterpillar would deem her unworthy of carrying it. That yet another piece of her childhood would be lost to her. But it acclimated to the scent of her in another moment, and its feet tickled as it traded Carmen's scarlet-taloned finger for her own plain, short-nailed one.

"So," said Carmen when it was settled, turning to the mess the bushes had made of her normally glossy hair. "You were going to tell me what to laugh at you for." She paused, wincing as a thorny branch took several strands of hair with it. "Today, anyway."

Dani sighed, every inch the girl whose beloved hadn't returned her favor, though she'd never experienced the feeling herself. "I know it's not . . . proper," she began, pretending to watch the caterpillar but really watching Carmen's face for cues. "But he was a gardener at school. He was always outside my window, and Primeras aren't supposed to . . . well, I was curious, I guess."

Carmen snorted. "You could have aimed a little higher."

Dani felt anger twisting in her stomach; of *course* Carmen Santos would judge a man just by the uniform he wore or the money he made. "Anyway," she said, "it was harmless. I never spoke to him. I never thought I'd see him again. But today I was having café with Señora Garcia and . . ."

"And there he was," said Carmen after a shower of leaves fell to the ground at her feet. "The future head gardener of your dreams."

"He . . . recognized me," Dani said, the caterpillar exploring her other hand now, its long green hairs tickling her wrist. "He said hello. And I'd always wondered . . . Well, anyway, he offered to show me this place, and I thought there wouldn't be any harm in it."

"He didn't try anything?" Carmen asked, mischief dancing in her eyes. "Come on, you really expect me to believe that?"

You mean besides trying to get me to spy on the Primera of the vice president's son? "Carmen!" Dani said aloud, scandalized. "As if I could ever . . ." She spluttered herself into silence, not entirely fabricating her discomfort.

"You never know with boys, huh?"

Dani folded her arms, shoving out the unbidden thought that Mateo had been the reason for her comment. That he'd tried something more than Carmen had bargained for.

"Hey!" Carmen shouted. "Look out for Hermanito!"

"What?" Dani asked in a panic, unfolding her arms and spinning around.

"The caterpillar!" she said, stepping closer, pulling the wriggling creature off the front of Dani's dress, Carmen's hands brushing her collarbones as she pulled away.

This time, Dani didn't have to fake her blush. She was exhausted. Things were starting to slip through the cracks. "When did you *name* him?" she muttered, trying to draw attention away from her glowing cheeks.

"Just now, obviously. Doesn't he deserve a name?"

Dani didn't say that apparently the gardener hadn't. "Listen, please promise you won't say anything," she said, pulling at the last vestiges of her patience, her feigned innocence. "It won't happen again."

"Sure, sure," said Carmen, returning Hermanito to a safer leaf.

Dani exhaled for the first time in what felt like an hour. "Thanks," she said, finding she meant it. She turned back toward the house before she could make any more messes, but Carmen wasn't finished.

"Oh, Daniela?" she said.

"Yeah?"

"You're pretty good." She winked. "But I still have my eye

on you." And Carmen meandered off toward the east side of the house, leaving Dani to walk the long way around, wondering what on earth she had meant.

She was back in her room, about to lie down and try to forget the world, when she realized she had only an hour to get ready for the Reyeses' dinner party.

It was already time to don another one of those hundred shades.

This one was as simple as zipping up the floor-length black gown she'd found hanging in her closet. Sleeveless, high necked, it was fashionable without sacrificing modesty. That's what Dani would have to be tonight. The green Primera at her first social event. The proud girl on the arm of the city's most decorated former bachelor. The trusted ex-roommate of Jasmín Flores.

She needed something well-executed. Something that would paint a thick layer over the truth: that she was, as of an hour ago, a resistance spy being blackmailed by La Voz.

"Señora?" came a voice from the hallway. "The car has arrived."

"I'll be right down," Dani replied, looking at herself in the mirror one last time. The cheeks that still hadn't given up their roundness. The lower lip that was always fuller than the top—her mama said it was from worrying at it with her teeth so much.

She smiled at the memory, tucked her cropped hair behind her ears, and closed her eyes for a moment. *The dutiful*

Primera, she told herself. Trying to contain her excitement at attending her first society party. Sharp-witted, but prone to a wandering gaze that took in the splendor around her and laughed self-deprecatingly at her own wonder.

A hundred shades of a girl . . . She'd never admit it to Sota, but it had a nice ring to it.

In the entryway, she adjusted her dress, lingering for just long enough to register that she was looking for Carmen. Dani scoffed at the empty room. She only wanted her rival to see her dressed as a perfect Primera, she told herself. To replace the view of her sheepishly exiting the bushes on the heels of a gardener.

But she wouldn't get the chance tonight.

"Good evening, Daniela," said Mateo, standing beside the car with her door open wide. "You look . . . nice."

Dani dropped her hand at the sound of his voice. No fidgeting. No nerves. She belonged in this dress. With the strange weight of the watch he'd given her on her wrist. She belonged with this man, his pale linen suit cutting handsome lines against the night.

Whether he believed it or not.

"Good evening to you as well, señor." She took his hand, allowing him to help her into the back seat. "The peach was a bold choice."

"I'm nothing if not bold," he said, with a wink that made her want to cringe.

She leaned against the back of her seat instead, focusing

on the trees and the purple dusk of the sky beyond, thankful for the quiet.

But too soon, they were pulling up the Reyeses' drive, their house illuminating the jungle surrounding it. "Are you ready?" asked Mateo, and Dani paused for a moment, as if she were steeling herself. In reality, she was testing the coverage of tonight's shade. Making sure nothing of the truth shone through.

"Yes," she said at last, her voice ringing.

"Well, we'll see about that," he replied, smirking as though attending a dinner party was something far above her level of qualification.

Remembering Señora Garcia's words, Dani didn't stay silent this time. "Señor, with all due respect, I deserve a lot more credit than you're giving me. If you want me to waste away filing invitations for the rest of our lives, it'll be your loss as well as mine."

Something gleamed in his eye, and in the dark of the car Dani couldn't tell if he was impressed or furious. "Well," he said, his voice inscrutable, "I guess we'll see about that, too."

When he turned to climb out of the car, Dani allowed herself a small smile. She wasn't sure why, but she felt she had gained some ground tonight.

Inside, they were greeted by a maid, who took Dani's handbag and escorted her and Mateo into the reception room, where the other guests were milling around with pre-dinner drinks. It was best to arrive slightly late, Mateo had said in the car: to make the room receive you, instead of the other way around.

Dani could feel her training glinting on top of her skin like a set of armor. This was a world she knew how to navigate. *Stay close to your husband until you've been introduced to everyone new. Make sure they see the two of you together. Break away just after, to show that you're independent, self-motivated, educated on your husband's positions politically, professionally, and socially, and ready to speak with his voice should the need arise.*

She had only heard about these parties. The ones where laws were unofficially passed, where deals were brokered over wine and appetizers and signed into being the next morning. Where the real currents of power flowed among people who had earned their places at the table.

Together, Dani and Mateo became the crowd's new center of gravity. He outranked everyone present, and Dani absorbed his status. He'd paid enough for the privilege of her company, after all.

"Oh, what a delight it is to see you finally settled, Mateo!" said their hostess, Señora Reyes, when they approached the bar. "And with such a well-regarded Primera. You must be overjoyed."

Jasmín's señora. Dani made a note of her dress—a dark red—and her hairstyle—a tasteful knot at the nape of her neck. She'd have to keep an eye on Señora Reyes *and* her daughter once Jasmín arrived. Whatever Sota had said of her, Dani knew better than to think a Primera would ever discuss something like this with a Segunda—even if the one in question happened to be her mama.

"Daniela was the top of her class at the Medio School for Girls," Mateo said to their hostess. "Highest marks in every subject. Her headmatron said she'd never seen someone so determined in all her years of teaching." Dani smiled at him, accepting the compliment, though she knew it was meant more for himself than her.

Once she'd been introduced around, Dani took her leave from her husband, approaching a pair of Primeras at the appetizer table to make some friendly small talk until the remaining guests arrived.

But she hadn't made it halfway across the room when she heard it: that wind-chime voice so familiar from her first four years at school. The young Señor Flores had arrived, Jasmín beside him, and Dani was no longer a guest at this party, but an enemy.

She'd only have to make sure no one knew it but her.

"Daniela!" Jasmín exclaimed the moment she spotted her. "Oh, Rodolfo, this is my old friend and roommate from school, the one I told you about!"

Dani smiled as warmly as was appropriate, greeting Jasmín with a kiss near her cheek and her husband with a deferential nod. "It's lovely to see you," she said when Rodolfo Flores had been swept away. "It's only been a year, but it must seem like much longer to you."

"A lifetime," agreed Jasmín, who couldn't have been aware that Dani was searching her for tension around the eyes, a falseness in her tone, anything to indicate she had something to hide. "But then again, it's like no time at all. You haven't changed a bit, Dani!"

"Neither have you," she said with a smile, but she didn't let her awareness falter. Did Jasmín's eyes suspiciously dart toward her señora? Did she seem eager to end this conversation—perhaps sneak into an alcove for a secret confession?

"Well, I should say hello to the others," said Jasmín, when the silence stretched a beat too long. "So glad we'll be seeing more of each other. And congrats on the catch." She winked in Mateo's direction before squeezing Dani's shoulder and winding into the crowd.

When Jasmín was gone, Dani realized her heart was racing, her palms sweating slightly against the slippery folds of her dress. Primera training had covered the repression and masking of emotion, but their exercises had never included a secret as big as this one.

She needed to get it together, and soon. They would be sitting down to dinner in a few minutes, and there would be eyes on her. Judging her worthiness to occupy the seat beside Mateo.

"Excuse me," she asked a Primera whose name she'd uncharacteristically forgotten. "Can you point me toward a washroom?"

"Through there, second door on the right," said the older girl, pointing, and Dani smiled in genuine gratitude, slipping into the hallway before she could be stopped again, opening the washroom door with fingers that trembled on the handle.

Get it together, Vargas, she told her reflection, the mirror set in a mosaic of glinting black stones and glittering tin pieces. Within the frame, Dani looked pale and frightened, moments from disappearing under the weight of all her lies.

Beneath it all was a moment captured in her memory like a photograph: Jasmín, the night of her graduation just over a year ago, dizzy with drink from the Segundas' legendary last-night party. She'd been loose and smiling, drunk on her own triumph as much as the rose wine. On the window seat, the full moon making a halo of her hair, she'd tipped back her head and laughed. A child's laugh. A simple, joyful sound.

This is it, she'd told Dani in a voice like silk and smoke. *This is the moment my life begins.*

And now Dani was going to try to take it all away from her.

The wine she'd had when she arrived tossed in her stomach like an angry sea. She couldn't do this. What would spying on Jasmín really do for the children starving across the wall? This was Sota's agenda, not hers. Did she even trust him to know what was right?

She would tell him he'd been mistaken. That Jasmín had never been alone with either woman. He wasn't here himself; how would he ever know? If she wanted to make change, she would find her own way.

Taking a fortifying breath that expanded her lungs to the point of bursting, Dani smiled at herself once in the mirror, just to make sure it looked natural. She was back to herself. Stone and ice. In control.

Before she could fully open the door, however, Dani stopped. There were voices coming from the dimly lit hallway outside.

"What is this about?" asked a gruff voice.

A second voice. A whisper of wind chimes. One she recognized right away. "I'm sorry, but it can't wait. Not anymore."

"Make it quick, then," snapped Señora Reyes, and Dani thought she could feel the air in the hallway thin as Jasmín steeled herself for what was next.

"I'm in trouble," she said. "I need your help."

Another pause. No answer from her señora.

Stop them, Dani beseeched the goddess of secrets and shadows. *Move them into another room where I can't follow.*

"It was months ago when it happened. Someone approached me, a girl from across the border. She asked me to . . ." Jasmín swallowed, hard. "She asked me to take Rodolfo's schedule. Copy it. Bring it back to her."

"You didn't!" gasped the señora, and Dani was all too familiar with the weight of her fear. The military boots. The windowless sympathizer cells.

"Of course not," Jasmín snapped. "But they've been back. They're very . . . persistent."

"We'll turn them in," said Señora Reyes. "We'll go out and tell young Señor Garcia this instant. He's heading the initiative to . . ."

"Stop," said Jasmín. "That's not all." Another deep breath.

Dani wished again that they'd go. Be interrupted. Save her from the choice she was about to have to make. But when had she ever gotten what she wished for?

"They . . . know something. About me," Jasmín said. "Something I'm not proud of, from back in school. Something that calls my Primera qualifications into question."

Dani felt the señora's heart sink along with her own. Apparently, blackmail was La Voz's preferred mode of operation.

"They say if I don't help them, they'll tell Rodolfo about Juan Felipe. The affair while I was at school. They'll tell the whole family. They'll ruin me."

She sounded close to tears, but her mother shushed her quickly. "Can you go to Rodolfo?" her mother asked. "Surely after a year he's invested enough not to throw you over for a youthful mistake."

Jasmín said nothing, but her expression must have spoken for her.

"Niña, I need you to listen to me carefully," said Señora Reyes, and for a moment Dani was stunned by the force of her envy. To have the woman who raised you nearby to turn to when things got difficult? Dani's mama wouldn't have known the first thing about what she was going through.

Yet another way in which legacy upper-class wives held the advantage. Absurdly, she recalled Señora Garcia's viper's nest. She was certainly the most venomous one here, though the señora would likely be less than thrilled to find out why.

"Do not do anything," said Señora Reyes. "Do not speak of this to anyone. I will discuss it with your father, and we will find a solution. Until then, you *will* act as if this never happened. You will avoid these people, run from them if they approach you again. Do you understand?"

"Yes." Jasmín sniffed. "Thank you, Mother."

"Don't thank me yet," she answered darkly. "Now go clean yourself up. Dinner is starting in a few minutes, and people whispering about your puffy eyes is the last thing we want."

Jasmín's footsteps were immediately audible. There was no time for Dani to escape. She could only ease the door closed, turn the faucet on full blast, and pray no one suspected she'd been listening.

A minute later, there came a tap on the door, and Dani layered every shadow she had into a new lie.

Dani took a deep breath.

"Oh, Jasmín!" she said when she opened the door, pretending not to notice the slight widening of the other girl's eyes, the fear like an aura around her. "I'm so sorry to hold you up, I just . . ." She sighed. "I needed a moment. It's a lot, in there."

The fear in her face thawed by degrees. "I remember," she said cautiously. "I spent half my first fund-raising event as a Primera hyperventilating in an upstairs coat closet."

Dani chuckled, as though this were helpful. "Thank you," she said. "I needed that. I'll get out of your way."

Jasmín ducked into the now empty doorway. "Hey," she said, before closing the door. "Give me just a minute to clean up. I'll head back with you, be your wingwoman in there."

Plus, you'll give yourself a solid alibi. "You wouldn't mind?" she asked instead.

"Not a bit," said Jasmín, a hint of that carefree, midnight smile on her lips.

Though a new wife's roots will always inform her, the moment the marriage contract is signed, her loyalty belongs to her new family. To her husband, her household, and someday, her children.
— *Medio School for Girls Handbook,* 14th edition

⊹⊱✳⊰⊹

IN THE DAYS FOLLOWING THE party, Dani's life felt like the careful defusing of a bomb. There were no instructions, and if she cut the wrong wire, the whole thing would explode.

At the center, the ticking clock was the fact that Sota had been right. Jasmín had given up La Voz. Her señora was looking for a way to undo the damage she'd done by daring to have a secret. Dani was supposed to be the obstacle in her path, but she still had a choice. She could say she hadn't seen anything, lie to the boy she was supposed to be lying for.

But what then? He'd find another contrived way to get them in the same room. He'd make her try again. And if Señora Reyes found a way to get back at La Voz for targeting her daughter, Sota would know she'd failed. He'd have every reason to turn her in. Endanger her family.

His inevitable return hung over Dani's life like a storm cloud. When the flowering vines outside her bedroom whipped against the window, she was up all night. When a new kitchen boy kept his back to her during dinner, she didn't stop staring until he turned around, revealing a stranger's face.

When Carmen watched her from across the dinner table, those dark eyes inscrutable, Dani sometimes imagined she'd given it all away. That Carmen knew she'd betrayed her family and her country, betrayed them all.

But Carmen never said a word, and Sota didn't return.

By the third day, it had become a kind of torture. There had been no word. No sight of him. All the glimpses she'd gotten had been her own mind inventing enemies where there were none, and she was left wondering if she'd dreamed the whole encounter.

But then, on the fourth night, when she turned down her sheets, there it was. Right in the place he'd left his first note. A card, looking completely foreign amid the pristine order of her room. It took her a moment to realize what it was, but when she did at last, tears sprang unbidden to her eyes.

This was no ordinary playing card. Not this far inland, anyway. Here, the playing cards sat unused in lacquered boxes, simple shapes and numbers inlaid on their surfaces in gold foil. They came out when the men at a party got too deep in their expensive liquor and one of them had something to prove.

But the card in Dani's hand was worn at the corners, its colors slightly faded from use. It spoke of the fine grit of the dirt near the border. The kind that stained more things than it grew.

As she took in the image of a tall, commanding robed man—blue cape tossed over his shoulder with the careless-ness afforded to the powerful, sword held loosely in one hand—the meaning came back as if the past ten years had folded into an hour. A minute.

This is El Rey de Espadas, she heard in her mama's deep, even voice. A person of strength, intellect, and ambition. A person who got things accomplished, who didn't hesitate. Two tears fell, making dark splotches on the dusky purple of Dani's dress. One and then the other before she got them in check.

In Polvo, the only work available was for the men. Hard, manual labor that left their backs stooped and their joints aching far too young. Women stayed at home. Cared for the children. Prepared the meager meals. But Dani's mother hadn't been content to sit and wait for her husband to arrive home. She had wanted to do her part. So she carried the cards, wrapped in a rough cotton scarf she said still smelled like her own mother. With her apron pocket bulging around the deck, she took Dani on social calls, where the children would play while her mother laid the cards out patiently in long rows, their beautiful pictures enchanting Dani before she even knew what they meant.

Her mama told the women of the town of small illnesses that were coming: a jealous eye on a child; a husband growing too fond of the fermented pineapple rind most families brewed in the dirt patches beside their houses.

She brought good news, too, like a new baby coming or a letter from home. She gave the women of the town a feeling that they were ready for what came. When she whistled for Dani at the end of a session, her pockets were always a little heavier than when she arrived. Two speckled, blue eggs from the Moreno's small coop; a chunk of honeycomb wrapped in wax paper; strips of dried meat pried from beneath Tía Elisa's floorboard, where they'd been stored for hard times.

Dani's favorite was always the candy. Coarse brown sugar melted and hardened again and again into a flat, round disk that stayed sweet on Dani's tongue for an hour.

When she was old enough, she'd asked her mama to tell her how the cards worked, and they'd sat on the floor in the long evening hours while beans cooked on the little stove. The squat clubs of the Bastos, the round, golden coins of the Oros. By the time she was eight she knew their meanings by heart.

But the card she now held in her hand didn't look exactly like Dani remembered it. Over the top of the king's pointed crown, an eye had been painted. Below that, in letters almost too small to see, two words: *Get free.*

Only someone who had been reading the cards her whole life would have noticed the difference. Sota had been doing his homework.

Dani sat cross-legged on her bed and slid into the meditative state that her mother said helped you hear what the cards were telling you. The whispers of ancestors long passed, the goddess in the stars; the gods in the clouds, trees, and soil that would guide you toward the truth.

A person of ambition and intellect. An all-seeing eye. *Get free.* The whispers were loud enough, even after five years away from home. In order to move forward, Dani would have to be alone—alone enough for La Voz to find her.

And they would be watching.

Dani slid the card between her mattress and the frame of her bed, feeling the edge of Sota's first note when she did. It was a safe enough place for now. Before tonight, it had seemed like such a hard decision. To ruin the life of a girl who had once been friendly to her, or to lie. To walk away from the bargain La Voz had forced her to strike.

Now, with the card beating the rhythm of her past into the mattress, Dani knew there had never been a choice. Not really. Her mama had read these cards so Dani's father didn't go hungry, so Dani herself would be healthy and strong when the time came to leave her family behind.

La Voz knew where her parents were—Sota had told her as much. And what would happen to them if the government found out who she was? What she was? Dani was guilty of everything that had happened since she left for school, but her parents had been the ones to purchase the forgeries, to smuggle Dani over the border into Polvo when she was just four years old. They had pretended to be just another border-town family for more than a decade now, but the truth was out there. What would happen to them if someone found it?

Nothing, she told herself. Nothing would happen to them, because Dani would make sure it didn't. She owed them that much. She owed them so much more. Maybe she didn't believe Sota could save the starving children across the wall, but it didn't matter. It had never been about what Dani wanted. How could she have forgotten?

With the card still whispering to her from below the mattress, Dani closed her eyes and said a silent prayer to all the gods that had protected the outer island. The god of the trees outside the window, the god in the cackling creek down the hidden dirt path. The god in Dani herself, keeping her heart beating strong.

I'm sorry, she told them, for whatever would become of Jasmín. But she would do what it took to survive. To keep her family safe. It was what she had always done. And if she could earn Mateo's trust and his confidence, maybe Dani's role could someday allow her to help Jasmín, if the worst happened. Maybe this one action wouldn't define her.

That night, for the first time since the Reyeses' dinner party, Dani fell into a sound sleep, and didn't wake until sunrise.

"Good morning," Mateo said when she finally made her way to the patio, the sun already three fingers up from the horizon. "I hope you don't mind, I started without you."

The food was already strewn across the table, and Mateo ate carelessly, missing the miracle that was delivered to him every morning on a tray. Maybe it was her decision to betray him, but this morning it took all Dani's restraint not to remind him of all the privileges he took for granted.

She sat instead, knowing it was more important than ever that she give him nothing to suspect. "It looks nice," she said, and he grunted in acknowledgment.

At least there was one good thing about this morning, Dani thought. If the food was here, that meant she'd already missed Carmen.

Cheered slightly by the thought, she ate with a Primera's sharp proficiency, gratified by the thought that she no longer had to reach for the persona that pleased her husband. She was learning. Fitting in. She was belonging.

But was she glad for her own sake? Or for the sake of what she had to do for La Voz? Already the line was growing blurry.

"Oh, I forgot to tell you," said Mateo, looking up from

his newspaper. "The kitchen girls are going into the capital tomorrow. You can make a list of anything special you'd like, and they'll fetch it for you while they're there."

"Like what?" Dani asked, genuinely puzzled. What could she possibly need that wasn't already in this house? She didn't even need three-fourths of the things that *were* in it.

"Oh, a specific book, a new pen, a dress or shoes for an event." He chuckled as Dani passed off her judgmental expression for wide-eyed innocence. "If they sell it in the capital, it's yours for the taking."

The anger was back. Dani smiled, layering gratitude over its jagged edges. She wanted to tell him how ungrateful he was for everything he had. How there were people where Dani was born who died for lack of medicine while he was sending kitchen girls to the city for gold pens.

But how would he even understand? He had only ever left this hill to direct men pointing rifles toward Dani's home, guarding the land of the wealthy from the land of the cursed.

"Is everything alright, Daniela?"

"Of course, señor," she said. "I was only thinking . . ."

His expression was attentive, curious, and Dani's mind was blank. She needed a shade, and fast. The stress of this many secrets was making her careless.

"Just, speaking of the girls going into the city . . ."

"Yes?"

A wick caught in Dani's mind then, and just in time. A way to solve two problems at once. "Well, why have the staff do it? I certainly wouldn't mind a trip into the city."

Mateo laughed. "Daniela, whatever for? You can take the car whenever you like and see the sights. Why would you want to do servants' work?"

"Aren't you a politico?" she asked, a little more edge in her voice than she should have allowed. "And aren't I your partner? Shouldn't we know how the people we serve live, if we hope to represent them well?"

Her husband's laugh softened into a strange smile. "That's quite a revolutionary sentiment, Daniela," he said, and Dani flinched at the word.

"I don't think so," she said, taking care to smile. "It's a new world now; we can't hope to govern it as our parents do, can we?"

Mateo's smile turned from amused to thoughtful. They hadn't yet discussed the presidency, or Mateo's aspirations, but Dani could tell he heard her talk of governing as belief that he had a chance.

Whether or not that was true, she could count on his ego to obscure the truth: that she needed to get to a crowded place to meet her La Voz contact.

"You're absolutely right," he said. "It's not as if you're going down to those awful border shantytowns or anything extreme. Why shouldn't we understand the hearts and minds of the capital's residents? I'm nothing if not progressive, you know."

"Of course," Dani managed. "Have one of the girls deliver

the list to my office this evening. I'll go tomorrow morning, early, and report back. Sound alright?" She stood to leave him, her appetite long gone.

"Sounds wonderful," he said with a greedy smile. "So long as you allow José to drive you and accompany you through the streets."

Inwardly, Dani groaned. Ditching an escort in her husband's employ was a nuisance she would have rather avoided. But she would take what she could get.

"And, Daniela?" called Mateo before Dani could reach the peace of the doorway.

"Yes?"

"See that you wear something bright. And tell the other Primeras once you've done it. I'd like people to know about this. To know we did it *first*." He winked, and Dani couldn't stomach more than a nod in his direction.

So, señoras, Dani thought on her way back to her room. *I did the most interesting and* progressive *thing last week. You see, I took the place of one of our house's kitchen girls to pass illegal information about one of our friends to a spy from La Voz! Mateo for president!*

This time, alone in the hallway, she couldn't help but laugh aloud.

As a Primera, the causes you choose to champion can cement your position in society. Choose wisely.

—*Medio School for Girls Handbook,* 14th edition

✠⊱✱⊰✠

WHEN THE CAPITAL CAME INTO view the next morning, hectic and chaotic as ever, Dani allowed herself a small smile. The car drove in, leaving the quiet and order of the complex behind.

Today, she wanted the chaos for more than just her own enjoyment: Dani had a plan. She just hoped Sota would be there to see her. Even if it worked, she wouldn't get much time.

The list of the day's errands was short. A nervous girl Dani remembered as Mia had delivered it to her office the evening before, looking utterly puzzled by the new arrangement.

Dani wondered if a Primera had ever run a house's errands before in the history of Medio.

"We'll need to hurry today, José," Dani called up to the front of the car. "I have a desk full of staff schedules, social calendars, and invitations back home."

José's shoulders tensed. The sides of the road were jammed with parked cars and waiting cars for hire, drivers shouting at each other to hurry, move, scoot up. Dani had gambled that the stoic driver would consider himself above rolling the window down to heckle the locals, and she wasn't disappointed.

"Can't we just pull over and leave it idling while we dart in?"

"No," he barked, his voice gruff until Dani raised an eyebrow in the rearview mirror to remind him who he was driving. "Apologies, señora," he said, just as gruff, but not as angry. "But this car is worth more than I am; I won't leave it unattended."

Too easy. "If the car's so valuable," Dani said, like she'd just come up with the idea, "why not just stay with it and let me go alone? I won't be long."

He opened his mouth to object, but Dani didn't give him the chance. "Look, José, I know you're used to a certain kind of girl, right? Upper-class ladies who can't find their own way out of a tea party?" Dani could see his cheek lift in a grudging sort of smile. "You know I was born outside the capital." Just *how far* outside, she would leave to his imagination. "I grew up throwing elbows in the border marketplaces. I can handle it."

"Señor won't like it," he grumbled.

"He wanted progressive," Dani said with a shrug. "Let's give him what he wants, huh? That's what he pays us for."

It was bold, brazen even, to speak of herself like the hired help. But it paid off. He chuckled reluctantly and pulled the car over to the side of the crowded street.

A symphony of horns blared to life behind them. José reached his arm out the driver's side window and waved them around with a sharp jerk that prompted a harmony of curses over the honking.

"You're an odd one," he said. "Be back in thirty minutes. No elbows."

"Surely this list is long enough to warrant an hour?" she asked, wheedling.

"If you're not back here in forty-five minutes, I won't be the only one who's unhappy about it. Understand?"

Dani saluted him and pushed her way out of the car quickly, before he could change his mind. The momentary high of victory didn't last long, however. The marketplace was massive, and she had no idea where Sota would be. If he was even here.

"Might as well start with the errands," she mumbled to herself, pulling out the list and choosing an item at random.

Sweet melons and agave nectar, that should be easy enough, Dani thought, pushing toward the largest produce stall in sight. But when she got there, ready to stand in line with the others, she realized they'd all parted to make room.

"It's really alright," she said, waving them back. "I don't mind waiting."

But they wouldn't budge. Women with babies wrapped on their backs, barefoot girls around Dani's age with coins and long lists clutched in sweaty palms. They waited for her to take her place at the front of the line, and eventually she did what they expected just to save them all any more of a wait.

"Señora!" said the girl behind the counter. "It's so nice to see you down here; to what do we owe the pleasure?"

How do they know? Dani wondered. Her forest-green dress was knee length and modest, undoubtedly expensive, but it was nothing so outlandish that it would set her apart. Her face had come from her mother and father, not from the high breeding on top of the hill.

Finally, the sun caught the face of her watch—Mateo's gift—and she understood. The band was royal blue and black, and with the silver it completed the Garcia family's colors. It wasn't just a gift. It was a brand.

"Just out doing some shopping for the house!" she said at last, realizing she'd been quiet for too long. People were starting to stare.

"Has . . . something happened to your market girl, señora?" she asked. "We don't normally have Primeras doing the shopping!" She giggled, and Dani smiled with her.

"My husband and I believe in staying in touch with what's happening outside the gate," she said, loud enough for the people behind her in line to hear without appearing to perform. "You can get used to seeing me here, and next time I expect you to let me wait in line." She turned to smile at the people behind her, and to her surprise, most of them were smiling back.

"That's a . . . unique approach, señora," said the girl behind the counter.

Dani shrugged. "There's only one way to change things," she said, hoping it would be the last they had to speak of it.

It was the same at the book stall, where Mateo had requested a rare volume on the rulers of early Medio, and the textile shop, where Carmen needed a bolt of custom-embroidered linen for the Garcia tailors. The eyebrows went up, the lines melted away, and the stall and shopkeepers fell all over themselves to be helpful.

The speech she'd delivered at the market stall got more notice at the book stall, and by the time she reached the textile shop, people were already whispering, her reputation preceding her. Mateo had certainly gotten what he wanted today, and if Sota or any other La Voz contacts were in the market, they would know Dani was here.

And that she was alone.

By the time the errands were finished, only twenty of her forty-five minutes had elapsed. She slipped her watch into a pocket of her sensible dress before returning to the streets. For the next portion of this adventure, it would be better not to be recognized.

The orders she'd made would be shipped to the house, so she was unencumbered as she crossed the marketplace purposefully, wanting to put some distance between where she'd made a name for herself and where she'd have to attract Sota's attention.

Dani stared too long at everyone with the right height or coloring. Was he a stooped-shouldered boy in rough cotton, haggling over the price of chickens? A vendor of glittering spun sugar in whimsical shapes?

Most importantly, if he didn't find her, would he consider it her failure or his own?

Passing a crushed-ice stall with a hundred flavored syrups, Dani joined the line, and this time no one seemed to recognize her. She rubbed absentmindedly at the place where the watch's familiar weight was missing; how quickly she'd grown used to it.

"Excuse me," came a low voice from behind her. "But you've taken my place in line."

Dani turned to lock eyes with a girl a little older than herself—tall, leanly muscled, her loose, black pants and close-fitted top giving no indication of her social standing.

Her eyes were startling, the flat silver of a weathered coin. Dani thought they weren't a pair of eyes you were likely to forget.

"Pardon?" she asked, a prickling at the back of her neck telling her this situation was more than met the eye.

"I *said* you've stolen my place," the girl repeated, louder now.

But Dani had been alone at the end of the line, and she knew she hadn't seen the girl. Her heart picked up speed. José had expressly forbidden her from throwing an elbow, but the girl was walking closer now, and the expression in those strange eyes meant business.

"Listen," the girl said, her voice low and menacing. People were starting to stare, but the girl was close enough now that they couldn't hear the words she whispered. "He's in the women's washroom near the north entrance. Hurry."

Dani locked eyes with her and nodded once, a short, sharp thing. "I don't want any trouble," she said for the benefit of the crowd, backing away slowly. "You can have my spot in line, will that solve it? There are plenty of places to buy a shaved ice."

"See that you find one," the wolf-eyed girl said coolly, and turned her back on Dani.

She had fifteen minutes left, and she wanted to waste as few as possible navigating the busy aisles. The watch was out of the question, so Dani felt herself sliding back into the persona that felt most like herself. The resourceful, scrappy girl from Polvo who could slip through a crowded street festival unnoticed and come back with eyes shining and pockets full of sweets and pennies.

Elbows pressed reluctantly to her sides, Dani made her

way through the crowd like a fish against the tide, the seconds slipping away faster than she liked, her heart racing at the prospect of what she was about to do.

Treason. The word echoed in every footstep. She'd been approached, yes. She'd already failed to turn in a known member of the country's most notorious criminal organization. But today would be different. Today, she was willingly passing information about an inner-islander to a criminal. Today, she was a criminal herself, in deed, not just by birth.

Outside the market's public washroom, a janitor stooped over a dustpan, and Dani's heart seized. But before she could panic, he looked up and winked, gesturing through the door before returning to his sweeping.

Inside, the gray stone of the walls was illuminated by shafts of bright sunlight from high windows. Sota stood in the center of one, his face turned up, a vulpine smirk on his face. "You made it," he said with a measure of pride.

"It wasn't easy," Dani replied, her voice clipped. Now that she'd accomplished the impossible, the reality of the situation was setting in.

Treason, came the whisper again. There was no going back after this.

"There was no going back even before you met me," Sota said idly, his face still turned up toward the light. Dani didn't let herself wonder if he could hear her thoughts. She had worries enough as it was. "You were a criminal the moment you were born, and surviving every day has multiplied those crimes a hundred times."

"I thought we had a conversation once about you explaining my own life to me."

"We did," he acknowledged with a smile. "Old habits."

"So tell me something true," she said. "Something that makes you more than just a phantom who appears at key moments and tells me who I am."

"We hardly have time—" he began, but Dani interrupted.

"Then you better speak quickly." She was through letting him have the upper hand. Even if it made her late, it was time to show him she couldn't be bullied.

Sota's eyes went dark for a moment, then he raised them to hers unflinchingly. "My parents were killed trying to cross the wall. Killed because my father was sick and dying and my mother tried to get him to a hospital. Shot down. Like dogs. Because they needed medicine, and the men on the other side decided they were too unseemly to deserve it."

Dani had often turned her face to stone in her short life, but never like this. Never from shock, and sadness. Never involuntarily. No word or gesture seemed right. Sota's eyes hid nothing of his pain, and he didn't look away, forcing Dani to confront it.

"I was eight years old," he said. "I waited. They never came back."

"I'm sorry," Dani said softly, finding she meant it. She

barely remembered her own crossing, but what she did remember was the fear in her father's eyes. The knowledge, even as a boisterous, small child, that she had to stay quiet and still no matter what.

"Don't be sorry," he said, the door closing behind his eyes as quickly as it had opened. "Be useful."

For a moment, he had been human. Just a boy, not much older than Dani, who had suffered at the hands of the same people. But facing her now, he was an agent of La Voz, and he was here for her intel.

"We're almost out of time," Sota said, almost gently. "I gave you what you asked for. Now it's my turn. What did you hear at the party?"

Last chance, Dani told herself. To lie and buy Jasmín some time. To put off the moment of her lost innocence. No matter what Sota said, no matter what the police believed, Dani knew there was a difference. Between what you couldn't help and what you did by choice. It was the choices that changed you.

"Dani . . . ," Sota said, a question and a warning.

She closed her eyes, asking for strength, for forgiveness. There was enough divinity in the sunbeams alone for her to know her mother's gods were here, watching. She sent a silent promise to them that this wasn't the end. That she would make this right, one way or another.

"It was just like you said," she told him. Choosing. For her parents? For the people suffering? For eight-year-old

Sota, and so many like him, who had lost everything? She didn't know. Maybe she never would. "Jasmín told her señora everything at the party. The girl who approached her, the blackmail La Voz is holding over her. She said she didn't want to risk her husband finding out about her youthful indiscretions, and she didn't know how much longer she could hold out before doing what you asked of her."

"What did her mother say?" Sota asked, eyes closed again, like he was trying to see her memories.

"She told Jasmín to tell her husband. Come clean. Turn her contact in. But Jasmín doesn't trust him not to throw her over and take away her whole life."

"So what's the plan, then?" he asked, opening his eyes, looking right into Dani's.

"I don't know the specifics," Dani admitted. "Señora Reyes just said she'd take care of everything, and not to worry."

Sota nodded. "That's all?"

Dani held his gaze for a moment before returning his nod, her jaw clenched, already thinking of how she could move higher in Mateo's estimation, gain a foothold so she could be heard. So what had happened to Jasmín never had to happen to anyone else.

Breaking into Dani's thoughts, Sota took a step closer to her, halving the distance between them.

The marketplace was in full swing outside. No one knew she was here.

He took another step, out of the light now, his face cut

with shadow. She could see every one of his eyelashes—long for a boy's, she thought deliriously. Much too long.

"Tell me again," he said, his voice husky and low.

"What?" she stuttered. "Tell you what?"

"Tell me again what happened with Jasmín. What you did. What you heard."

No one will hear you scream.

She told him. Haltingly, second-guessing each sentence to make sure it was the absolute truth. There was no trace of the boy he had been when he spoke of his parents. He emanated the power of the organization he represented, and Dani was afraid.

When she had finished, he stepped closer again. There was almost nothing between them now. A scant few inches of shadowed room and clothing separating skin from skin, pulse from pulse. Dani had never been so close to a boy before—not even her husband. It was against the rules, and more than that, she'd never wanted to. Never even been curious.

But there was a dark power to closeness, and it was here, between them. Dani hardly dared to breathe.

"Daniela," Sota said, his voice low and hypnotic. "I need you to be very, very honest with me right now, do you understand?"

She nodded. Dust motes floated down through the shafts of light. Everything was unbearably still.

"Did you tell anyone else about this? About Jasmín?

About me, or our visits, or your work for La Voz? Even a single word?"

"No," Dani said, just a whisper. Barely a breath. "No one."

"Tell me again," he said, leaning in a fraction of an inch.

Dani found herself leaning closer, too, pursuing the source of this strange, shadowy force that had sprung to life between them. "I didn't tell anyone," she said, her voice stronger.

Sota breathed in, deep, like he could smell the truth or lie in her words on the air. Whatever he sensed there must have been enough, because the spell broke, the dust motes scattering around him as he stepped back into the light, leaving Dani breathless in the shadows.

"Thank you," he said, his voice businesslike again. "For your help, and for your discretion."

Dani straightened herself with as much dignity as she could muster, but Sota wasn't finished. "Your husband and his father are taking a trip to survey the border sometime next week," he said without preamble, reaching into his jacket for a tiny drawstring bag. "There have been more incidents involving La Voz than usual, more protests, and it's their job to suggest the necessary modifications to security protocol. When they return home, we'll need to know—"

"Wait, wait," Dani interrupted, holding up a hand. "What are you doing? You did me a favor. I did you a favor. We're done. This is over." She turned to walk away, but the heaviness in her chest told her she wouldn't get far.

Sota was in front of her before she even heard him move, the door behind his eyes opening again, a fraction of the light shining through. "Haven't we been having the same conversation here, Dani?" he asked, and his voice sounded tired. "Could you really walk away? Knowing what's at stake? Knowing you could help, if you wanted to?"

Dani knew her time was running short, if it wasn't already up. But a million images were flashing through her mind, from her fractured memories of crossing the border to her childhood in Polvo, where so many went without food and the military terrorized anyone suspected of crossing. Every one of Carmen's pointed barbs. The visceral fear Dani had felt the night of the riot at school.

The way Sota's note had trembled in her fingers at the thought of everything the Garcias took for granted.

The growing resentment she felt for her husband, who controlled everything and wanted for nothing.

"We need the exact date of the border visit," Sota said, though Dani still hadn't answered. "The schedules of the higher-ups, especially regarding travel that could be compromised, are locked up tighter than the cell we'll both be in if anyone finds out about this. When you get the date, you'll place stones on your windowsill corresponding with the day: one for Lunes, two for Martes, et cetera." He rattled the bag in his hand.

"What are you going to do with it?" Dani asked, mostly to buy herself some time. "The date, I mean."

Sota raised an eyebrow. "Your intel will serve the same purpose all our efforts serve," he said. "The liberation of those who have been unfairly oppressed. The upset of a power structure that prioritizes the wealthy and leaves the rest to suffer. We're fairly consistent in that regard." He held out the bag, but Dani wasn't ready to take it.

"That's all fine and well," Dani said. "But what does it have to do with me? Or Mateo? Or his father?"

Sota sighed, his eyes rolling back in exasperation. "Your husband's father has been at the president's side for a decade, doing all the things the man himself can't for fear of losing popular approval. The president is the only person in the government elected by the popular vote, so—"

"I'm familiar with the basic structure of my own government, thank you," Dani said, not bothering to hide her irritation. But Sota didn't even slow.

"Who do you think is responsible for the militarization of the border?" he asked. "For the shoot-on-sight policy regarding border crossers?"

Her mind flashed back to Sota's parents. To the fear in her father's eyes as they followed a flashlight's beam to safety. This time she didn't interrupt, but her face, for once, must have spoken for her.

"If you think that's bad," Sota said, "have a chat with Mateo about his plans for the future. We need you, Dani, and if you understood what he was capable of, I think you'd feel differently about your role." He waited, but in vain. Dani didn't know what to say. "All I ask is that you keep your eyes open," he said, setting the bag of stones on the lip of the sink.

Dani took it, weighing it in her hand, listening to the stones clicking together.

"We know the trip is happening sometime next week, so you have three days to get us the info in time for us to use it," Sota said, catching her eye. "This is your chance. To do more than sit idly by as people are rewarded for doing wrong."

When he climbed up and out the high window, she barely noticed. He'd left something much worse in his place.

A true Primera is not concerned with the physical. She lives in the realm of order, of reason, and she must stay there at all costs.
—*Medio School for Girls Handbook,* 14th edition

⊢⟩✳⟨⊣

"SO, HOW DID IT GO in the marketplace today?" Mateo asked over dinner.

Dani stopped surreptitiously watching Carmen for long enough to catch the speculative gleam in his eye. "It was fine," she said. "Excellent melons."

Carmen snorted into her soup, then passed it off as a cough.

"I couldn't care less about the melons," Mateo replied impatiently. "Were you seen? Were you talked about? What did people say?"

Dani fought the urge to roll her eyes. After the day she'd had, she wasn't in the mood to feed Mateo's insatiable ego. Unfortunately, that particular obligation was on page one of the Garcia household manual—in so many words.

"They were quite impressed, I assure you," she said lightly, and no more.

Mateo's expression soured. "I want *details*," he said tersely. "I sent you out there as my representative. To elevate our image in the eyes of the capital's citizens. You've been clamoring for more responsibilities, haven't you? I want to know how it went."

"I held up my end of the bargain, Mateo," Dani assured him. "I said the family name aloud as many times as I could manage. I fielded a thousand questions about how we'd chosen to break from tradition. I spoke of your interest in the welfare of the capital's citizens at length with *actual citizens* of the capital." *I met in secret with a member of La Voz to pass information about friends of the family. In a women's bathroom. I felt his breath against my neck . . .*

"Well, why didn't you just say it that way?" Mateo asked with a laugh. "Women, I'll never understand them."

With only his Primera and Segunda present, there was no one in the room to laugh at his joke. While he was busy congratulating himself on it, Carmen shot Dani a look over her napkin. It almost looked . . . conspiratorial.

Little as Dani enjoyed Carmen normally, the way she subdued herself in their husband's presence was nothing short of disappointing. Who was Carmen without the sharp edge of her wit? Her immediate retorts?

Mostly giggling and hair tossing, as it turned out. Not even a worthy opponent.

Dani shook herself mentally. She didn't have time to debate with herself about Carmen's masks or motives.

All through the drive home from the capital, and during the first course of dinner, she'd been hearing Sota's words again and again in her head. About Mateo and his father. Their views. Their contributions to the hell that was life at the border.

Dani didn't know much about Mateo beyond his tendency to be condescending and cold, unconcerned with the happiness of those around him. She didn't trust him, but she didn't trust Sota, either. In a battle between two men trying to control her, she'd chosen herself. She'd draw her own conclusions before risking her life to work against her husband.

But that meant learning more about Mateo, and that was something he'd actively worked against since she arrived.

"Mateo, how was work today?" she asked casually. In any other household, it would have been an appropriate question for a Primera to ask. She needed to be knowledgable about her husband's career in order to champion him in society. Mateo took a long time looking up from his dish, his muscles rigid beneath his expensive shirt.

"It was very busy," he said at last, and his tone said not to press further.

But it was Dani's job to press further, and tonight she wasn't willing to let him stop her.

"I'm afraid I don't know much about what you do, day to day," Dani said, ignoring the tension rising between them. "What's your favorite part about it? Do you work with your father much?" *Are you helping him pass laws that get innocent people killed?*

"It's quite complicated," he said, each word clipped. "I assist a great many important people in doing important things, and I don't like to be bothered about it at the dinner table."

"I don't mean to be a bother," Dani said, knowing she was on thin ice, continuing anyway. "But I'm your Primera. I'd like to be part of your life."

"You'll be exactly as much a part of my life as I tell you to be, when I deem it necessary," he said, and there was anger in his words now, not just dismissal. He knew he was acting strangely, leaving her out of the loop, and his defensiveness proved it. Had Sota been right about him? Was he behind the ruthless policies keeping her people sick and starving?

Either way, Dani had pushed enough for one night. Any further and she might not recover. "Apologies, señor," she said, looking down at her plate. "Just naturally curious, I suppose."

Mateo didn't reply.

They returned to their dinner in silence, Dani's mind racing with possibilities, Carmen taking advantage of his momentary distraction to stare unabashedly at Dani, like she was a mostly finished puzzle with a piece out of place. They continued this way until Mateo dropped his fork noisily on his plate.

"Well, ladies," he said. "I must retire to my office for the night." His eyes were cold on Dani's as he said it. He wanted her to know her behavior had angered him. But he wouldn't be rid of her that easily. "Enjoy your evening," he said, but this time he looked at Carmen.

When he was gone, Dani sank even deeper into her spiraling thoughts. He had certainly been cold before, but he was making a habit of avoiding her questions about his work, his life. He was actively preventing her from doing the job his family had chosen her for.

Deviating from the standard marriage structure was frowned upon on the inner island; if people found out he was hiding things from the woman who was supposed to be his partner, eyebrows would no doubt be raised. What was he hiding that was worth that?

"Are you . . . okay, Daniela?" Carmen asked, when they'd been sitting in silence for far too long. "You don't seem your normal prim and boring self tonight."

"What does it matter to you?" Dani asked wearily.

Carmen only shrugged. "Just wondering, that's all. You don't have to talk to me if you don't want to."

Dani's head spun with exhaustion. Since when did Carmen say anything to her that wasn't laced with ridicule? Was this some kind of a trick? Was she trying to uncover the reason for Dani's distraction so she could use it against her later? She stopped herself before she could take it any further. She didn't have the energy to figure out Carmen's motivations tonight.

"I don't really feel like talking to anyone," she said, settling for neutral as she placed her napkin on her plate and stood. "But . . . thanks," she said as an afterthought, not daring to meet Carmen's eyes when she did.

The next morning, Mia tapped on the door to summon Dani to breakfast.

"Will you please tell señor I have a headache?" Dani asked through the door, trying to make her voice sound as pitiful as possible. "I'll join him tonight for dinner."

"Of course, señora," said the muffled voice from the other side. "But Señor Mateo won't be at home this evening. I'll send your regrets."

Dani thanked her and settled gratefully back into bed. She would take this time to gather her thoughts. The stones were well hidden in a desk drawer behind her extra ink, but they weighed heavily on her mind. After the mess she'd made of things at dinner, she didn't dare question him directly again. The last thing she needed was for him to become suspicious.

But that left just one course of action, and it wasn't an idea Dani relished.

Outside, low clouds made the day muggy and strange. There was a restless static in the air, like the moment before a lightning strike. Dani watched the sun travel behind the clouds for most of the morning, the sky changing from silver to the storm-yellow of an old bruise. She would have to wait for the perfect time, and right now they all seemed equally dangerous.

When another tap came at the door, Dani groaned into her pillow. "I'm sorry, but I have a headache today," she called. "I'll be down for dinner!"

"Please," said a voice from outside. "Save it for someone who believes you."

Carmen. Dani jumped out of bed, shock motivating her where nothing else had. She crossed to the door in her dressing gown, feeling suddenly self-conscious.

Carmen was never underdressed—unless you counted too much bare skin. Today's dress was plunging, the deep purple of a summer night's sky. How did her skin just . . . glow against any color?

"What are you doing here?" Dani asked. Carmen had never visited her rooms before.

"Thought we'd spend the day together," Carmen deadpanned. "Paint our nails, talk about hair care and boys?" When Dani didn't respond, she rolled her eyes. "The Garcia tailor is here to do our fittings. I'm supposed to bring you to my room."

"Oh." Dani cleared her throat, dispelling the strange illusion Carmen's sarcasm had cast. One where they were the kind of people who could spend the day together. What was wrong with her? "I'll just get dressed and meet you down there."

"No point," said Carmen, already turning away. "She's just gonna undress you again anyway, right? Come on."

Walking through the house midmorning in a dressing gown with bare feet was not one of the more decorous moments of Dani's life. Two of the cleaning girls stared openly until Carmen clucked her tongue at them.

"I wish you had let me get dressed," Dani muttered under her breath.

Carmen shrugged in a way that was becoming troublingly familiar. "You're still wearing more than me."

That much, at least, couldn't be disputed.

When they arrived at Carmen's suite, she pushed the doors open like there was nothing special beyond them, but Dani had to tighten her jaw to keep it from dropping. The room was the opposite of her own in every way. The carpet swallowed Dani's bare foot nearly to the ankle, and opposite a large window overlooking the garden, a gilded, three-paneled mirror took up an entire wall.

It was a luxurious suite, fit for a luxurious girl, and Carmen moved in it like she'd never expected less, at home in her surroundings in a way Dani feared she could never be.

"She'll be here in a minute," Carmen said, wandering into a closet the size of the houses in Polvo. "Make yourself at home."

Dani almost scoffed aloud at that. Was there a place in the world she could possibly feel less at home? The most she could manage was to perch on the corner of a royal-blue settee and wait for Carmen to return, or for the tailor to arrive and this strange sojourn into another world to end.

As she waited, Dani looked around the room, searching for clues beyond her bad attitude to tell her what kind of person Carmen was. But everything seemed standard issue. There were no photos of her family or friends, nothing that looked sentimental. Even in five years at school, Dani had never learned anything personal about the Segunda, though rumors had certainly followed wherever she went.

Dani had done her best to stay away from gossip, but sharing a hall with twelve other girls, she hadn't been able to help picking things up here and there.

Once, she'd heard Carmen was the illegitimate daughter of Medio's president. The next time, it was that she'd grown up on the outer island, barely crossing the border in time for selection. Three separate times, Dani had heard Carmen was in love with another Segunda. The most drastic one of these involved a desertion pact, where Carmen and her secret lover had vowed to run away before graduation, rather than be parted and forced to marry anyone but each other.

The rumors functioned as any others—easy to pass along and impossible to prove—but as Dani watched Carmen saunter back into the room and adjust the lighting to her preference, she could be absolutely certain of one thing: Carmen had never set foot on the outer island. This was not a girl who knew what lacking felt like.

"I thought it would be easier in here," she said, gesturing toward the massive mirror. "Better lighting than that prison cell of yours."

Her choice of words made Dani's heart stutter. She kept her face casual as she watched Carmen out of the corner of her eye, searching for any hint that her remark had been more than just a dismissive turn of phrase.

But Carmen's face showed nothing besides her usual haughtiness, and as Dani relaxed, another thought pushed Carmen's suspicions (or lack thereof) from her mind entirely.

She was going to be undressing here. Measured mostly naked in front of Carmen with her dewy skin and topaz curves and that slightly snide smirk on her face.

It was too late now to back out without making a scene and inviting more ridicule. Instead, she prayed to the god who gathered shadows to conceal her as well as he could, the goddess who lived between her heartbeats to keep them slow and steady.

It would be bad enough without Dani going to pieces.

"Morning," said the tailor, taking in Dani's discomfort and Carmen's nonchalance. She was a tiny woman, barely reaching Carmen's shoulder, her short hair just brushing her chin. "My name is Lara," she said. "Let me guess . . ." She pointed to Dani. "You're Señora Daniela, and you're Mistress Carmen?"

Carmen smirked. "What gave her away, the abject terror?"

So much for avoiding ridicule. "Where would you like us?" Dani asked in her chilliest tone. "I don't have all day."

"In front of the mirror is fine, señora," Lara said, bustling over with a box of supplies and returning to the hallway for fabric samples. "Feel free to get undressed; I'll be back in a moment."

Dani shifted from foot to foot uncomfortably as Carmen slid the straps of her dress over her shoulders without a thought. Like it was nothing. Like she did it all the time. Had Dani ever undressed in front of someone before? Carmen reached for the zipper at her side in slow motion as she considered it.

She thought she remembered playing in the mud with some neighbor kids once; she'd been six, maybe seven. But even then, her mother had made her leave her shirt on to protect her shoulders from the sun.

Carmen's dress made an expensive sound as it slid down her body and settled at her feet. Dani kept her eyes straight ahead, trying to avoid the sight of her undressed, but of course there was the mirror, reflecting everything back in perfect, well-lit detail.

Dani's fingers froze on her zipper. Carmen in clothes was ridiculous enough, but in nothing but her underwear she was, objectively, a work of art. She was all circles and curves, all dark amber and soft edges. Her shoulders flowed effortlessly to an ample chest, her waist thick with hips that demanded notice and a belly that fit like a puzzle piece between them.

She's evenly bronzed all over, Dani thought, delirious. *How does she . . .* But the answer occurred to her then, and she wanted to bury her face in her hands to blot out the image it invited.

"Need any help with that zipper?" Carmen asked, bringing Dani back into the moment reluctantly.

"I'm fine," she snapped, thankful for the sound of the tailor coming back in, for the puncture in the terrible tension that apparently only Dani had noticed.

Dani jerked her zipper down, trying to leave her body completely before she bared it in front of strangers. The dress was over her shoulders. Around her waist. With a deep breath to steady herself, she slid it over her nonexistent hips and lowered it to her ankles, ignoring the uncomfortable, fluttery feeling in her stomach.

She was sure Carmen would be staring, smirking, maybe outright laughing, and she braced herself for it. But she and the tailor were preoccupied. No one was looking at her.

Unfortunately, Dani couldn't help but look at herself. Narrow shoulders and hips; long, spindly legs. Her skin was the brown of a branch, a stone. She was a solid presence, without adornment. There was nothing wrong with the way she looked, Dani thought, but there was nothing special about it, either, and it had never been more obvious than it was now, with Carmen glinting and glittering beside her. Alluring in a way Dani's dry kneecaps and uneven tan lines couldn't possibly equal.

She shook herself. Primeras weren't supposed to concern themselves with the fleeting trivialities of beauty. That much had been beaten into them during every lesson for five years. Let Carmen have the skin and the curves and the sparkle. Dani had . . . other things. Which she was sure she'd remember later.

"Arms out," said Lara, who attacked them with measuring tape, muttering numbers under her breath.

She took no notes, apparently memorizing every measurement before moving on to the next. Dani tried to get swept up in her capable attitude, in the feeling that this was nothing stranger than a checkup at the physician. But even with her eyes closed, Carmen's curves pulled on the tide of her blush like a honey moon.

A true Segunda, Carmen was not quiet during the process. She suggested cuts and colors, expressed preferences for necklines and hem lengths. Once, Lara looked to Dani for similar instruction, but she could only shake her head, distrustful of even her voice. Not to mention her knowledge of high-society fashion.

Carmen rolled her eyes. "High waists," she said. "Long

lines at the leg, high collars."

Lara nodded again, a curt, efficient gesture. "Colors?" she asked, and Carmen looked at Dani again, thoughtful but not critical.

"Black for formalwear," Carmen said, like Dani wasn't there. "But for daywear, maybe earth tones. Some deep blues, a forest green or two."

More nodding, more bustling. Carmen had made all the choices Dani would have made for herself. How had she known?

"Okay, I think we've got it!" Lara said, tossing the tape measure into her box. "Thank you, ladies, you'll have your garments the moment they're ready."

"Do thank Mama Garcia for us when you see her," Carmen said, making no move to pick up her dress, though the fitting was clearly finished.

Desperate as she was to cover herself, Dani felt that to reach first would count as a loss in this unspoken competition with Carmen. And the only thing she hated more than exposure was losing.

"Good day, Primera," said Lara as she backed out with her things.

Dani managed a nod in her direction.

Surely Carmen would reach for her dress now. Put them both out of this misery. Dani willed her toward it, looking harder than was necessary at the hand now reaching up to smooth her plum lip stain.

"So, *Primera*," said Carmen, leaning forward into her reflection.

Dani cleared her throat, ignoring the ways that leaning changed Carmen's shape in the mirror. "Yes?"

"What were you really talking to the gardener about that day?" Quick as a striking snake, she'd turned to face Dani, her eyes locked in.

Dani's throat went dry. She couldn't look away. Her mind was entirely blank of everything but stupid comparisons between her own body and Carmen's. All she could think was how ridiculous it was that her cover was going to be blown at last, in a Segunda's room, in her underwear. It was the twin god and goddess of lies she thought of now, hoping they would honey her tongue.

"He hasn't been back since," Carmen continued relentlessly. "I know, because I've been looking for him. What you said about having a schoolgirl crush on him isn't true, because I've watched you. You don't have a romantic bone in your body."

Dani swallowed hard, her mind spinning with absolutely nothing useful. If only she hadn't been so fixated on their reflections. On the way Carmen's skin glowed like there was a setting sun behind it . . .

"It was you," she blurted, the twin deities coming to her rescue after all. "I had to let him go . . . because of you."

Carmen's gaze went from predatory to calculating. "Oh?"

"The señora and I were having breakfast, and I heard him

talking about you. About your figure in your dress and how he'd like to . . ." Another hard swallow. "Well, you get the point."

Something almost joyful danced in Carmen's eyes. "Oh, go on, Primera, entertain me."

Dani drew herself up with as much dignity as she could, considering she was still mostly naked. "I'm not going to repeat the filth traded around by the help," she said. "It's beneath us both. I let him go for saying inappropriate things, and that's final. He won't be back."

"So why lie?" Carmen asked, seeming genuinely curious. "Why not just tell me?"

"First off, to save myself this exact conversation," Dani said, rolling her eyes. "And second, because I didn't want you to feel . . . unsafe. I thought I'd just take care of it and that would be all."

"And the secluded walk down the garden path?"

"It's unseemly to terminate an employee in front of their peers," she said, in a voice as dry as the Medio School for Girls handbook. "Also, I'd never done it before. I didn't know if he was going to throw a fit."

Carmen raised her eyebrows, looking momentarily impressed. "I guess that explains the look on his face when he stormed off," she said.

"He wasn't happy about being fired by someone younger than him," she said with a self-deprecating smile. "Or . . . less male, either."

"Typical," said Carmen, and Dani found herself silently chuckling.

Finally—*finally*—Carmen reached for her clothes, sending Dani lunging for her pajamas and dressing gown. They dressed in almost companionable silence.

"Anyway," said Dani, zipping herself up. "Sorry you had to find out."

"You know," Carmen said, "you've been kind of a pleasant surprise. I figured this job was gonna be a bore, but here you go making it interesting."

Without the first clue what she meant, Dani just smiled—an unpracticed thing—and started toward the door. "Well, see you around," she said, but then she turned back. "Carmen?"

"Yes?"

"Why the change of heart?" She wasn't sure she even wanted to know, but her mind was too full of mysteries to add another to her plate. "You hated me so much in school, but now . . ."

Carmen looked almost sad, or maybe it was a trick of the light. "It's a conversation for another time," she said. "But trust me, it had nothing to do with you."

How was that possible? She wanted to ask, but she felt she'd pushed her luck enough for one day. Without answering, she gave Carmen a nod and padded across the rug to the door.

"Hey, Dani?" Carmen called after her. It was the first time she'd ever used her name, and Dani felt a strange thrill at the sound of it. "I really will tell you sometime, if you want. And in the meantime, if you ever need anything, you can consider me a friend."

"Oh," Dani said, completely taken aback. "Sure, okay. Um, thanks."

Carmen just laughed and shook her head. "Okay, make your escape," she said, with an eye roll that might have been more affectionate than mocking.

Dani hurried out before she could change her mind.

As Primera, you will be your husband's first line of defense against detractors, including himself. Be strong, reassure him, support him always.

—*Medio School for Girls Handbook,* 14th edition

⊹⟩✳⟨⊹

THE HALLWAY AIR WAS COOL as the sun set, and Dani wandered the house, knowing what she had to do but unwilling, for the moment, to do it.

Her thoughts were scattered, her dedication to the mission Sota had given her waning in the face of her afternoon on the south side of the house, her mind wandering to Carmen's reflection in the mirror, the strange confession that buzzed in Dani's ears even now.

Could she possibly have meant it? Was there a reason for everything she had put Dani through in school? One that didn't involve reflexive disdain for the lower class?

And what did it mean if there was?

Dani shook herself mentally when she reached the library, ducking inside for some privacy while she pulled herself together. The last thing she needed was the house staff reporting to Mateo that they'd seen his Primera behaving oddly. She couldn't afford to raise suspicion now, when so much depended on him remaining in the dark.

She had two days to find out when Mateo's secret trip to the border was happening. That had to be her first priority. Nothing Carmen could do or say was important enough to distract her from her duty to her parents, or what was at stake if she failed.

In the mirror on the library wall, Dani looked into her own wide brown eyes and glared. *The impossible is impossible*, she said to the part of her still lingering on Carmen's words. *Fulfill your obligation to Sota. Stay vigilant. Stay alive.*

Her reflection nodded its agreement, and together they left the library, leaving the distractions of the day behind in the darkened room.

With renewed purpose, Dani's feet took her east, into the wing of the house that held Mateo's bedroom and private office. She'd been warned by the household manual on her first day as a Garcia never to enter it, and that warning had only been reinforced by not-so-casual comments from the man himself since then, but what choice did Dani have at this point?

The hallways were empty, with Mateo gone for the night and the staff preparing for dinner, and Dani found her way to the dark-wood double doors without incident, their polished gold handles so different from any of the others in the house.

Though the moment deserved gravity, there was no time. Dani gripped the left handle and pushed, her heart in her throat. She was almost surprised when it gave way. Was Mateo truly arrogant enough to trust a verbal warning to protect this place?

There was a hush inside that Dani had never found anywhere else in the house. Everything about this room screamed that she didn't belong. This kind of quiet seemed to say that important decisions would be made in this room. That the walls trusted the man they bore witness to, to be just, and fair, and to do what was right.

Dani shook herself slightly, dispelling her flight of fancy. Whatever these walls had seen of the man she married, she doubted it had been justice. Maybe he knew he could never be the kind of leader a room like this deserved, Dani thought as she stepped toward the desk. Maybe that was why he was so cruel.

The desk was the most likely place to find a schedule, and so Dani started there. The first few drawers opened easily, noiselessly, almost welcoming her to peruse their contents. But there was little in these drawers besides blank paper and pens. Dani's own desk had more secrets to offer than this one.

The seconds ticked by, and though Mateo wasn't due back until after dinner, Dani found her heart racing along with them. She forced her hands to stay steady. To replace every item exactly where she had found it.

She was about to give up when she noticed a panel on the back of the desk that was slightly less polished than the rest of its gleaming parts. She crawled underneath and pressed, jumping back when it sprang out at her touch.

This was where he would keep the things he didn't want seen, she thought as she slid the panel aside to reveal a cabinet with a shiny brass lock. It didn't give when she tried to slide it aside. She should have known better than to think it would be that easy.

She returned to one of the unlocked drawers for a letter opener, thankful for Berto, her neighbor's son in Polvo who had taught her to pick locks on a lazy summer day. Her mama had chased them around the dirt yard with one of her woven sandals for an hour when she discovered what they were doing, Dani remembered, smiling despite the circumstances.

The sharp point of the tool slid easily into the lock, and Dani let her memories melt away as she focused on the lock's mechanism, closing her eyes like he had taught her, barely moving until she could sense all its parts, probing for the little catch that would let her inside.

"*Yes!*" she whispered when it finally swung open, the word swallowed by the luxurious room. Inside the cabinet were

leather-bound notebooks, loose sheets of paper, ledgers—all
the things that had been missing from the unlocked drawers.

But Dani had been in this office too long, and there was
so much to look through. Her heart picked up speed as she
rifled carefully through papers and folders, looking for anything promising, anything that could tell her what Sota
needed to know.

Calm down, she told the hairs standing up on her arms,
the goose bumps warning her that something was wrong. *He
won't be back until after dinner, and no one else is allowed in this
room.* She was safe. She just had to be careful.

In one folder was a stack of letters with Medio's official
seal at the top, and Dani slid it carefully out, opening it in her
lap, skimming the contents until something caught her eye.

It was a letter from the desk of Medio's president, signed
in bold strokes by his own hand. An invitation to accompany
him on a tour of the south segment of the border wall to
"assess failings in border security in light of recent events."

Sota had told her this much. Protests after the death of
a man attempting to cross the wall. Government property
damaged or destroyed. Apparently, the men in uniform with
guns and the towering border wall weren't enough anymore.
Dani shuddered to think what would come next.

The date was clearly printed midway down the page. Two
days away. Dani had barely made it. It was time to get back
to her room, where Sota's bag of stones was waiting beneath

her mattress with the cards he'd left her.

Her task finally accomplished, she felt lighter than she had in a week as she carefully returned the letter and closed the cabinet door. But before she could take the letter opener to the lock again, she heard it. Footsteps. Loud ones. Coming down the hall.

Dani could feel her heart beating in every vein, her hands shaking as she tried to lock the cabinet door again. But the footsteps were getting closer. Maybe it was just a member of the staff, she thought frantically, as the opener failed again and again to find the catch. Maybe the footsteps would continue on past. . . .

But deep down, she knew better. The only person who could be so unaware of the racket he was making in the hallway, at this hour, was her husband. No servant would ever dare to walk so loudly.

Finally, Dani gave up, replacing the panel over the still-unlocked secret door, setting the letter opener back into its drawer. It was too late to worry about locks. She had to get out of here.

It was much too late to leave through the door, but she darted to the window, which was open to tempt the evening breeze. The drop was dizzying. Two stories onto the flagged stone driveway, with nothing to cling to on the way down and nothing to break her fall.

Dani swore under her breath. She'd survive the drop, but

walking away from it was far less likely, and then where would she be? There were no gods who could keep her bones safe from an impact like that.

The bookshelves were mounted, all but the small one in the corner, and Dani wasn't sure she'd be able to fit in the space behind it, even narrow as she was.

She was running out of options. The footsteps had stopped in front of the door.

The only other feature in the room was the gleaming bar cart, with bottles of liquor and intimate glass settings. Dani thought of hiding behind it, waiting him out, but the door-knob was turning and she closed her eyes instead, throwing herself into her least believable persona yet, and the one she most needed him to swallow whole.

The doors opened slowly, the hand on them unhurried or weary. Dani fastened on her mask with iron hooks, and turned to face her husband half in shadow.

"What are you doing in here?" he asked, his voice low and dangerous as he walked toward her.

"I know I shouldn't have come," Dani said with a small quaver in her voice that she didn't entirely have to fake. "But I feel like I've upset you lately, and I wanted to explain." She looked into his eyes, hard and suspicious, and despite the screaming of adrenaline through her veins, she held them. "I didn't think it would be appropriate to wait in your bedroom, and you seemed upset when I spoke to you at dinner and . . ."

"You're here now," he said, his vowels a little too long, his consonants sloppy. "Spit it out."

He was drunk. The closer he moved to her the more obvious it was. His movements were strange and loose, and his eyes focused on her face, unfocused, then focused again. It was subtle, but it was there, and Dani could use it.

"I just . . . get so nervous," she said, breathing around the words, like a weight was being taken from her in the saying of them. She took a step toward him on feet that longed to flee instead. "So desperate to prove I can be useful to you, give you another perspective like my maestras said I should."

Mateo had stopped moving forward, and was she imagining it? Or had one corner of his mouth turned up in a smirk? "Go on," he said.

"You know that I come from a very different background than you," she said, and it felt like a confession, even though he knew exactly where her papers said she was from. "I was worried I'd be behind, without the experience that you, and even Carmen, have with this world. I'm alone here without you on my side, Mateo, and no one knows more about navigating these waters than you do. I just want to do what you do. I want to be as good as you are."

Mateo smiled, baring his teeth. A predator displaying dominance. "Well, I'm not sure that's possible," he said. "But I applaud the effort."

Dani's blood boiled at the readiness with which he accepted

the flattery. The bald-faced lies that were her only path out of this room alive.

"I feel like I started all wrong," she said, her voice even smaller now. "Asked too many questions. Pushed too hard. I just want you to know I'm willing to earn my place in your confidence. I'm willing to learn from you."

"Let's have a drink," he said, a challenge in his eyes that told her she'd better accept.

I want to punch you in your smug face, she thought. "I'd love that," she said instead.

Mateo walked to the bar cart Dani had so recently considered hiding behind, and he poured two heavy tumblers with a clear liquid that smelled like an open flame when she breathed it in.

"What is it?" she asked, a wrinkle in her nose.

"What is it!" Mateo repeated. "Daniela, you haven't lived." He leaned over his glass, taking a deep breath in, gesturing for her to do the same.

She coughed, recognizing the scent at last. It had wafted off enough of her neighbors growing up. Sad-eyed men who walked miles through the dust to forget their troubles. Dani's father had staunchly refused to keep anything stronger than the customary sangria in the house.

Mateo laughed, a fake, booming thing that made the glasses clink on the cart. "Okay, now a sip, just a small one, and swish it around your mouth." He demonstrated, closing his eyes and moaning in a way that made Dani's stomach turn.

But she had gotten herself this far. If drinking liquor would keep her secret safe, what choice did she have? Even her father couldn't begrudge her this, she thought as she took a mouthful. But before she could swish, she choked, barely managing to get it down, coming up with streaming eyes.

The taste had been bundles of herbs aflame, the smoke seeping into her mouth and nose until she felt she'd caught fire, too.

"That's it!" Mateo practically shouted. "I can't believe this is your first. Although I suppose women don't often appreciate the finer things in life, do they? Not like men do, anyway."

The heat from the liquor spread, her anger not far behind. She took another sip just for something to do, and this time her mouth was ready for it. This time the liquor tasted like home. The spiny plants her mother grew out back for all sorts of purposes, the salt in the air, the smoke of a bonfire when someone had something to celebrate nearby.

This time, the tears filling Dani's eyes weren't just from the burn.

"I swear I'd be glad to see the whole outer island go up in flames if it weren't for this stuff," Mateo was saying, half his glass already gone, the slurring more pronounced. "I've tried to have it distilled inland, but it's just not the same."

"They make this beyond the wall?" Dani asked, trying to

pass off this falling feeling as mild curiosity.

"*Near* the wall," Mateo corrected her. "We buy it from the right side, of course. Importing from over the wall is illegal." He winked. Dani wanted to toss her liquor in his face. She'd seen him evasive and condescending, but she'd never seen him like this.

She took another mouthful, saying silent thanks to the people who had been growing and cutting and mashing and fermenting for centuries, only to have their humanity insulted by the people enjoying the fruits of their labor.

This time, the anger didn't cool.

"I have to say," said Mateo, draining the rest of his glass, "I was surprised to see you tonight. And I'm glad to hear you're committed to emulating those who excel in this world. One thing that school is rather lax on, in my opinion, is respect for one's betters."

The pleasant buzz of alcohol was the only thing that kept her from committing an act of physical violence. It was like the smoke had enveloped her, whispering with the voices of home that she should stay safe. Save her retaliation for when it would do more than doom her.

"You'll do what I ask you to do," Mateo was saying now, his eyes tracing her jaw, her collarbone. She wanted to crawl out of her skin. "You'll know what I deem you worthy of knowing. If someone asks a question in public you don't know the answer to, you'll play dumb. It'll hardly be a stretch."

The heat was everywhere now. She thought of the betrayal she would commit the moment she left this room, and this time she felt proud.

"For now, you'll tell the plebeians where to put my newspapers and you'll answer my invitations and you'll rest assured that my father and I are doing everything we can to stop the cursed trash on the fringes of this country from destroying us all." He smiled a little, as if proud of his answer.

"Yes, señor," Dani said, and her voice was small and still, even while an inferno raged in her chest.

Mateo was quiet for a while, and Dani drank, and she thought of stones, and protests, and Sota. She thought of her neighbors and friends at the border and the way he had just reduced them to nothing.

"The older generation may be afraid to send a message," Mateo said after a long moment, drawing Dani from her heat-crazed thoughts. "But I'm not. It's about bringing this country into an era that utilizes its full potential. No more softness. No more forgiveness." There was a faraway look in his eyes now, like he was seeing a future only he could bring to bear.

Did he even remember she was there? He seemed like he was continuing another conversation. One she hadn't been a part of. She hardly dared to breathe.

"If it takes extreme measures," he said, his eyes still unfocused and dreamy, "so be it. There's no room for disobedience in the future I'm planning. And if they fear us for a little while, they will obey for generations."

"Like animals . . . ," Dani said, almost without meaning to. She steeled herself for his anger, but he smiled instead, draining his drink and setting it on the table with a clunk.

"Now you're starting to understand."

"You know," said Dani, rapidly forgetting the importance of survival, "I think I'll head to bed. I'm feeling a little light-headed."

"Not so fast," Mateo said, filling his glass again, a little slopping over the side. He leaned forward and filled Dani's as well, not bothering to ask permission. He drank deeply before continuing. "Don't think I've forgotten that you disobeyed me by coming here."

"No, señor," Dani said, sipping again when he stared pointedly at her glass.

"I'm not an unreasonable man, Daniela," he said, leaning so close that she could smell the liquor on his breath. "But I do expect something from you. . . ."

This time, it was as if a thousand spiders were crawling across her flesh. It was all Dani could do not to pull away in revulsion.

"Do you know what it is?" he asked, moving closer still. Dani's mind jumped, inexplicably, to Carmen. How often had she been close to him like this? Had she enjoyed it? Or had she held still and borne it like Dani was doing now?

It doesn't matter, she told herself, forcing her awareness back into the moment, where Mateo's eyes were glittering in the lamplight, his thin lips stretched around a smirk, like he could taste her fear, and he was savoring it.

"N-no, señor," she said.

"Obedience," he whispered, snakelike. "Complete obedience. Is that clear?"

His long, pale fingers were on her chair arm now, just inches from her hand. She didn't move. She met his eyes and hoped that a little of her anger showed. Enough to keep her safe.

"Yes," she said, her voice small in a way she hated.

He moved closer one last time, his body taking up too much space, his mouth taking in too much of her air. Dani felt light-headed as he lifted a finger and grazed her cheek.

"Good," he said, and she could taste the word. His sour breath. The liquor's flame. She could taste everything that would come next if he decided to ignore the rules.

The moment stretched, the fear coiling in Dani's belly as he pinned her in place with his beetle-black eyes. Then his mouth curled into a smirk, and she felt them balanced on a knife's edge, about to fall off one side or another.

"Get out of my office," he said, choosing at last. "And don't you *dare* come back."

Dani didn't have to be told twice. She stood on unsteady legs and walked as quickly as she could to the door, stumbling a little on the edge of the carpet. The last thing she heard before the door closed behind her was the clinking of glass on glass, and the sound of Mateo's laughter.

When she stepped into the dark silence of her own room, the sliver moon barely making shadows on the floor, Dani felt her hands begin to shake. She closed the door behind her, locking it even though she knew it was futile. There's no way he would allow her to have a room he couldn't access.

The shaking spread as she sat on the edge of her bed, unable to stop herself from allowing every fear she'd shut out in his presence from surfacing, clawing up her throat, stealing her breath. He could have had her arrested. He could have had her killed. But all she could think about now was the way he'd come too close, the way he'd used his body and the authority its strength gave him to make her comply.

With that thought, anger replaced her fear. How dare he? With all the authority he already had, to use something so much more sinister to control her? She had wondered if Sota was exaggerating, trying to win her loyalty, but at that moment she didn't care what he had said. She only cared about what she had seen, what she had felt.

Dani pulled the stones from their hiding place and weighed the bag in her hand. Mateo thought she was powerless. That he could reduce her to a trembling victim with some harsh words and the scent of his breath on her face.

But she wasn't powerless. And if she played her cards right, she would never have to be again.

Her parents had dreamed of a better life, but they had

never sat across from Mateo Garcia and seen the cruelty in his eyes. What would they say if they knew staying safe meant putting a man like that in power? Sitting by while he destroyed lives and oppressed people just because he could?

Walking toward the window, Dani let two stones fall into her palm and peered into the dark, tropical garden outside. When she placed the first stone with a satisfying click, Dani thought of the towns like Polvo, being burned to the ground because of "suspicious activity." She thought of the people shot at the wall, deemed criminals because desperation forced them to cross a border they hadn't built or consented to. She thought of the children, sent back to starve for being born on the wrong side of that line, or forced—like her—to live with lies and ghosts trailing them all their lives.

When she placed the second stone, she didn't think of blackmail, or her parents.

She thought of Mateo, and how no amount of privilege or safety was worth letting him win.

✣✦✱✦✣

AFTER THE EVENTS OF THE previous night, the last thing Dani felt like doing was getting dressed up and attending a Primera salon. But as Mateo had so often reminded them, the schedule was not a suggestion.

She had barely escaped disaster in that office. Tonight, she would have to be perfect. In the car on the way there, she took deep, steadying breaths, relishing the few moments she had to herself.

To think I spent years in school looking forward to my first salon, she thought, almost smiling at the image of that naive girl. The one who would never have dreamed her top priority at her first all-Primera event would be to watch her mark for signs that she suspected something.

The same mark who had told her what to expect from a salon just last year . . .

Dani shook herself as the car pulled into the steep driveway. Nostalgia wasn't helpful for a spy *or* a Primera. *Watch Jasmín, and don't raise suspicion*, she told herself as the car stopped. There was no room for anything else tonight.

The Soto house was similar in size and scope to Dani's own, though the stone was a deep blue, the roof tiles dazzlingly white in the moonlight. Inside, the floor plan was open, blue walls set off by accents of sun-bright yellow and the occasional crimson.

Everyone congregated in the informal living room, trays of appetizers on tables and sparkling rosé wine beside the customary clay jugs of sangria.

"Good evening, Primera!" said Ana Soto, another of Dani's old classmates. "So glad you could be here tonight."

"I wouldn't have missed it," Dani assured her, moving through several more greetings, careful not to display her impatience until she finally caught sight of Jasmín.

Her hair was shoulder length and smooth, her dress a deep red almost daring for a Primera, even a young one. But most importantly, she seemed undisturbed, a glass of wine the same color as her dress resting between relaxed fingers as she laughed at some joke, tossing back her head.

Dani felt her shoulders relax a fraction of an inch. Jasmín

was safe. Laughing. Enjoying the evening. All she had to do now was keep her distance. Watch, but not get too close.

"Good evening, Daniela," said a voice from behind her. She turned to find herself face-to-face with the elder Señora García, who held water instead of wine and pursed her lips as a shorter-than-strictly-appropriate hemline passed her on the way to the appetizer table.

"Good evening to you as well, señora." She offered her hand to her mother-in-law for a firm handshake. "Having a good time?"

"Oh, yes. After the four hundredth salon, they only get more thrilling."

Dani smiled and grabbed a glass of iced lemon water from a passing tray. Señora García looked around the room, and for a moment Dani thought back to Jasmín at the dinner party, the way she'd felt safe telling her mother everything, no matter how bad it seemed.

As difficult as it was to imagine her own mama here, Dani found her in everything Señora García was not. In the harsh angles of her posture and the slight downward turn of her mouth. In the way she seemed to repel confidence rather than inviting it.

"Now don't waste your time lurking in this corner with an old woman; go on and mingle," the señora said. "Is that a friend of yours over there waving?"

Dani's smile felt painted on. Of *course* it was Jasmín waving, just after she'd decided to give her a wide berth tonight.

And was it just Dani's imagination, or was there an extra edge in Señora Garcia's voice?

"Oh. Yes, Jasmín. We were roommates at school, though I don't know her well."

Did she raise her eyebrow higher? Was she skeptical? "Well, I suppose now's your chance, isn't it?"

"Yes, señora," Dani said. "Thank you; enjoy the party."

Walk normally, she told herself as she headed for Jasmín. *Not too fast, not too slow.*

"Jasmín," Dani said as she reached the other girl, still feeling—or imagining—the señora's eyes on her back. "Lovely to see you." As Jasmín shook her hand, Dani watched her closely for anything that would betray an undercurrent of tension. But Jasmín was a Primera, too. There was nothing but her smile.

"How have you been?" asked Jasmín when they'd dropped each other's hands. "How's life with Carmen Santos?" There was a smirk on her lips Dani wasn't quite sure how to interpret, so she merely shrugged.

"She chatters constantly, but other than that she's no more than I expected."

Jasmín's eyes glinted with mischief. "You're very diplomatic as usual," she said. "But I remember Carmen from school, and I'm quite sure that's not the whole story."

Try as she might to keep the mask in place, a rueful smile broke through Dani's armor, Jasmín's comments bringing back the fitting, and Carmen's strange remarks about their time in school. After Mateo's performance in the office, she'd had little time to dwell on it.

Jasmín laughed triumphantly. "I knew it," she said. "I know you won't tell me a word of it, you bore, but let's at least get you a drink to take the sting out of whatever she's done."

On their way to the bar, Dani felt the prickling feeling of being watched fade away. She wondered what it would feel like to really talk to Jasmín. About the fitting, and Carmen's confession, about the way Dani had begun to look for Carmen in the hallways. About the idea that, despite it all, she wanted to know the Segunda better. To figure out what she was hiding in those mysterious smiles . . .

It was nice to forget Mateo's threats for a moment. To think about something that made her smile instead of shake.

"Well, if you won't talk, I will," Jasmín said, pulling Dani toward the wall nearest the front door, where she slumped dramatically. "*My* Segunda has taken to discussing the future of our husband's career with him! As if that's not a gross breach of our responsibility divide."

Tongue loosened by wine, Dani exclaimed in offense. "Who does she think she is?" she asked. "Did she take too many naps in school? We learned that the first day!"

Jasmín nearly choked on surprised laughter. "We need to get many, many more of these in you," she said, tapping at Dani's wineglass with an unpolished fingernail. "You're much funnier when you relax. I feel cheated that I didn't think to feed you wine years ago."

Despite herself, Dani laughed. Jasmín had enough stories about her awful Segunda to keep them laughing into their glasses, and the house staff milling around didn't seem content to let either of those glasses stay empty.

So lost in their conversation were they, Dani and Jasmín didn't hear the first knock at the front door.

The second was impossible to miss.

This was not the polite knock of a latecomer to the party but the loud, large-fisted knock of someone on a mission. Conversations around them sputtered and stalled. All eyes followed the young Señora Soto as she crossed to the door, shrugging her shoulders at anyone who raised an eyebrow.

A numbness had started to creep through Dani: a reaction to the pounding, the whispers, the fear. She remembered knocks like those from her childhood. The ones that would send her diving beneath the blankets while her father walked stiffly toward the front of the house.

Ana Soto answered the door, pretending the attention of every Primera in the room wasn't on her. Dani didn't lose her breath until she saw the silhouettes of two military officers standing in the dark outside, and the slimmer figure of her husband between them, stepping into the light.

She should have known she wouldn't be able to escape him. Even for an hour.

The whispers caught like an oil-soaked wick, but Dani didn't take her eyes off Mateo. Whatever was happening here, he was at the center of it, and if the cold determination on his face was any indication, it was nothing good.

She could feel Jasmín tensing beside her, ripples forming in her wine as her fingers trembled on the stem. Dani forced herself not to look, terrified she'd give something away with her eyes. She was a politely curious Primera, she told herself, in no danger of course, though she'd been placed slightly on edge by the presence of armed officers at a salon. Who wouldn't be?

Even though her heart was a faulty engine in her chest, she had to remember that to Daniela Garcia, Primera to the capital's most up-and-coming politico, the police were allies, keeping her safe from the threat beyond the wall.

"Isn't that your husband?" Jasmín whispered as Mateo stepped the rest of the way into the entry hall and spoke in hushed tones to Ana. His cold expression had thawed, replaced by fake concern that was visible from across the room.

Dani felt ill. "Yes," she said lightly. "Though I can't imagine what he's doing here." *Or which one of us he's here to arrest.* The moment the thought had landed, it took flight again, along with Dani's vision of the secret cabinet left unlocked beneath his desk. Mateo's image was at the forefront of his motivations. Should his wife be involved in a scandal, the last thing he'd want would be to handle it publicly.

"Curious," Jasmín said, a beat too late, and Dani chanced a look at her. There was something more than polite interest woven into her mask, and after five years at the Medio School for Girls, Dani knew just how to read it.

Fear, in the slight widening of her eyes. Determination, in the set of her jaw.

Dani clearly wasn't the only person here who knew something she shouldn't.

"I should go talk to him," Dani said. "Find out what's going on . . ." But before she could finish the thought, Mateo nodded regretfully to Señora Soto and began to walk toward them. Without even a beckoning gesture, the officers accompanied him, hulking shadows that made Dani shiver.

Compared to the ruthlessness in every line of Mateo's face, the large men looked almost tame.

"Ladies," he said, as though he needed to address them to get their attention. No one had said a word since he'd stepped inside, too consumed with trying to overhear his low conversation with their hostess. "I'm so sorry to interrupt your party, but I'm afraid we have some business to attend to." He gestured to the men flanking him.

Dani was holding her breath, she realized dimly, but she couldn't seem to let go of it.

"Jasmín Flores, will you please step forward?"

Glancing sideways at the girl who was not quite her friend, Dani tried to look innocent, surprised, giving up her own gods for the moment and beseeching Constancia, who had apparently marked her a Primera at birth, not to let her fail. "What's this all about?" she asked, but Jasmín only shook her head, her mouth a grim line as she stepped toward the men waiting for her.

I'm sorry, Dani thought. *I'm so, so sorry*. There had been no time for Jasmín's señora to find a solution, and when Sota learned Dani's information he must have decided mere social ostracization wasn't good enough. This was her fault. She felt it in her bones. This was the price Jasmín would pay for telling her señora about the blackmail. For trusting that the hallway was empty when the enemy was lurking just out of sight.

It was the same thing Sota had threatened Dani with, in the beginning. A threat that still hung over her head every moment. She would obey, and keep her mouth shut, or the Median government would find out where her papers came from.

This was what it looked like when you disobeyed.

The officers moved to meet Jasmín, taking her by the wrists as Mateo spoke in a voice loud enough for anyone in the room to hear him clearly. "Señora Flores, you are charged with rebel sympathizing, and with passing information to spies from across the border. You will be remanded immediately into custody for questioning, and to await formal charges of treason."

Jasmín didn't struggle. She didn't even appear to hear him. Her eyes were closed, and her face looked almost peaceful. It was a mark of the seriousness of the situation that the room remained utterly silent.

Mateo, clearly looking to make a scene, wasn't pleased with her response. "Did you hear me, Flores?" he asked, the chill in his voice deepening. "You're a traitor to this country. You're going to prison. Did you hear me?"

Jasmín didn't speak. She didn't even acknowledge him.

For a brief, mad moment, Dani wanted to applaud. But the look on Mateo's face was nothing short of dangerous.

"Take her," Mateo finally spat.

The officers whirled around with Jasmín hanging between them, looking impossibly small and bright in her red dress.

I will make this right, Dani thought, staring so hard at Mateo she wondered if he could feel it. *One way or another. As long as it takes.*

Now, finally, the whispers began.

"Do you think she really did it?"

"Even if she didn't, it's over for her."

"Of course! Rodolfo can't afford a Primera tainted by accusations . . ."

"Her poor father, he worked so hard."

"Her poor madres, can you imagine the shame?"

Mateo lingered in the doorway, smirking, listening to the whispers of Jasmín's dreams dying. As the officers dragged her past him, he stepped closer, and Dani recognized his posture. She'd been the victim of it just last night. The way he bent toward her, blocking out her vision, his body almost pressed against her own.

I own you now, his body language said. But Jasmín stood

perfectly still. Dani moved to one side, desperate to hear what he was saying to her, but when his face came into view his mouth was still, a strange light dancing in his eyes. Something predatory and out of control.

"Looking forward to your cell, you traitorous bitch?" he asked with a sneer, pressing even closer. The officers held her limp wrists, looking away. Behind her, the Primeras were too busy buzzing with the scandal to hear him, but Dani read the shape of the quiet words on his lips.

Dani didn't know if she was in the Sotos' lounge or the dim light of Mateo's office. Was that Jasmín's ear he was whispering in, or her own? Her control slipped, and she moved toward him before she knew what she was doing. She couldn't let him get away with it. With making another helpless person feel the way she had felt . . .

But before she could reach him, an iron hand clamped down on her upper arm and steered her toward the wall. "What on earth do you think you're doing?" asked Señora Garcia. "I know the girl was your roommate, but this is *not* behavior befitting a Primera of your station."

"Did you hear what he called her?" Dani asked, her heart still racing, her legs begging to carry her over to her sneering husband so she could give him a piece of her mind.

"Mateo is young, and . . . potentially overzealous," his mother allowed. "But it is his job to root out sympathizers and punish them, Daniela, and it is your job to support him."

Dani opened her mouth to argue again, but she stopped

short at the look on Señora Garcia's face.

"I'd like you to think very carefully about what happens next," she said, her tone light as Jasmín disappeared into the darkness outside the door. "Either you charge out there like a madwoman and embarrass your husband and yourself while defending an accused sympathizer . . ." She paused, raising an eyebrow. "Or you turn around, have some fruit and cheese, and express your polite and bland sympathies about how things transpired here tonight."

Dani didn't say a word.

"I *strongly* suggest you choose the second option, Daniela."

Then she was gone. Into the chattering crowd to take her own advice. And Dani, biting the inside of her cheek so hard she tasted blood, had no choice at all except to join her.

But as her body obeyed, her mind was racing. She wasn't certain she could trust Sota, or La Voz, and she had little enough power in this world with Mateo keeping her in the dark. But one way or another, Jasmín would be freed, and Mateo would pay.

Dani planned to make sure of it.

When Dani arrived home hours later, the entryway was quiet, the only light coming from the fireplace in the front room. Mateo had personally escorted Jasmín to her new four-by-four concrete home and still hadn't returned. Dani didn't let herself shut out the images of what she feared was happening now. About what she'd set in motion to keep her own secrets safe.

You don't deserve to hide, she told herself. She would face it until she could fix it.

She'd been lost in thought in the entryway for a few minutes when footsteps sounded from the darkened hallway. Even amid her guilt and her determination, Dani's traitorous heart leapt into her throat, trying to convince herself she wasn't hoping for Carmen. The strange gravity of her situation had been reawakened by Jasmín's questions tonight, but the silhouette that came into view wasn't Carmen's.

Dani froze along the wall of the front room, partially hidden by a glossy bookcase, as Mama Garcia came in, clutching a piece of paper to her chest.

Still unaware of Dani's presence, she veered left to stand before the fireplace, lit against the unseasonal chill outside. She glanced once more at the page before tossing it into the flames. Muttering to herself, too low to hear from Dani's vantage point, she walked out the front door and into the night.

With her natural suspicion kicking into overdrive, Dani stole quietly to the fireplace, where the paper Mama Garcia had tried to burn was only half in the flames. She pulled it out and blew frantically as the glow crawled along the paper's edges, turning more and more of Mama Garcia's secrets to ash. When it was finally extinguished, less than half of the page remained.

"Dani?"

Hurried movements will always betray the emotions beneath them, said the maestra's voice in her head as she slid the paper smoothly into the neck of her dress and turned to face Carmen.

"If you're looking for Mama Garcia, she's already gone," Dani said.

Carmen's eyebrows drew together. "Mama Garcia? What are you talking about? And why do you look so pale? What happened?"

With the mystery fading, and Carmen seeing more than she should, the reality of Dani's night came crashing back down. This time, she didn't rein it in. Maybe she was just exhausted, or tired of pretending. Maybe she wanted to see what Carmen would do with a little honesty.

Whatever the reason, she let her shoulders fall under the weight of Mateo's behavior the night before. Jasmín being taken. The secrets she'd whispered. The fear that she'd be next. She let her face move in response to the memories, the feelings. Her mouth crumpled in distress, and she didn't stop it.

Carmen moved closer, though she still left a yard of space between them. "Dani, are you okay? Seriously, you look awful." For once, it didn't sound like an insult. She sounded concerned.

"It was . . . Mateo," Dani said, still not sure how much she was ready to confess. "A girl at the party was accused of rebel sympathizing. He came with police and arrested her in front of everyone. And the way he did it . . . It was terrifying."

"Sun and skies," Carmen said. "That must have been awful." She paused, and the only sound was the crackling of the flames. The darkness swallowed Dani's fear, and her curiosity about the letter, and everything but the fact that Carmen's heart was beating just a few feet away. They stood in silence for much longer than was appropriate for either of them, but tonight, Dani didn't care.

"Dani . . . ," Carmen said at last, looking down, looking back up.

"Yeah?"

"It was because I was afraid."

"What?"

"That's why I told people where you were from . . . why I made fun of you. I know it doesn't excuse it, but I wanted you to know. I just needed them to target someone else."

"But why would anyone have made fun of you? You were already perfect."

Carmen smiled, but it was a sad smile. "Didn't you ever wonder why I was on the bus from the capital, and not in some fancy car from a house in the government complex?"

Dani hadn't. But a tiny, hopeful sun was rising in her chest. "You're not from here?"

"Not even the capital."

"But then . . . where?"

Carmen took a deep breath, like she was steeling herself. For once she wasn't polished and shining, looking down from her pedestal. She'd never looked so much like the girl Dani met on the bus five years ago.

"Mar de Sal," she almost whispered, and Dani's jaw dropped.

"But that's almost to the border! So you . . ."

"I pretended," she said with a shrug. "I was young and afraid, and when they started looking at us like we didn't belong, I panicked. I was selfish and stupid, and I always wanted to take it back, but by then it was too late."

"So you didn't hate me?" Dani asked in a small voice. She should have been furious that Carmen had used her that way, but hadn't she been twelve and scared, too? Wouldn't she have done anything to make her parents proud?

"You were the only real friend I ever made," Carmen said, her voice just as small. "The rest of them knew the lie. You were the only one who saw the real me. Even for a minute."

Dani didn't know what to say. She was relieved. She was scared. She was looking right into Carmen's eyes.

"I'm sorry, Dani," she said. "I've been waiting five years to say it. I'm so, so sorry."

"It's okay." It was barely a whisper, but she meant it. She understood. "I forgive you."

Was Dani just dizzy? Or was the space between them

closing? She blinked, hard, but Carmen didn't stop until they were less than an arm's distance apart. Until they could have reached out and touched each other.

Dani knew she should pull away, leave this room, but after Mateo's threatening presence, there was something healing about inviting someone to share her space. Someone she wanted there, even if she shouldn't. Didn't she deserve that feeling?

Carmen's eyes were still on hers. She could feel the gaze in the tips of her toes. Something was happening to her breath; it was shallow and strange in her throat. The air between them was charged, and Carmen's eyes darted down, sending goose bumps across Dani's skin like a wildfire.

Without thinking, for once, Dani stepped closer, so close that her breath stirred Carmen's hair when she exhaled, and she could see the flickering of the fire in her eyes.

What are you doing? asked a shrill voice in her head, but it was a million miles away as Carmen's breath hitched in her throat and she reached out, brushing a wayward strand of hair out of Dani's eye where it had fallen as she bent over the flames. Was this what the goddess of hearts did when she wasn't tending to steady beats? Dani had never known her, the rosy-cheeked girl from her mama's stories, but she felt her in the room tonight.

The darkness and the quiet had cast a spell, and Dani felt like she was moving through a dream as she let her gaze flicker downward to Carmen's full lips, then back to her eyes.

Somewhere in the back of her mind, a maestra's voice was screaming. Alarm bells were ringing. But Dani couldn't bring herself to care. The heat building in her chest began to spread beneath her skin, and her thoughts licked like flames against every wall of ice she'd been trained to put up.

Between them, the moment hung until it grew ripe and full, and Dani thought she'd burst into bloom with wondering. But just as it swelled to its peak, to a point when the only options would be dive or retreat, a door closed deep in the house and footfalls echoed down the hallway.

Their closeness seemed suddenly dangerous, stupid, the spell the darkness and firelight had woven unraveling with the presence of someone who would draw their own conclusions from what they saw.

"Go," Dani whispered, and Carmen opened her mouth to argue. "Go!" she said again, and this time Carmen did as she asked, not looking up before whirling in a cloud of perfumed silk and hair and running out the patio door.

Dani had to remember how to breathe. The room was airless without Carmen, the letter in the fire and Mateo's cruelty and this strange fizzing in her bloodstream forming a wave inside her that crested and crashed. But the footsteps faded, going in the direction of the kitchen, probably just a member of the staff setting the fire in Mateo's room before his return.

When the house had gone silent again, the tension fizzled out in Dani's blood, leaving exhaustion, deep and dark, in its wake. It was all she could do to drag herself and her secrets to her room, but when she pulled the letter out of her dress at last, she'd never felt more awake.

At the bottom of Mama Garcia's letter, two incomplete sentences spelled out Dani's fate in bold script:

. . . have proof she's been in contact. It's time to neutralize the threa . . .

Though a wife must obey her husband, a husband must respect his wife. In this way, they remain equals in the household, and peace is kept.

—*Medio School for Girls Handbook,* 14th edition

⊹‡✦✳✦‡⊹

DANI SPENT THE DAY BEFORE Mateo's trip to the border watching everyone very closely, sleeping little, and thinking about death.

Whoever she had been talking to, Mama Garcia suspected Dani, and it sounded like she was ready to take drastic measures to make sure she couldn't harm the family.

What had given her away? Dani wondered for the hundredth time. It was the morning of the trip, and Dani was on her way to catch up on reading in the library, thankful to avoid the breakfast table for once.

In the hush of her favorite room in the house, she sank into an armchair and tried to quiet her thoughts with the heavy volume in her hands: *A Hundred Years of Faith—Religion and Culture in Medio.* But her mind wouldn't stay put.

Had it been the unlocked cabinet door in the office? she asked herself. If so, Mateo knew, too, and Dani couldn't imagine him keeping quiet about it. But a full day had passed, and nothing out of the ordinary had happened. So maybe it had been something else. . . .

Whatever it had been, there were a hundred ways to dispose of a girl who'd committed treason, and as a Garcia, Mateo's mama must have known them all. So why wait? Why leave Dani to her own devices, run the risk that she might be gathering more information, or passing it?

She thumped her pillow against her mattress in frustration, for once aware of the gaps her training had left in her view of the world. To want to eliminate a threat to one's family was logical, to seek help in doing it even more so. But to be aware of a threat? To identify it and plan to eliminate it and then . . . do nothing?

It was outside the realm of logic, and illogical things were hard to predict.

On her way down to breakfast, Dani busied herself with the arduous task of forgetting her dreams. The stomping of military boots always welcomed her to sleep, followed by Jasmín's wind-chime voice screaming as Dani pounded against a locked door. But those visions were only half the problem.

There was also the dream where Carmen moved closer to her across a ballroom with a lacquered floor, removing clothing until she revealed a glittering serpent's tail, her forked tongue flickering as she leaned in closer to Dani. . . .

"Good morning, Daniela," came a voice much too close to Dani's chair. She jumped a little, the open book in her lap closing with a thump.

Dani's heart kicked into a gallop when she looked up to find Mama Garcia, half in shadow and holding a tea tray. Had she been wrong to expect her to strike at night? Dani wondered hysterically. Why not the middle of the day? Why not now? She forced herself to take even, measured breaths.

"Good morning, Mama Garcia," she said, pleased with her voice for remaining steady. "To what do I owe the pleasure?"

"Oh, it's just been a while since you and I got a chance to *chat*," she said, sitting down in the chair opposite Dani without being invited and pouring tea for them both. Was it her dreams spilling into waking, or was there a sharper gleam in Mama Garcia's eye than usual?

"Well, I appreciate the company with Mateo gone," Dani said, careful not to avoid eye contact or to watch her too closely. The letter seemed to emit a faint alarm bell from its new hiding place in her desk, but Dani was trapped.

"Agosta mentioned some unpleasantness at the last Primera salon," the elder Segunda said, using the señora's given name in an attempt to seem casual, Dani supposed. But beneath her tone, Dani sensed tension. This was the reason she had come, and she'd just given it away too early.

It was a mistake that would have earned her bad marks in year one of Primera training.

"Yes, so regrettable," Dani said, stirring agave nectar into her cup. She faked a sip before setting it down. Poison wouldn't be very subtle, but it was easy to play off as an illness, and Dani wasn't about to let her get away with something that simple. "I'm just so glad Mateo is taking his duties so seriously," she continued. "I'm sure it will take us all some time to recover from the shock." Dani paused to shake her head. "To think, she was just walking among us all this time . . ."

"Yes," said Mama Garcia. "And from what I hear, she was walking rather close to you."

Dani let the silence grow teeth between them. Mama Garcia didn't drop her gaze, but Dani didn't look away, either. "Was there a question you wanted to ask me, Mama?" she asked, her tone light but her words warning. She was new to the house, but she was still a Primera. She needed to show Mateo's mama that she couldn't be intimidated.

"No need to get *defensive*, Daniela," she said. "I merely wanted to convey that it would be a pity for a member of this family to be tainted with any . . . questionable associations. Especially considering the roles my husband, and yours, fill in our government."

"It seems Jasmín Flores has been fooling a lot of people for a long time," Dani said, still careful to keep her voice even, though she wasn't sure her knees would hold her if she stood. "I assure you that I, like everyone else, have seen her for what she really is and count myself lucky that she's behind bars, where she belongs." The lie had sharp edges, and Dani felt it cutting her tongue to ribbons on the way out.

Abruptly, she remembered Sota's words in the closet on the first night she met him:

Think about the crimes your precious government condones, not just the ones they punish. Then you can talk to me about who the real criminals are.

Mama Garcia laughed, though her eyes stayed cold. "Well, I certainly wasn't looking for a blood oath, Daniela, but I'm glad to see you're taking the matter seriously. We can't be too careful who we trust, after all."

"That's true," Dani said, raising her cup in a salute and setting it down without even the pretense of a sip. It was insulting, to toast without drinking, and Mama Garcia's eyes flashed.

With a last, lingering look, Mama Garcia drained her teacup. "Well, I'm expected at home for lunch," she said, as if they'd been discussing the weather and not Dani's loyalties. She smiled, but the gesture wasn't kind, and Dani felt as though an ice cube had been dropped down the back of her dress.

Whatever she had said today, Dani knew things weren't over between them.

In fact, they had probably just begun.

"Thank you again for coming by," Dani said, standing to kiss the air beside each of Mama Garcia's cheeks. Her smell was strange up close, floral perfume too thick over something metallic.

"Enjoy your day," she replied.

"You as well."

She left the tea tray, with Dani's untouched cup growing cold beside a bowl of figs. Dani had never been less hungry. As the fear subsided, she turned her thoughts to La Voz, the border trip, and the fierce hope that some obstacle was being placed in Mateo's path not to mention his family's.

Giving up on her reading, Dani wandered back into the hallway at loose ends, craving a distraction from everything outside her control. She didn't realize she was heading for Carmen's rooms until she was already in the south section of the house, and by then, she reasoned, it was too late to turn around.

Had it really been so short a time ago that Dani had considered Carmen to be the worst thing that had ever happened to her? So short a time since she'd been free of the preoccupation caused by hair and curves, her sleep unbothered by dreams of serpent girls? Primeras didn't think in terms of bodies. Of dreams. These were dangerous thoughts even with a husband at their center. But a Segunda?

It was unthinkable. Unheard-of.

More unheard-of than passing information to La Voz? Dani asked herself, pleased when the disapproving maestra's voice in her head seemed to have no answer.

Dani knocked on Carmen's door before she could talk herself out of it. She needed to quiet her thoughts, that was all. And hadn't Carmen once said Dani could consider her a friend?

"Come in!" she called, and Dani hesitated. Was she really doing this? And what did it mean if she was? Taking a deep breath, she pushed open the door, leaving her train of thought mercifully unfinished.

Carmen's suite was the same as it had been the last time Dani had been here, the gilded mirror still reflecting every part of the scene back at her. The only thing that had changed was Dani, who felt much different about the idea of Carmen's reflection than she had that day.

You're here as a friend, she reminded herself sharply.

In front of the window, in a silk wrapper that slipped off one shoulder, Carmen was deep in concentration over a flower arrangement, clipping the stems of plate-sized scarlet blossoms with curling indigo tongues, taming them into a glass vase like she was a magician from a story, the blossoms some unruly flame.

"Dani!" said Carmen, her scissors slipping on the flower stem. She hissed in pain and Dani crossed the room before she could give herself permission, bending over Carmen's thumb, where a bead of too-red blood was just welling up.

"I'm sorry," she said. "I didn't mean to startle you. Do you need anything? A bandage?"

Carmen stuck the wounded digit in her mouth and pulled it out again with a satisfied smacking sound. "Nope," she said. "All better."

Great, Dani thought, *now I'm hovering this close for no reason at all.*

"So," Carmen said, returning to her flowers, increasing the space between them with predictable grace. "What brings you to my humble abode?" Her lips quirked on the word *humble,* and Dani found herself laughing.

She should have expected the question, but somehow, she didn't have an answer. What *was* she doing here? "Honestly?" she said, when too much time had passed. "I don't know. Primera social season shut down after Jasmín's arrest, and having only Mateo to talk to for days is just . . ." She trailed off, realizing she was rambling, and looked at her hands as she waited for Carmen to say something. Anything.

But for a minute or more, she didn't say a word. Dani regretted everything in that minute. Coming here, being so cavalier about wanting to spend time with her, ever being born. She prayed to the gods in the clockwork to take her back ten minutes, even though she knew it was impossible.

But after a moment, Carmen smiled, a mischievous thing that showed her sharpest teeth. "If I have to hear him go on about the dawn of Medio's new, Mateo-centric era for one more minute, sometimes I think I'll scream just to stop him."

They were shocking words from the mouth of a high-society wife, but Dani found she wasn't shocked at all. In fact, she was nodding in agreement before she could think better of it.

"How lucky we are," she deadpanned. "To be the simple dogs of the world, and he our benevolent kennel master."

Carmen's laughter came in a short burst. "You surprise me, Primera."

"What, you've never met a funny Primera?"

"Once," Carmen said. "But she wasn't irreverent, too."

Dani bowed with a flourish. She felt loose and light, like she might float away. If she was actively working against her husband's agenda but under suspicion of sympathizing by his awful mama, what was the use of being proper anymore?

Dani had never felt more free.

"One of a kind, then, I suppose," she replied at last.

"You certainly are," Carmen said, and her eyes lingered.

Dani didn't look away, and the space Carmen had so deftly put between them suddenly felt like not enough and far, far too much. The strange intensity from the night of the party had returned, and Dani had to stop her eyes from wandering down. . . .

"You know what?" Carmen dropped the last of the flowers into the vase. A perfect bouquet.

"What?" Dani asked, her voice slightly hoarse.

"Let's have an adventure. Go somewhere fun. You up for it?"

It was the word *fun* that caused Dani to pull back. It wasn't the most hated word in the Primera lexicon, but it was close, and her reaction was instinctual, borne from years of conditioning against this very danger. "It's probably not a good idea," she said, though something bubbling and sun-bright inside her was urging her to say yes, and damn the consequences.

"Come on!" Carmen pleaded, whirling around, not noticing the way her robe gaped at the thigh. "It would be irresponsible to let me go alone, wouldn't it? All the way to the marketplace where who-knows-what is lying in wait?"

Dani began to thaw.

"It would be perfectly proper," she said. "A Primera chaperone to make sure a flighty Segunda doesn't run amok while their husband is away."

Her low, persuasive tone was quickly eroding Dani's objections. She knew she was supposed to refuse, but at that moment she couldn't for the life of her remember why.

"We'll stay inside the gate. Just for an hour," Carmen promised. "Please, Dani?"

The way she looked up through her lashes sealed it. She could have asked for anything.

"People don't say no to you, do they?" Dani finally replied, fighting the smile that threatened to stretch her pursed lips apart.

"Not if they want to live." Carmen threw Dani a mock sinister look before standing and slinging an arm around her shoulder. "Thank you, Primera," she said. "You won't regret it."

Overwhelmed by the closeness of her, the scent of her hair, Dani could only nod.

Carmen dressed quickly—in the privacy of her closet, thankfully—and before Dani could think better of it, they were walking down the driveway in the blazing sun.

"No car?" Dani asked, and Carmen laughed, skipping ahead, swinging her arms.

"Walking is part of the *experience,*" she said. "Get on board!"

"I'm on board," Dani mumbled. That smile kept returning at the most inconvenient times.

On the road to the complex's plaza, Dani's loose black dress was fitting for a chaperone, but Carmen flaunted curve-hugging, sky-blue silk, drawing stares of admiration and more as she passed. She ignored them all, humming and twirling and looking altogether oblivious to the effect she had on people.

As the residents of the gated community stared, Dani imagined taking Carmen's hand. Walking arm in arm. It was absurd, of course, this far inland. A fantasy.

In Polvo, and other villages like it, there was the occasional couple that broke tradition, living woman with woman or man with man, and some who eschewed the confines of their gender altogether. Old men muttered about it being unnatural, uptight mothers gave *those* houses a wide berth when they walked to the wells with their children, but in a place where marriage was based on love and there were still gods in everything, people were mostly allowed to live in peace.

Here, though, marriage was a business transaction. Wives were bought and paid for. Even if the bearded Sun God had ever condoned two women in love, or two men, it simply wasn't good for business.

Dani was forced to leave her musings behind as the pop-up marketplace came into view in the town square. It was nothing like the markets she had visited in her childhood—this one was more entertainment than function—but Dani found herself as breathless as she'd been in the capital. Intoxicated by the bustling feeling of people moving and living, of hearts beating in tandem. At the top of the plaza's steps, a woman in a sweeping embroidered skirt played a painted guitar as if she had twelve fingers on her left hand alone. The notes drifted over the small crowd, adding a magic to the moment that wasn't lost on Carmen.

When she tossed her head back to laugh, spinning in circles to the rhythm, Dani found herself smiling, her dark thoughts drifting away. When she laughed, the sound was hesitant, but it felt good leaving her body. It left a weightlessness in its wake.

She didn't notice Carmen watching her until it was too late.

"You should laugh more often," said Carmen, almost shyly.

"Happiness suits you." Her eyes lingered a moment, and Dani's cheeks bloomed with a warmth that was becoming all too familiar. Maybe it was a fantasy, but today, she didn't care that they had no future. She just wanted to live in this moment for a little longer, where she and Carmen could lock eyes and share a blush. Where every note of every song had meaning and the very air was electric.

"Come on," Carmen said at last, breaking eye contact, dispelling the worst of the tension. "Let's shop."

She took Dani's hand in hers, and though she knew she should, Dani didn't protest. Carmen had long fingers and a strong grip, and Dani let herself be propelled by Carmen's energy. This force-of-nature girl who was on a mission to see and touch everything in her path.

Carmen trailed the fingertips of her free hand along wide turquoise disks hanging from braided leather bands; she scooped a handful of tiny, glittering obsidian beads from an open cloth sack and let them fall back one by one, clicking against one another. In the next booth, she pulled at the corner of a woven blanket, rubbing it first across her own cheek and then Dani's.

"Isn't this the softest thing you've ever felt?" she asked, her eyes bright.

But with Carmen's hand still in hers, she found she couldn't agree.

Carmen dropped Dani's hand then, needing both of her

own to lift a giant polished horn and peer inside. The old man running the booth only smiled when Dani looked at him in alarm. No one could say no to Carmen.

"I'm *starving*," she exclaimed when she'd returned the horn. "Come on!" and she bumped Dani's hip with her own before darting off toward a row of tiny food stands, mouth-watering smells mingling in the air before them.

From a green-and-gold-striped tent, Carmen ordered for both of them. White, flaky fish grilled with citrus and herbs, a heap of scarlet pickled onions, a stack of little flour tortillas like clouds.

They sat at a tiny table in the middle of the commotion, and their food came with paper cups of white wine that tasted like a sunbeam. Caught up in the day, Dani shed her Primera propriety and groaned with her first bite. Carmen stared, and Dani tried unsuccessfully not to stare back.

Things grew quieter for a moment, as they ate and sipped and caught each other looking. A small but brilliant flame was catching in Dani's chest, and she felt the presence of the heart goddess again, turning the air warm and the sunlight liquid.

Was it possible that she wasn't the only one feeling the terrifying things she was feeling?

And what did it mean if Carmen felt them, too?

She was cruel to you in school, said the increasingly desperate voice of the maestra in her head. But the accusation floated away. It was old news, and Dani understood what desperation felt like. She couldn't blame Carmen for surviving. Hadn't she done things she never expected to do for the very same reason?

It's against the rules!

What about Mateo?

Sota?

Your parents?

But none of them were here, and Dani was, and her skin was alive like it had never been, her heart thudding too hard in a way that wasn't quite unpleasant. When Carmen's plate and cup were empty, it was Dani's turn to say, "Come on."

She walked away from the crowd, ignoring a knot of people gathering for some midday attraction nearby. She sensed, rather than saw, that Carmen had stayed close. They followed a winding walking trail until they could hear the chattering of a creek, fed by the freshwater spring that kept this part of the island green, so different from the salt-bleached landscape where Dani had cut her teeth.

Where Carmen had cut hers.

Where was this boldness coming from? Dani wondered as she left the trail, pushing into the trees until she could see the plate-sized pools with their glinting silver fish.

She stopped.

Carmen stopped.

There were gods everywhere here, and Dani knew without

212

a doubt that whether or not her feelings were lawful, they weren't wrong. Nothing that felt like this could be. She was working up the courage to turn and face Carmen when she felt a soft hand on her wrist, the pressure fainter than before.

It gave her the bravery she needed.

The enthusiasm Carmen had been buzzing with all day wasn't gone, but it was quieter somehow. Softer. She didn't let go of Dani, just slid her hand down until their fingers tangled between them.

"Dani," Carmen said, and the way she said it made Dani sure.

"Yes," she answered in a whisper. "Yes."

Carmen's answering smile could have rivaled the moon that had blessed her for brightness.

Dani stepped closer, her flat shoes whispering through the vines at their feet until there was less than an inch between them. The silk of Carmen's dress brushed her bare knee, and she shivered.

"Cold?" Carmen asked, her breath against Dani's face. She could only shake her head in response. "Is this okay?" Her nose grazed Dani's, her lips not far behind.

"Yes," Dani said again, breath sending strands of Carmen's hair dancing.

"How about this?" she asked, sliding her thumb along Dani's cheekbone.

"Mhm." Dani closed her eyes against the feeling. But

there were things she wanted to feel, too. Things she'd been dreaming of feeling for weeks.

Hesitantly, she lifted the hand that wasn't holding Carmen's and slid it into her hair. "Okay?" she asked, and Carmen sighed a contented little sigh.

"Yes."

Dani thought of the day she'd found Carmen in the bushes, untangling of the twig from the back of her curls as Hermanito the caterpillar crawled across their palms. She'd thought Carmen's hair seemed alive that day, but she hadn't known anything then.

Carmen's hair had a pulse. A weight. A magic to it that made Dani feel like her bloodstream was full of tiny bubbles. Carmen had traced Dani's cheekbone and was now running a hand down her neck, leaving goose bumps in the wake of her fingers.

Their eyes locked, their breathing synced and heavy, their pupils blown wide as they took each other in, unhurried for the first time.

"Okay?" they asked together, then laughed. But they didn't stop.

Carmen sighed. Dani brushed her hair off her forehead. Their noses bumped, corrected, and passed like ships in a channel, making just enough room.

Dani's heartbeat was like gunfire, she thought through a dreamy haze, but when Carmen screamed and dropped to the ground, she realized:

It hadn't been her heart at all.

It had been actual gunfire.

"Dani, *get down*," Carmen said, pulling at Dani's hand until she was on her knees beside her, suddenly breathless for another reason.

"What's going on?" she asked.

"I don't know," Carmen said, a shadow passing over her eyes.

The stones. Mateo's trip.

This was La Voz, Dani realized, and she had drawn them here.

"We need to get out of here," she said, standing up and pulling Carmen with her. "This place is about to be crawling with officers and we're not . . . exactly . . ." She gestured helplessly at the scene they'd painted. Scandal scented the air for a mile around them.

"Right, okay." Carmen let go of Dani's hand and shook her head like there was a fly buzzing around it. "How?"

"If we get back on the path, we can take it away from the marketplace and back up the road to the house," Dani said, already moving, but Carmen didn't follow. "Come on!" Dani said, impatient now. "They'll be combing this whole area any minute!"

"I don't think we should run," Carmen said, quiet but fierce.

"What. Are. You. Talking about?"

She stepped closer, scattering Dani's concentration again.

"Think about it. You know what it's like at the border, even on the right side. People are dying. Starving. Even here, they're being dragged out of parties and arrested. We've gotten close to talking about it, haven't we? Saying what a pity it is? But let's be honest here, Dani, we both know who's out there. If we care even a little . . . shouldn't we be brave enough to witness it?"

Dani's mouth was hanging open, and there was nothing she could do about it. She had seen hints of this. Wondered. Even hoped. But here was the proof, right in front of her. Carmen understood, and Dani had never wanted to kiss her more.

"I know we can't help," Carmen said, taking Dani's silence for disagreement. "Not without going to prison. But can't we at least be there? Can't we do that much?"

There was no time for kissing now. Not the way Dani wanted to do it. So she stepped forward and hugged Carmen fiercely. Just for a moment. "Of course we can," she said into her hair.

They held hands all the way back up the path to the marketplace, walking too close, shoulders and hips bumping with every step.

They didn't let go until the first uniform backs came into view.

*A Primera with strong principles, iron-clad restraint, and a
thirst for knowledge will never be led astray.*
— *Medio School for Girls Handbook,* 14th edition

⊹⧓✳⧓⊹

THE SCENE IN THE MARKETPLACE had gone from
casual to chaos.

Merchants ducked behind their stalls, and a crowd had
congregated at the top of the road that led back to the residences, blocked from returning home by the demonstration.

The gunfire had ceased for the moment, and Dani battled
her way through a crowd trying desperately to move away
from the source of the commotion. Carmen stayed close—
but not too close—behind her, and the occasional brush of
her hand against Dani's made her feel brave.

Military officers had arrived, clogging the street, guns at their shoulders; their boots stomped in a way that made Dani's knees unsteady. But unlike the inspections of her childhood, or the riot at school before graduation, this time there was something bigger than Dani's fear.

"There they are," Carmen said, speaking softly into Dani's ear so she wouldn't be heard. How, in the midst of a revolution, could she still change the focus of every cell in Dani's body with a whisper?

Up ahead, through a tangle of gun barrels and toppled tents and endless limbs, they could just make out the protesters. Dani saw Sota first, his angular face proud, his chin jutting upward. Beside him was the wolf-eyed girl from the marketplace. They were two of at least twenty. Around their waists, chains glinted in the afternoon sun.

For one panicked second, Dani thought they had been arrested. That they were chained together as some sort of spectacle, to be made an example of. The thought of watching Sota die, watching any of them die, wrenched at something that had just been born in her chest. She stepped forward without thinking of the consequences.

Carmen caught her before she could make it far. "They're okay," she said. "Look."

She was right. In addition to the chains, they were all holding hands. Blocking the road to the government buildings and the elite residences. They were forming a human obstruction, forcing the people in the market to bear witness to their pain.

"Come with us peacefully, or you will be arrested for treason," came a booming voice from behind them. The officers of Medio's military didn't need amplification—they were trained to be heard.

"*We are the voice of the voiceless*," said the protesters as one. No one moved a muscle.

"Do not force us to make this a confrontation," said the officer's voice. "If you agree to return to the outer island without violence, you will be treated with mercy."

At the center of the human chain, one of the women got to her feet. "The violence has already begun," she said, in a calm, clear voice that didn't need to rise to be heard. Dani thought she could feel it echoing inside her chest, alongside her heart. "The violence is committed every day you defend that wall and let citizens of Medio starve."

Beside her, a bearded man stood, and the woman pressed her palm to his before returning to her seat. "We protest for lack of shelter. We protest for lack of medical care. We protest because our children are hungry, and you, with all this excess, would rather kill them than feed them."

Tears sprang to Dani's eyes, and around her, the crowd was quieting, turning to listen.

The man turned to the wolf-eyed girl, her black hair glinting in the midday sun. She looked so fierce, so brave.

Dani felt Carmen straighten her shoulders, saw her lift her chin.

"This violence has been fifteen years in the making," she said, forcing the crowd to grow softer to hear her.

They did.

"The government claims the wall exists to keep you safe from the threat beyond it, but ask yourselves: When has there ever been true protest without injustice? Who really cast the first stone? Who is attacking, and who is bleeding?"

When she turned to Sota, she pressed both palms to his and bowed her head before taking her seat amid the clinking of chains.

"Your newspapers paint us as criminals," he said, and though the sun was in his eyes, Dani felt as though he was looking right at her. "And how easy it is for them to judge. With two beautiful wives for every undeserving husband. With enough fresh food that it goes bad before they can eat it all. With doctors and hospitals and shoes with soles. With healthy children that are allowed to grow thick before they grow tall."

The crowd was silent, and beneath their silence Dani thought she could sense the god of guilt spreading his shadow across their hearts. Guilt they'd never admit to their neighbors, but that burrowed into the secret places. Some red-faced folks had stalked off angry to stand behind the line of officers, but far more had stayed.

Out of fear or curiosity, who could say? But they had stayed.

Dani's heart was a paper kite, soaring on the wind of the protesters' words, on the change she could almost feel. Like the swell of a wave before it breaks.

"But what would you do?" Sota asked, softer now. "If all that were gone. If your children were stretching thinner and your wives cried at night from hunger. If the streets were thick with criminals, stealing your meager garden's bounty and selling it for more money than you could ever hope to make?"

He took a deep breath, emotion choking him. "What would you do then? If you were desperate, and every day a simple, treatable illness took another of your friends? Your children? Would you stay at home? Would you be silent? Would you remember the rules?"

In front of them, the officers had begun to mutter among themselves. They didn't dare open fire now, not with so many witnesses to the peaceful nature of the protesters. These were Medio's most notorious gossips. Whatever happened here would spread.

"They're lying to you about who we are," Sota said, somehow making eye contact with everyone at once. "We only want to live."

Behind him, one of the protesters began to hum. A low, pervasive sound that grew louder as the rest joined their voices to his. It was twenty separate tones. It was a hundred. It was one. It vibrated through Dani's teeth and jaw, in the space between her ribs, growing somehow louder still, and she thought—for the second time today—that she could feel the gods watching.

Some people said this conflict, the one they would not officially call a war, had started thousands of years ago during a falling-out between two brother-gods. But here, today, Dani could see that was just a fanciful story, perpetuated to give people an easy answer. The real answer was harder. Prejudice. Privilege. Hatred.

Maybe the Sun and Salt Gods *had* walked with mortals all those years ago. Maybe one had betrayed the other. But there was nothing left of that story here today. This was politics. This was humanity, and the refusal to recognize it. The realization felt like another small chip coming off the foundation Dani had always trusted to remain solid beneath her.

Then, at the edge of her vision, she saw an officer break away from the group. Consumed with the spectacle before them, no one else seemed to notice. Dani elbowed Carmen, but she turned too late. The officer had disappeared into the trees.

The hopeful feeling she'd had just a moment ago was quickly evaporating in the face of a sinister fear that filled Dani up like smoke.

She pushed through the crowd at her side, hoping to find a better vantage point, but she'd only made it two feet from Carmen when an explosion cracked the air and sent earth flying just past the treeline. The vibration stopped, the low hum replaced with screams and curses from both sides.

"They're firing!" shouted an officer in front of Dani, and the call was echoed down the line. "They've hidden explosives! We're under attack!"

"No!" Dani shouted, but another blast went off on the other side of the road, swallowing her cry.

"Take them alive if possible, but do not let them escape!" shouted an officer.

The first gunshot went off seconds later, and Dani screamed, not caring if her anger was mistaken for fear. She charged toward the front, thinking of nothing but the injustice of it all. The fact that all of these people had come here at great personal risk to promote a message of tolerance and understanding, and they were about to pay the ultimate price for it.

In the commotion, she could have slipped through the rough, uniformed bodies trying to restrain her, but a moment later she was being held from behind by two much softer, warmer arms.

"We can't," Carmen said in her ear, pulling her back, holding her close against her chest. "Not now, do you understand? Not right now."

Her voice calmed Dani, though she had no idea what the words meant. Carmen repeated them, something of the protesters' hum in her tone as she walked Dani backward into the crowd of terrified onlookers who had, just a moment ago, seemed willing to listen.

"Did they have the bombs set up in the trees?" shrieked a voice on the edge of hysteria.

"They lured us in with that speech! They were going to kill us all!"

"Criminals!"

"Rioters!"

"Illegals!"

Dani turned to Carmen, her eyes wide as she wordlessly pleaded for understanding.

"I know." Carmen looked like she'd swallowed something bitter that was taking a long time to go down.

"Carmen, they didn't—"

"I know."

"It was the officers. They—"

"I *know*, Dani. I know."

Her eyes said what her words couldn't. That it didn't matter if they knew. There was nothing they could do about it. Not today.

The gunfire finally died down, and soon cars sped down the hill with the bodies of protesters, living and dead. Even the living wouldn't last long, not in those cells, and Dani's body felt suddenly boneless.

She'd been a hungry child. A criminal, moments from arrest or death. She'd been a daughter who couldn't do enough to save her parents, and a victim of blackmail, and a girl who dreamed of kissing a Segunda in a sun-filled glade.

But until this moment, she'd never been so completely helpless.

Carmen stood steady and strong, letting Dani slump against her as they walked slowly up the newly cleared mouth of the road toward home. For once, they didn't have to worry about how it looked. Even strange as it was, no one was looking at them.

The moment they walked through the front door of the massive house, they were descended upon by frantic house staff, who checked them for injuries and asked questions faster than Dani could even begin to answer them.

She looked for Carmen in the commotion, and she was there, her eyes steady as they held Dani's. She heard the words she'd whispered at the scene again.

Not now. . . .

She wondered again what they'd meant, but before she could think of a way to get Carmen alone, the maids were separating them, bundling them off to their respective rooms to be treated for scrapes and bruises.

The long, shallow scratches on her neck were the least of Dani's worries. There had been blood on the pavement as they'd left the marketplace. . . .

What if it was Sota's? Did anyone else know about their arrangement? She'd been so busy pushing back during their meetings she had never thought to ask. A few weeks ago, the idea of being free of La Voz, no strings attached, would have been the answer to a prayer.

But now?

She thought about her life as it would unfold without her connection to the resistance. A life of parties and staff schedules. A life of luxury beyond what she'd ever dreamed, built on her husband's belief that people like Dani's family didn't deserve to live.

A life of watching Carmen disappear into his bedroom every night, educating the children they made together behind those ornate doors when they grew old enough. Pretending to be an unfeeling, uncaring hunk of stone while the world went on killing people and she became bitter and resentful.

Despite her best efforts, the tears were back in a moment. Between Carmen and the protest, this day had put a crack in her perfect restraint, and she wasn't sure it was fixable. Dani sent the maid out with less tact than she normally would have employed, and breathed in the minty, herbal scent of the salve on her scratches as her thoughts continued to spiral.

She remembered so clearly now, the things she'd said to Sota the first day they met. About how she shouldn't be expected to fight for the cause just because she happened to have been born in the wrong place. About how survival was the most important thing.

But right now, after what she'd seen, survival felt less guaranteed than ever, and more than that, it felt small. Selfish and mean. What right had she ever had to hide away in this rose stone mansion, cloaking herself in safety when she *knew* what it felt like to want? To need. To be denied.

If we're not all free, none of us are free, Sota had said that day. And wasn't it true?

Today, La Voz had tried to tell the truth, and Medio's military had put them *all* in danger just to make sure that message was never received. She'd thought they were protecting her, once. That if she learned to imitate the elite well enough, one day she would be one of them.

But there was no safety in wartime. There was no protection. Not for people like her. She had done what she needed to do to survive, but even now, at least one member of the family she'd counted on to protect her wanted her imprisoned or killed. What would come next?

And if every part of her was a lie, what would be left of Dani?

She felt dizzy with the realization, her life so far wobbling on a foundation that had been slowly eroding since graduation and was now crumbling beneath her feet.

The maid came back with dinner sometime later, and Dani ate ravenously, her body exhausted though her mind had never been more awake. She stayed up long after the sky went dark and the house went silent, wrestling with her thoughts and history.

The police had tried to erase the truth Sota and the others had spoken from the minds of every onlooker with their underhanded trick, but they could never make Dani forget what she'd seen. This house felt stifling, her role in it even more so. She felt restless and strange, on the precipice of a decision she wasn't sure she trusted herself to make.

I need to see Sota, she thought, surprising herself. But was it really so surprising? During their meetings, Dani had always had a single objective: *Do the least possible damage, and get out before anyone realizes what you've done.* But what would it feel like to take matters into her own hands? To volunteer? To make a choice to do what was right instead of what was safe?

The thought filled her with a cold, biting fear. Today's events had pushed her visit with Mama Garcia to the back of her mind, but her suspicion was still there, like a knife against Dani's throat. Even so, there was something bigger than fear inside her today.

As the sky began to turn pink at the horizon, Dani left behind her sadness and reformed her anger into something diamond hard and sharp. At her desk, she took a piece of stationery and a pen from her drawer and gritted her teeth.

She had a plan. Now she just had to hope it didn't get her killed.

As a Primera, you will need the ability to assess situations quickly, to become an expert on any subject in as long as it takes to finish an appetizer or cocktail.

—*Media School for Girls Handbook,* 14th edition

⊹⊱✳⊰⊹

JUST BEFORE BREAKFAST, DANI SNUCK out her patio door and clung to the shadows beside the house, an envelope clutched in her trembling hand.

She met no one on her way to the front of the house, where she lurked out of sight as two maids who had just finished the pre-breakfast table setting walked down the driveway toward the servants' quarters.

When the coast was clear, Dani approached the front door, trying to look casual even though no one was there to notice her posture. Whispering a prayer to the gods in the shadows, the gods in her own coiled-to-spring muscles, she slid her envelope under the door and bolted back to her bedroom patio.

No one had seen her. Phase one was complete.

Taking a deep breath, Dani made sure her desk was clear of evidence, stuffing the page below the one she'd written on into the back of her desk drawer with the cards. If even the impression of those words was noticed, it would be over for her, and she wasn't going to be caught burning things in the garden before breakfast. Not when Mama Garcia might already be onto her.

With the coast clear, she let her Primera calm settle. She'd been through an ordeal the day before, her mask told the world. She was tired. But nothing else was out of the ordinary.

Until a knock sounded on her door. Dani jumped before throwing herself into her desk chair and trying to look like she'd been there for hours.

Mateo didn't wait for her to invite him in, pushing the door open harder than was necessary. It banged against the wall behind it as he strode in, his normally well-ordered hair disheveled, his eyes open a little too wide.

Dani's body reacted to the sight of him, rage heating her from the inside. His wide shoulders and his long arms, the body he'd used to intimidate her, to terrify Jasmín when she was already doomed. She hated him and everything he stood for, but she had to prevent him from finding that out at all costs.

"Daniela," he said, barely looking at her. "I've doubled down on security. No more of those monsters will be getting in through the gate or anywhere else."

"Thank you, Mateo," Dani said, the grateful wife and her heroic husband. Like he hadn't startled her nearly out of her skin by barging in here. Like there was nothing to hide in this room. "I'm alright," she said when he didn't reply. "Just a little shaken up."

By the thugs you employ as military police.

"Understandably so. To attack us here, at home . . ." He shook his head and turned his eyes on her at last. They were bloodshot. A little wild. Like he'd hardly slept. "I never would have forgiven myself if something had happened to you or Carmen."

"Luckily we were well out of the way of the blast," she said, seething at the way his mouth wrapped possessively around Carmen's name. Mateo was agitated about something, that much was clear enough, but she'd bet the contents of her secret drawer that it didn't have anything to do with the safety of his family.

She could only hope the wheels she'd set in motion this morning were rolling in the right direction.

As if on cue, Mia appeared in the open doorway, Dani's envelope in her hand. "I'm so sorry to bother you, señor, señora," she said. "But this letter has just arrived. It's addressed to both of you and it's marked 'urgent,' so I thought you'd want to see it right away."

"Give it here," Mateo said, holding out his hand, not making eye contact with the girl. "That'll be all."

He ripped into the letter as if it was addressed to him alone, which was exactly what Dani had been counting on. She sat idly before him, fighting the urge to check that her drawer was securely closed, tension in every muscle that she could not let him see.

After a minute that lasted far too long, Mateo set the letter down and looked at her pityingly, the wildness gone from his eyes for the moment.

"Everything alright?" she asked, as casually as she could.

"I'm afraid not," he said, leaning down to place his hand on her shoulder. It was all Dani could do not to physically recoil. "The letter is from your mother. It seems your father has fallen ill and is now being treated at the hospital in the capital." He passed her the letter, and she took the excuse to shrug out from under his heavy hand, pretending to read the letter she'd written herself just after dawn.

"Oh no," she said, her face falling, the concerned daughter mask sliding into place. "My poor papa. And my mama all alone." Dani let the letter fall and covered her mouth.

"The capital's hospital has the best doctors outside the complex," said Mateo, his voice detached rather than comforting. This was an unwelcome distraction from his vendetta. "I'm sure he'll make a full recovery."

"Of course, señor," Dani replied, hesitating for just long enough to get his attention. "It's only . . . my mother isn't from the city. They've never been to the capital, let alone a hospital that size. I wish they had someone to navigate things for them, to ensure he's getting the best care." She looked up at him with pleading eyes, as if this was a problem she couldn't possibly solve on her own.

Mateo stroked his chin. "Normally, I would say *you* should go and be with them," he said. "But with the riot yesterday . . . ," he continued, already shaking his head.

"José can drive me," Dani said, trying not to sound too eager. "It might startle them to see me with a bodyguard, but perhaps he could . . . leave me at the hospital doors? I swear to you, I won't leave the building until he returns."

On your honor, she thought.

Mateo was impatient to return to his diatribe against La Voz, but Dani was pitiful, and more than that, she knew he wouldn't like the story spreading that he'd refused her the opportunity to see her ailing father.

"Go," he said at last. "But José will have to remain with you; that part is nonnegotiable."

"Of course, señor," Dani said again. "Thank you." It wasn't perfect, but it would have to do for now. She'd find a way to shake José when they arrived. It wasn't like it would be the first time. She forced a smile and got to her feet. Mateo made no move to go. "I'll . . . need to get ready," she said, eyeing the door.

There was a flash of something distrustful and cold in his eyes, but it was gone in an instant. "I hope your father recovers quickly," he said, and then he was gone.

Dani was ready in moments. In the driveway, she sent the doorman scurrying for José and waited, the feeling of a ticking clock making feel her jumpy and strange. When the car pulled up, Dani exhaled, and within its dark interior she relaxed for the first time.

"Sorry to hear of your father, señora," said José perfunctorily. "To the hospital?"

"To the hospital," she agreed, feeling for the first time like she might actually get away with this.

The feeling didn't last long.

Air rushed into the back seat as the door was pulled open from outside. Dani's heart stuttered to twice its normal speed, and then seemed to stop completely when she heard a familiar voice.

"I'm coming with you."

Carmen was sliding into the seat beside Dani, her magenta skirt settling around her as she made herself comfortable for a long ride. "Are you okay?" she asked Dani once her seat belt was buckled. "I heard your father was ill, and I just thought . . . maybe you could use some company." A strand of hair fell into her eyes, and she peered around it with a shy smile that almost broke Dani's heart right there.

"Okay, señora?" José asked, but Dani turned to Carmen.

"You shouldn't," she said. "Mateo's already upset about the riot. He didn't want to let me leave the complex. I wouldn't want to get you—"

Carmen interrupted her with a wave of her hand. "I already cleared it with Mateo. He said as long as we don't leave the hospital and we're on the road by sundown, it would be nice for you to have the company."

But Dani had never planned on staying in the hospital, and she already had José to contend with. "I just don't know," she said. "My mama is fragile right now, and I don't know how bad things are there. It might be best if we just . . ."

"Dani," said Carmen matter-of-factly. "I'm not going anywhere. I'm great with parents. You're obviously upset, and I'm not going to let you guilt yourself out of a little comfort on a difficult day, so can we just go? We don't have much time as it is."

One argument, then another and another died on Dani's lips before she could speak them aloud. Carmen's mouth was set, her eyes were concerned but somehow still sparkling, and short of being physically thrown from the vehicle, she really didn't seem to be going anywhere.

"Just say thank you," Carmen said with a smirk, settling into her seat.

"Thank you?" Dani gestured at José to drive, not at all sure what she'd do when they reached the hospital and her father was nowhere to be found.

Of course, the ride to the capital had never passed so quickly, and Dani spent it watching Carmen out of the corner of her eye, but not for the reasons she usually watched her. The way she'd charged into the car wasn't uncharacteristic of her, but the way she'd insisted on staying struck an odd chord in Dani. Why had Carmen been so determined to accompany her despite Dani's reservations?

Something was off, and little as Dani liked to distrust the only friend she had in the world, she found her mind wandering back to the morning after graduation. When she'd watched the growing closeness between Carmen and Mama Garcia in the car, thinking she shouldn't trust either of them. One apology from Carmen and she'd been so quick to forget it all. . . . But hadn't Carmen already proven that she would sell Dani out if it meant protecting herself?

Then there had been the night of Jasmín's arrest, when Mama Garcia had tried to burn the letter. Lost in everything that happened next, Dani had barely registered the way Carmen had denied knowing the elder Segunda was in the house. But she had been the only one home. Who else could Mama Garcia have been meeting?

Dani had never thought to be suspicious, especially after their day in the marketplace. The almost-kiss. The way Carmen had encouraged her to stay and watch when the protests began. She'd been so sure that day, that Carmen was sympathetic to the cause, that there was so much more to her than Dani had ever thought.

But hadn't she behaved exactly like someone trying to gain Dani's trust? Someone trying to lower a Primera's famous guard so she would admit something incriminating?

This time, she looked at Carmen directly. When she looked back, something twisted and flipped in Dani's stomach. A combination of attraction and apprehension. Carmen smiled as their eyes met. Was it the smile of someone who could sell her out? Who would follow her into the capital to spy for Mama Garcia?

Was it the smile of someone who could almost kiss her one day and then get her killed the next?

She was so lost in thoughts of kissing and loyalty, they were pulling up to the hospital doors before Dani decided what to do about Carmen, not to mention José.

Carmen slid out first, stepping out of the car and into the oppressive heat of the capital. Dani stalled a moment, making sure José's eyes were averted before undoing the clasp on her watch and letting it fall silently to the floor of the car.

She'd pretend to look for it tomorrow, claim it had slipped from her narrow wrist. But the last thing she needed today was a brand.

Out on the street, Carmen and José stood beside her, and Dani had no choice but to walk through the front doors of the huge stucco building that housed Medio's largest hospital.

It was cooler inside, and Dani stopped in the lobby, everything inside her a knot that would not come untied. "I'll just see where his room is," Dani said, an idea coming to life just in time. She didn't wait for an answer, just walked up to the reception desk as if she did this every day. Thankfully, José and Carmen stayed put, out of earshot.

"Excuse me," Dani said, smiling. "My cousin and I are here to visit my father."

"Name?" she asked, and Dani hesitated, just a beat.

"Before we get that far, I just want to check something with you," Dani said, glancing back at José for effect. "Our uncle insisted on accompanying us, and while I know my father doesn't mind his criminal record or his tendency to get . . . boisterous in confined spaces, I just wanted to make sure the hospital didn't mind him coming to the room."

The woman paled a little, looking over Dani's shoulder at José's hulking silhouette. He stood at least a foot taller than Carmen, his arms crossed meanacingly across his chest.

"To clarify," Dani continued, drawing her attention before José could get suspicious. "He's not *dangerous* or anything, unless there's any sharp instruments around, or anyone makes direct eye contact with him. He gets a little . . ."

"I'm sorry," the woman interrupted. "But unfortunately, we only allow immediate family into the patient rooms."

"You don't say," Dani replied. "Well, if it's a *hospital rule*, I'm sure they'll understand."

She returned to José and Carmen to deliver the bad news. At first, she was sure José would cause a scene and demand to be sent with Dani, but thankfully he took a seat in the waiting area.

"Be back here by sundown," he said. "I'll be watching the entrance."

"Of course," she said. "Thank you."

She headed for the hallway, hoping she could find a side door and slip out unnoticed, but as she rounded the corner back to the reception desk, Carmen was right on her heels. "Dani, wait!"

It was all she could do not to groan aloud. "Look, they said . . ."

"Please," Carmen said, tossing her hair. "I've charmed my way into far more difficult situations than this. I told you, I'm coming with you."

Dani looked at her, every heartbeat evidence of the time she was losing. This was the moment of truth. Could she trust Carmen or not? She certainly hadn't expected to have to make this decision so soon.

"Do you know what room he's in?" Carmen asked, looking around for a sign to point them in the right direction.

Dani wished there were a sign to tell her what to do instead. She had her suspicions in one ear, telling her that Carmen couldn't possibly have changed her mind about Dani so quickly, that she had to have some ulterior motive, and whatever it was could be deadly.

But in the other ear was the whisper of a nearby creek, a nose grazing hers—a feeling that she could step forward into nothingness, and Carmen would hold out her arms and keep her from falling.

"Dani?" Carmen asked, an expectant look on her face.

Looking at her, Dani felt that pull the same as always. The pull she hadn't known at twelve years old meant more than just relief at finding a friend in a new place.

Carmen was beautiful, and mysterious, and fascinating, and Dani wanted so much to trust her. But at this unexpected moment of truth, she found some walls were just too high to be breached.

"I'm sorry," she said finally. "But I need to see my family alone."

Carmen smiled. "I know you're scared, but—"

"No," Dani said, freezing the word at the edges in a way that stopped Carmen in midsentence. "I'm saying I don't *want* you to come with me. It won't help. It'll only make things worse."

This time, the lie hit its mark. Carmen's face fell, but only a little. "Is this because of the other day?" she asked. "Because, Dani . . . if that wasn't . . ."

"It isn't about that," Dani said. There was no time to go down that road. Not with sunset only a few hours away. "It's about now. This is my family, they don't know you. I barely know you. And I don't need your help." Her voice was hard this time, and she didn't have to fake it. Every suspicion she'd courted in the car wove through her words like metal. "I'm sorry for wasting your day, but if you would wait here with José while I take care of this, I'd appreciate it."

"Sure," Carmen said, her voice small. "I'm sorry for pushing, I just . . . I thought you might need a friend."

Dani's heart squeezed in her chest. It was almost painful, how much she did need a friend, how much she wanted to believe Carmen meant it. But Dani had been burned once before, and she couldn't afford any more mistakes.

If Carmen was really working with Mama Garcia, she'd likely ask the woman at the desk the moment Dani was out of sight. She'd find out there was no Señor Vargas in this hospital. But at least she wouldn't know where Dani was going.

And if she wasn't spying . . . if she was really just here as a friend . . .

Dani shoved the thought aside. She had made her choice. She didn't have time to question it now.

"I'll be back as soon as I can," she said, trying not to meet Carmen's eyes and failing. The hurt in them seemed so genuine, but Dani knew all too well how emotions could be faked.

"Take your time," Carmen said, trying to smile. "I'll be here."

Dani hoped against hope that she really would. That Dani had it all wrong. But Carmen was definitely hiding something from her, and today was the wrong day to gamble on what it was.

"Thanks," she said, and then she was off, trying to look like someone who really had a sick father down one of these hallways. No one stopped her. As she walked deeper into the hospital, looking for a side or back entrance that couldn't be seen from the street, she tried to leave Carmen and everything she implied in the waiting area.

She would need all her focus if she was going to do what she needed to do.

Finally, a quiet hallway ended in a door that groaned when Dani pushed it open, and she found herself in a courtyard, surrounded by a low wall. The plant life just beyond it was beginning to take the area back, vines breaking through flagstones to reveal earth so alive it was almost red.

The hospital wasn't far from the marketplace, and Dani oriented herself as quickly as possible, avoiding the main street until the building was out of sight, trying not to think about how different this would be if she'd chosen differently in the waiting room. If she were hand in hand with Carmen right now, giggling as they pushed their way through the crowds Dani now navigated alone.

Irritated, Dani forced herself to focus. There would be plenty of time to second-guess her decisions when she was safely home. Right now, she needed to find Sota, or someone who knew what had happened to him.

It was a long shot, but it was the only one she had.

The first thing she'd have to do was find a way to rule

out the vast majority of the market's shoppers and loiterers. The narrower the window for observation, her maestras had always said, the greater the chances of getting it right. So, what would a La Voz agent be doing in the marketplace today?

Too carefree, she thought, passing a group of young women with crushed ice and syrup from the stand where Dani had once gotten into a fake argument with the wolf-eyed girl.

A man charging past the lime stand was too determined, a scowl on his face. No La Voz agent would give away so much. Anyone here on resistance business would look relaxed but observant; they'd return to the same places more than once.

Dani started scanning faces she'd seen twice more closely, moving in small circles around the restroom where she'd once met Sota, assuming it hadn't been a random location. Not much about the way La Voz operated seemed random, after all.

Dani was on her third circuit when she realized she'd seen the same tunic on every pass. The girl wearing it was slight, brown skin warm against the cool gray. Three times past, and Dani hadn't seen her face, which meant she'd been circling around the post she now leaned against. Possibly avoiding Dani's eyes?

Silently, Dani moved closer, pausing at a stall full of stuffed children's toys in bright colors, picking one up and examining it in a way she hoped didn't look forced. Next, she fingered the fabric of a scarlet dress embroidered with bunches of vibrant bananas, as if considering the quality of the fiber, taking a look at the hemline.

She tried not to think about the last time she'd pretended to be interested in a market's wares, or the girl she'd been with that day, now sitting alone in a hospital waiting room. . . .

Hopefully.

Dani was close to her target now, and she shook herself for the second time. She needed to focus. She made sure not to stare too long or walk too straight. If the girl was intent on avoiding her, she'd be on high alert.

Slowly, painstakingly, she closed the yards between herself and the narrow-shouldered girl. It was too late now for her to melt back into the crowd. Dani felt a thrill of triumph as she reached out to touch her elbow. If it wasn't someone she recognized, or someone who recognized her, she'd keep walking, but she would have bet her priceless watch that this was a La Voz operative.

When the girl whirled around to face her at last, there was fire in her all-too-familiar gray eyes. It was the wolf girl from her first trip to the market, looking furious.

"Can't you take a hint?" she hissed.

Dani grabbed the other girl's arm, moving smoothly to avoid causing a scene. She only needed a second to plead her case. "I need to talk to Sota," she said, hoping the honest concern in her eyes would be enough.

"Shut. Up." There was alarm now where there had been anger. "Meet me in the bathroom in two minutes. If you're not there in two minutes, I will be gone. And you will not find me again."

Dani nodded her understanding, saying a silent prayer to the god of fate and chances that Sota was alive, and she would get the chance to tell him what she had realized that sleepless night after the riot. That she wanted to do more than exist on the fringes. That she wanted to fight back against the husband who thought he could control her, the government who thought they could decide who deserved to live and die.

That she wanted to make her own choices, and she was ready to start today.

For a new Primera, social alliances can be the key to success. Choose your friends carefully.
　　　　　　　　　　　—Medio School for Girls Handbook, 14th edition

‡‑‑☀‑‑‡

"IS HE ALIVE?"

"What do you think this is? A dominoes club?" the girl asked, her tone harsh and condescending. "If you're going to blow your cover and run down here every time there's a scuffle, you're even more useless than I've been telling him you are."

"I didn't blow my cover," Dani said. "I told him—"

"Sick papi, yeah, we know. Trust me, we'll have plenty of follow-up work to do on that one. I'm not sure you realize that if you ruin this, you're not the only person who suffers.

We would lose the closest spy we've had to the Garcias in years. It would be a huge setback for us. So . . . not everything is about you."

"I'm sorry," Dani said, though she wasn't sure she meant it. "I just have to talk to him. If he's . . ."

"Don't start crying on me, okay, this isn't a romance novel," snapped the other girl. "Yes. He's alive. But I barely got him out. And we were the only ones. Everyone else was arrested or killed."

Quick as it had lifted, the weight was back, ten times heavier than it had been just a moment ago. She saw their faces as they sat in their chains. Proud, brave. "I'm sorry," she said again. "It was terrible, the explosions and—"

"*We* didn't set off those explosions," snarled the girl in shadows across from her. "That was your friends in uniform."

"I know!" Dani said, too eager, cringing at the sound of her voice. "I saw them. That's what I wanted to talk to Sota about."

"Look, he's not in great shape for talking, but he'll be pissed if I don't take you to him, so whatever. Let's go. We need to get you back to that hospital as soon as possible, because if you give youself away over this I swear on everything I believe in—"

"I won't," Dani promised. "No one is expecting me until sundown." She failed to mention Carmen and José in the waiting room. That would be her secret.

"Great." The girl laced her hands together and held them out to Dani, who set a foot in gingerly, looking up at the window without enthusiasm.

"What's your name?" Dani asked on impulse. She could hardly call her "wolf girl" out loud, no matter how fitting a moniker it was.

"What do you think this is, a date? Get up there."

Dani's stomach dropped as she was hoisted to the windowsill. This was a joke you could make if you lived outside the repressive atmosphere of the inner island. If your entire romantic history hadn't consisted of being sold to the highest bidder, and an almost-kiss in the bushes with a Segunda who might be trying to have you killed.

"I'm Alex," she said, landing gracefully beside Dani on a low rooftop outside the bathroom window. She brushed off her hands like she'd done it a thousand times.

Dani nodded, trying not to break whatever moment had inspired her trust.

She followed Alex over the rooftops as the early afternoon turned late, the air growing heavy and muggy in their lungs. The city spread out below them like patchwork, lights glimmering to life as the tallest buildings cast short shadows across the bustling city.

"It's beautiful," Dani said, stopping for a moment, savoring the breeze that played across her face.

Alex didn't reply.

"There's a safe house just up here," she said after a few

more minutes. "That's where he's recovering. You'll only have a few minutes."

"I understand," Dani said. "And thank you."

Alex only rolled her eyes again, leading the way over a final rooftop and pulling back a tattered red curtain.

Inside was a poorly furnished room with several empty beds, sheets over holes in the crumbling walls. Against the back wall was Sota, alone, pale and reclined and looking like he'd been waiting for her.

"Look what the tides brought in," Alex said, and the familiarity of the phrase settled with an ache in Dani's chest. She hadn't heard it since she left home.

"I thought I might be seeing you today," said Sota with a wan smile.

"I'll give you two a moment," Alex said with yet another eye roll. Dani wondered if she ever got dizzy. "But *only* a moment," she said with a pointed look at Dani.

"Sundown. Cover intact," Dani said with a salute.

Sota laughed softly, and she walked toward him, careful, like even disturbing the air too much could hurt him.

"So, you were there," he said as Dani sat down on the bed beside his.

"I was."

"And?"

Dani took a deep breath and let it out slowly. All morning, she'd been trying to figure out what to say. How to explain why she hadn't been ready before, and why she was now.

"Your parents died," she said after a beat. Sota opened his mouth to reply, but Dani held up a hand. "Your parents died, and ever since, you've been doing your duty to them. To their memory."

He nodded and this time he didn't try to interrupt.

"My parents didn't die," she continued. "I don't know if that's fair, if it's right or wrong, if it's the goddess of luck or just a big damn coincidence. I don't know. But they lived, and they raised me to believe in the idea that my safety was the first priority. That no matter what I did, no matter how far it took me from them, it would be worth it if I could have a better life than they did."

"They love you," Sota said simply.

"Yes," said Dani, taking another deep breath. "But that love made their world shrink. It began and ended with me, and with the hope that I would be safe and prosper. I've been trying to honor their sacrifices, and their hopes, and their dreams for me, just like you've been trying to honor the memory of your parents."

Sota nodded again, looking thoughtful.

"It's right for parents to prioritize their children's lives. Their safety. Their happiness. But I've let their dreams for me become me. I've done everything they ever wanted, and it didn't make me safe. It only made me selfish."

Sota's eyes were bright now, some of the pain clearing from them. It was a mark of how far they'd both come, Dani thought, that he didn't interrupt or try to explain her feelings to her. That he waited for her to find her own words, in her own time.

"My parents wanted better for me, but I think the danger in that was that they believed the lies. That money and status and proximity make you *better.* That believing the Sun God chose you is *better* than hearing the whispers in the wind and feeling the pull of the million tiny divinities in everything. That being born with a certain name, and certain privileges, make you inherently higher quality."

Dani spoke slowly, haltingly, hearing the words as she spoke them, letting them warm her. Sota listened with patient eyes.

"They tell us about the curse of the Salt God because it's a simple story, but I don't think it's the real story. I think the real story is greed, and money, and politics. Privilege and prejudice. A system that was created thousands of years ago by people who wanted to reward those like them and punish everyone else."

"*Yes,*" Sota said, fierce, admiring.

"I'm not one of them," Dani said. "No matter how high I climb or how much I manage to grasp, I'm never going to be. And there's nothing wrong with that. There's nothing wrong with who I am." The words felt heavy spilling out, suffused with the same glow as the scarlet-tinged sky beyond the window.

Soon, the sun would set, and Dani would have to go.

But not yet.

"I know my parents love me," she said, finally ready to let go of the last piece. "But I want to live in a world where love doesn't mean fear. Where we can survive without forgetting who we are."

"Thrive, even," Sota said with a smile.

"Thrive," Dani agreed. "And . . ." She hesitated, but only for a moment. "I want to help build that world. Even if they don't understand. Even if it means I'm not safe or special. Even if I don't . . . survive. I want to fight it. Fight Mateo and everyone who believes him. Fight the men who framed you for those explosions."

"You saw that, too?"

"I'm a spy," Dani said with a smirk. "I see everything."

Sota laughed, but it quickly became a wince of pain.

"They shot you?" she asked, solemn now.

"Just a scratch," he said, but a complicated web of bandages spread across his chest and down his left arm, telling a more sinister story. "I'll be back at it in no time."

Dani's eyes stayed trained on the blood. She wanted to remember. Back in the rose stone house. Surrounded by vipers, just as Señora Garcia had told her during her first week. She wanted to remember the people who had died. Everything it had cost.

There was more, but Dani hesitated, letting Sota breathe through his pain. This was the part where she was supposed to confess Mama Garcia's suspicions. The letter. The strange way the Segunda had interrogated her over breakfast. It was the second piece. Total honesty.

But Sota trusted her. She could see it in his eyes. He believed she was one of them. And right then, with the glow of it still warm in her chest, she couldn't bring herself to break the spell. She could handle Mama Garcia, and she would. She would prove she was everything La Voz needed her to be.

"We knew it wouldn't be pretty," Sota said, gently bringing her back to the present. "And we were all willing to take the risk. We needed them to know we aren't going to stay in the shadows forever, that they're not safe behind the walls they build to keep us out."

"But now?" Dani asked, thinking of all the people they'd lost, the eloquent activists in chains who would never live to see the change they had given their lives for.

"Nothing has changed," Sota said without hesitation, though his eyes were sad. "That's what it means to fight. It means believing in the movement, and doing whatever it takes to further it, no matter what the consequences may be."

For once, Dani's determination was louder than her fear. She didn't want to dwell on the half-formed dangers of her past. She wanted to move forward. Now. As part of it all.

"So, what's next?" she asked, and Sota smiled, the brightness in his eyes kindling to a blaze.

"Listen," he said, shifting into a seated position as a mild breeze fluttered the curtains around them, showing off slices of the city and the orange sky. "This most recent scuffle isn't the worst thing the government has done to us by far. That's the first thing you need to understand."

"Please," Dani said, "I've been living in the belly of the beast for weeks." She thought of Jasmín, and Mateo. His commitment to creating a world free of protest, ruled by himself alone. "Whatever the worst thing is, it won't hold a candle to what's coming."

"Down on the lower parts of the island, even the people on the right side of the wall are getting restless," Sota said. "The curse they trapped us with isn't supposed to extend beyond the wall, but they don't live much better in the shadow of it. They're fed up with the excess, the gloating."

"Who can blame them?" Dani asked, before she realized what she was saying and smiled. She had blamed them herself, only a few short weeks ago.

But everything was different now.

"Mateo and his cronies won't stop until every last one of their dissenters has been silenced," he said. "And the more threatened the privileged feel, the more drastic the measures they'll be able to justify in the name of 'safety.'" Whether it was his injuries, or the shadows growing longer, Sota looked suddenly weary. "I don't know what they're capable of anymore. This new generation doesn't seem to play by any of the rules we've learned to fight against."

"What do you mean?" asked Dani. "I thought you said they'd done worse than the scene at the protest."

Sota looked at her now, appraising in the same way Carmen seemed to be sometimes. Like he was looking for a sign. Whatever it was, he seemed to have found it, because he went on after a minute.

"There's something else, Dani. The reaction to the protests is public, but this is something different. It's the thing we've been working to stop since I contacted you."

Her heart picked up speed. He was about to tell her something real. He was trusting her. Remembering Mama Garcia's note and the things she hadn't said, Dani felt a pang of guilt. But it didn't last long.

"It used to be that we knew what would happen when one of ours got arrested," he said. "It wasn't ideal, obviously, but it was predictable. Sometimes we could get them out, turn a guard on the inside, bribe the right people, take a transport van on the road. But when we couldn't, we could find some . . . closure. In knowing." He swallowed once, hard. How many had they already lost? How much closure had this boy who was barely a man needed to find in his life?

"But now?" Dani asked, unable to bear the silence any longer.

Sota looked her in the eye. The pain there was unmistakable, but his gaze was steady. "They're disappearing," he said. "Fifteen arrested La Voz members and suspected sympathizers in the past year. They're arrested in high-profile scenarios, but we have a source inside who's telling us they never arrive in the cells designated for them, and no one says a word." He hesitated, then steeled himself and pushed on. "The most recent disappearance was Jasmín Flores."

Dani's heart sank as fast as it had swelled at the thought that he trusted her to fight. "But Jasmín didn't even get a chance to tell you anything," she said. "What would they want with her?"

Sota smiled, shrugging with his good shoulder. "Who knows why they do what they do?"

But his tone was off, and Dani could tell. There was more to the story. A silence stretched between them, Dani waiting to see if he would offer more information, Sota acknowledging her distrust and refusing to placate her.

"So what do we do?" she asked, an edge to her tone that her maestras would have corrected in a heartbeat.

Sota adjusted his position again, trying to hide the pain. "We have things in motion that I can't tell you the details of."

Dani opened her mouth to argue, but he held up a hand to stop her.

"It's not personal," he assured her. "But you're in a precarious position. Behind enemy lines. If things go south, it's best that you know only what you need to know."

Dani clenched her jaw against the spike of fear and nodded her agreement.

"Just trust that we're working on it. For now, you've been asking a lot of questions at home, disappearing under strange circumstances. You need to go back. Lie low. Act natural. But watch *everything.* We're fairly certain the Garcias are the key to this whole thing, and we need to know all their pressure points. Anything we can use against them if it comes to that. We need to know schedules, times, the layout of the house, windows that open, entrances and exits. Even things that don't seem important, keep track of them."

Dani hesitated. She had come down here to pledge her allegiance. To make her choice, once and for all. She wanted to do more than attend dinner parties and keep her eyes open. She wanted to do something big and risky and heroic.

"Trust me," Sota said again, as if he could hear her reckless thoughts. "It's important. We have plenty of people willing to run around causing chaos, but none of them can waltz into the government complex and right into Mateo Garcia's mansion without arousing suspicion."

"I understand," Dani said, standing reluctantly, the sky deepening to red outside as the sun kissed the horizon. "And it starts with being back at the hospital by sundown, so how will I get the information to you?"

"We'll be in touch. Notes, cards, same as before. When it's safe to rendezvous, we'll let you know. Until then, just collect whatever you can."

Dani nodded, but she could feel the thrill of the visit

starting to wane as the sun sank. It was almost time to go back.

"Look, Dani," Sota said, sitting up, his knot of hair backlit by the rooftop sunset. "This is a pivotal time. We need people we can trust on our side, otherwise it all falls apart. If there's still *any* part of you that's thinking of this as blackmail . . . or wants out . . ."

The unspoken end of his sentence hung between them, like a fruit to be plucked, or left to rot.

"If we're not all free," she said, holding out a palm, like she'd seen the protesters do in their chains, "none of us are free."

With a smile that dazzled, Sota pressed his palm against hers.

"I'm glad," he said simply.

"Me too."

"As *adorable* as this all is," Alex said from the doorway, "it's time to go."

She disappeared back into the purpling night, and Dani turned to face Sota one last time.

"Goodbye," she said.

"It's not goodbye," Sota said. "It's 'get to work.'"

Dani cracked a smile, but it didn't stop the feeling that she was a butterfly about to climb back into her cocoon.

"Get to work," she whispered.

"Get to work."

"And don't die, okay?"

Sota chuckled weakly. "You either. And here." He reached out as far as he was able, and Dani met him there, taking a card from his hand.

The Cuatro de Bastos. Strength.

She pressed it to her chest for a brief moment, fighting with something heavy and warm and prickling inside her.

"Go," he said gently, and she did. Carmen was waiting, and there was work to be done.

When Dani pushed the crimson curtain aside, the city sky was on fire. From the rooftop, the dancing, shifting light bouncing off every reflective surface below, it was breathtaking. She whispered a thank-you to the gods in the light and the clouds for delivering such a good omen.

Alex led her back to the hospital in silence. Across ladders laid over gaps and steps set haphazardly into steep inclines. They were two shadows against the vivid sunset, moving toward home.

"Down these stairs," the other girl said, stopping after a few long minutes. "You'll be in the alley on the east side of the hospital. There should be an unlocked door in the back courtyard where no one will see you go in."

"I know it," Dani said quietly. "And thank you."

"You won't be thanking me if you take any more unauthorized trips into the city," she said, then turned back the way they'd come, moving much more quickly across the uneven terrain than she had with Dani in tow.

She watched her go for a minute, feeling like the last

traces of some strange magic were bleeding out through her fingertips. She had been a bright, certain-edged thing for an hour, but it was time to be a hundred shades again. There was more than her own survival riding on it now.

Back inside the hospital, Dani made her way to the front entrance, the last of the sun's rays staining the window above the door. The waiting area was empty, save for Carmen, who was asleep in a chair. For a moment Dani just looked at her, the soft lines of her sleeping body, the restless tangle of her hair.

"Your cousin is a loyal one," the woman at the reception desk said. "Stayed in that chair for hours, watching the door." She gestured toward the door Dani had disappeared through hours before.

"And my uncle?" Dani asked, seeing no sign of José.

"Visiting the restroom," she said, her eyes darting around in fear.

"And she didn't go anywhere?" Dani asked, gesturing toward Carmen, unable to help herself. "Talk to anyone?"

"I've been at this desk the whole time, just sorting through these donations," the woman said. "Never saw her move."

"I guess I'll have to thank her," Dani said in a low voice, the hint of a smile tugging at the corner of her mouth. Carmen hadn't sniffed around for information on Dani's father. She'd just waited. Like a friend would.

It wasn't proof of anything—not yet. But for now, it was enough.

She woke Carmen gently, and in the moment between her

eyes opening and her mind catching up, she smiled at the sight of Dani's face. "Hi," she said, and Dani couldn't help it; she smiled back.

"Hi."

"How's your father?"

"He's going to be okay," Dani said, sinking into the chair beside her.

"Listen," they both said together, and then they laughed, soft sounds that wound around each other in the spaces between their lips. "Go ahead," Dani said.

"I shouldn't have pushed it today," Carmen said. "You were obviously upset, and just because we've grown closer doesn't mean you have to trust me with something like this. I'm sorry."

Dani had been trained in the art of reading people, in discerning their motives, but there didn't seem to be anything at all lurking beneath Carmen's apology. "I'm sorry, too," she said. "I was scared, and I'm so used to hiding my parents. Where I come from . . ."

"I know the feeling," Carmen said, but this time it was there, a sharp glint at the edge of her confession that sent Dani's instincts into overdrive.

Their eyes locked, and despite her suspicions, Dani couldn't look away. The moment gathered intensity as it hung between them unbroken, and something warm pooled in her belly.

"When I was a kid," Carmen said, her voice low and a little

husky in a way that made Dani sure she wasn't alone in her feelings, "I used to ride with my family to deliver fruit to the marketplaces. There was this girl whose mama worked in one of the stalls, and she'd always hide behind piles of platanos when we got there."

Dani listened, never looking away, understanding that this story wasn't a logical continuation of their conversation. It was a confidence. An offering. Something Dani alone could keep.

"She was beautiful," Carmen said with a wistful smile. "I remember thinking all I wanted to do was hold her hand. Just to see what it felt like . . ." Whether unconsciously or not, her eyes darted down.

Dani had never been so aware of her fingers before.

"Anyway, one day I was helping stack lemons and she ran up and took one, right out of my hand. I chased her through the aisles, following that little spot of bright yellow, and when I finally caught her, I took the lemon back. But she didn't let go, so for a minute we just stood there, both our hands on the same lemon. And it felt like the world was opening up."

"So you knew," Dani said softly, glancing around the still-empty room. "Even then?"

"What?" Carmen asked, the tiniest lift at the corner of her lips. "That I wanted to hold hands with girls?"

The way Dani fidgeted slightly beneath the weight of the question was answer enough for Carmen, whose smile widened.

"Yes," she said, almost a whisper, and without thinking of

what was at stake, or what Carmen was planning, Dani slid her palm across the chair between them and into Carmen's waiting fingers.

They tangled there, just for a moment, and Dani's heart beat so hard she was sure Carmen could feel it in her palm. Her eyes drifted up Carmen's body, from their hands, laced together, to her eyes, which were still on Dani's face. There was nothing behind her eyes but wonder. Awe. How could one person be so open and so mysterious all at once?

When the men's room door creaked, they pulled apart guiltily.

But the feeling stayed.

Lust is not a word in the Primera lexicon.
—*Medio School for Girls Handbook,* 14th edition

⊹⟩✳⟨⊹

THE NEXT MORNING, DANI WAS walking the garden, trying to commit the dimensions of the house to memory, counting the windows and doors, paying special attention to any access point that wasn't in view of the street.

But when she passed Mateo's ground-floor suite, he was on the private patio, sneering at the newspaper. Dani reined in her calculating, measuring, and assessing and let her posture relax. A casual stroll through the garden. She hoped he wouldn't see her; between the knowledge that she was actively working against him and her confusing thoughts about Carmen, she had little mental energy to deal with Mateo's moods.

Not that she had a choice.

"Daniela, good," he called, waving her over. Her feet obeyed his beckoning hand reluctantly, like there were weights in the bottoms of her shoes. "I've had a letter from your father's doctor," said Mateo when she reached him, the crease still visible between his eyebrows. "Your father is being sent home in the morning to continue care, but he should recover." He was preoccupied, barely glancing at the letter, still engrossed in his paper.

The official hospital seal was visible on the discarded envelope, and Dani was grudgingly impressed with Alex's cover job. She could only hope Sota was as lucky as her fictional father.

"That's wonderful news," Dani said, layering the concerned, exhausted daughter over her amusement. "It was so helpful to them to have me there yesterday; thank you again."

"Mhm," Mateo replied, though she was certain he hadn't heard a word. "Anyway, there was a note from your parents as well. They asked that you don't risk another visit, given the climate, and I have to say I agree."

"Of course not, señor," she said demurely. "I did what I went there to do."

"Good," said Mateo. "Because with these miscreants on the loose . . ." He shook the newspaper at her, his eyes blazing. ". . . who knows what might happen next."

Dani watched Mateo, thinking of Sota's mission, trying to find any weak spots she hadn't already noted. He had been the last person to see Jasmín, as far as Dani knew, and if he was hiding something, La Voz would want to know. That was her job now. To know him. To know his secrets and his weaknesses.

To use them to make him pay for his cruelty.

"You should have seen those bumbling old idiots in the government building yesterday," he said, oblivious to Dani's traitorous thoughts, jerking his head at an empty chair. "They spend so much time waffling about what to do next."

Dani sat across from him, remembering what her maestras had told her. Silence was a weapon. She said nothing. If she played her cards right, this could be more useful than measuring the house by a long shot.

"As if it's not obvious what should come next," he said, the chill in his voice cracking, making way for his anger. "As if it hasn't been for a decade." His voice had a serrated edge to it again, the one that told Dani he was close to losing control.

Carmen and Sota faded in her thoughts as she sharpened her focus. She would have to tread very carefully here. "That must be frustrating," she said.

"Frustrating doesn't even begin to cover it," he said, abandoning his café to pace around the patio. "There were explosions, set off by a radical group, within the *government complex*. What more does it take to provoke a drastic response around here?"

"Well, they did kill or arrest all of them," Dani said, trying to keep her voice mild, looking down at her hands as if this were a typical conversation topic.

"Not *all* of them," Mateo said darkly. "And anyway, that's not what I mean."

Dani retreated back into her silence. He was clearly more interested in an audience than a conversation partner, but what he would get was a spy. Dani cataloged every movement, every twitch of the skin beside his eye. This was not the composed, cold man she had come to know. Something had changed. But what?

Mateo turned his attention to her, stopping the pacing, focusing on her in a way that made her skin crawl. His eyes were dark and hooded, like he hadn't slept in days. She had never seen him so disheveled.

"I'm talking about *really* going after them." His voice was low and dangerous, daring her to object. "Going on the offensive instead of just reacting when they attack us. I'm talking about *taking them all down.*"

Dani told herself to breathe normally, not to curl in on herself, to be a spy and not a scared girl from the wrong side of the wall. She had claimed a power over him, and he was none the wiser. She only had to stay still.

The god of steel was in her spine and her throat, and together, they waited.

Beyond the well-groomed lawn, all was calm, the leaves in their patch of jungle swaying gently in the breeze. *So strange*, Dani thought. *That the world can still be beautiful, even in the midst of all this.*

When Mateo stopped pacing, staring out into the trees, she stood slowly and crossed to stand beside him.

Up close, his eyes were more bloodshot than before, the skin around his lips dry and cracked. He stood perfectly still, looking straight. Then, as if something had erupted inside him, he clenched his firsts and let out a frustrated growl that echoed across the garden.

It took every ounce of Dani's restraint to keep from flinching.

"I've *told* my father what needs to be done! I've told them all! Right up to the president himself! Time and time again! I've told them that our god chose us. That he chose us to prosper and that he's never wrong!"

Dani's blood chilled at this. The sentiment wasn't new, but from the mouth of someone with real power to wield, in this ragged, almost hysterical tone, it was terrifying. She had never known Mateo to be religious, besides in the cursory way all inner-islanders masked their greed with worship for the Sun God. But something had clearly shifted. He needed a justification for whatever he was planning, and he had found one.

"They still resist," he muttered, running his hands through his hair until it stood on end. "They say it's all too *radical*, that the people won't support it. But *hang* the people! When have they ever known what was best for them?"

Dani stood very still, wondering if he remembered she was here. Wondering how much he'd say if he didn't.

"They've seen it now, though," he said, calming himself a little, smoothing his hair back into place. "They've seen the explosions; their wives and children have been in immediate danger. . . . Surely now they'll understand why I had to . . ."

But a stinging fly flew into Dani's face then, and she was forced to swat at it. Mateo glanced up with those wild eyes, realizing exactly what he was giving away, and to whom. In a typical marriage, a Primera would be privy to all these thoughts—would have input and influence, would be his partner. But that was never the way Mateo had operated, and Dani was more sure than ever: it was because he had something to hide.

His face closed off at once, becoming smooth and reflective again as he looked at her, and Dani knew she would get nothing else from him today.

"Well, it all goes over my head, of course, señor," she said. "I just hope the violence stops soon. I'd like to be able to visit the marketplace again without fear of being incinerated."

His face relaxed a little at this. It was just the sort of shallow concern he expected from her as a woman. She'd put him back at ease. "Well, Daniela," he said in an ominous tone that still managed to be condescending, "I have a feeling you won't have to wait long."

He was put together again, the wild edge gone from his voice and appearance. Mateo Garcia was just a man working hard for the safety of the people. A man losing sleep out of concern for his wives and the country he loved. A man with faith in his god and the power to create change.

A man people might listen to, if they were afraid enough.

At that moment, Dani wished she could kill him. Just take the glass-topped table and shatter it over his head. But there would only be another leader if she did, she reasoned. And one she couldn't watch so closely. She had to be smart.

Carmen walked up then, a flower behind her ear, unaware of the tension between them. Dani tried to focus on Carmen's expression, not to get lost in her lips, or the way her shoulder was escaping from her loose top. Did she glance at Mateo in any particular way? Did she seem at all like a girl plotting an assassination on behalf of her mother-in-law?

Mateo certainly noticed her. Was Dani imagining the way he angled his body toward her? The way he seemed to rake his eyes across her chest? The glass table caught the sun, and Dani had to calm her pulse. It would be so easy . . .

"Roberta gave me this," Carmen said. "Apparently it just came for you, señor." She held out a folded letter, and Dani watched it change hands, avoiding everyone's eyes.

Mateo unfolded the note, and only then did Dani allow herself to look at Carmen.

"Morning," she said.

"Primera," Carmen answered. "Lovely day."

"Beautiful . . ."

Mateo swore loudly, and Carmen released her lower lip from between her teeth. Dani looked up as she did, taking in the hard lines of Mateo's face gone solid as stone.

"Is everything alright?" Dani asked, taking a surreptitious step back.

But he didn't answer, just looked between the two of them like he'd never seen them before. Without a word, he stormed inside, the double doors to his room slamming behind him until the glass panes rattled.

Dani and Carmen stood, frozen, until they heard his car engine rev from the front of the house and the sound of tires squealing out of the driveway.

"What in the—" Carmen began, but Dani interrupted her with a wave of her hand and a shake of her head.

Mateo had always been prejudiced, cold, pickled in his own privilege. Sure, as of late there had been an edge to him, something that felt like a warning, but until this morning she had never thought him truly reckless. She could no longer predict what he would do, and that made him twice as dangerous.

Dani had been worried for her safety more than once since she arrived here, but today, with Mama Garcia an unknown, Mateo losing his composure, and Carmen's loyalties anyone's guess, Dani was starting to feel cornered. Afraid.

Part of her had hoped that committing to La Voz would put an end to the feeling that someone always had the power to hurt her. Ruin her. She was braver and more determined than ever, but the fear was still there. Maybe it would always be.

"I think I'll take breakfast in my room," she said.

"I'll bring it up?" Carmen asked, hopeful.

"Don't bother, just send one of the girls," Dani said with a wave of her hand, trying to ignore the disappointment that weighed down her smile. "You should take the morning off, too; who knows when he'll be back."

Carmen nodded once. "Good idea," she said. "I'll let them know to bring it up. Have a nice day, Primera."

"You too," Dani replied.

In her room, the walls were too close, the whispers of what could go wrong too loud. Was someone from La Voz watching her now? Sota was injured, and Alex was probably still in the city watching the safe house while he recovered. What was the protocol if Mateo had found her out? If Mama Garcia was getting closer to making a move to silence Dani? Would someone swoop in and pull her out before things could get too bad? Or would she be just another sympathizer arrested for treason?

Would she disappear on her way to prison, too? Like Jasmín? And if so, would she deserve it for everything she'd done?

Everything she hadn't. . . .

She paced until her legs grew tired, still sore from her scramble across the rooftops. There was nothing more to do. Mateo was gone doing gods knew what. Mama Garcia could be plotting her demise at this very moment with whoever the letter had been written to.

And Carmen . . .

Dani's body was wound like a watch and ticking too fast, and she wandered into her bedroom's private bathroom without deciding to.

The water in the shower was scalding, and it felt good against her palm. She rarely allowed herself the luxury of hot water—Primeras bathed in cold water that sharpened their minds; they didn't indulge in sensual pleasures.

When she climbed into the spray, her body was alive in every place the water touched it. The sensation was so overwhelming she nearly had to step away, but she forced herself to stay inside. To let the heat and pressure loosen the tension in her muscles.

Dani closed her eyes, seeing the pallor of Sota's face in his sickbed, her gory imagining of Mateo on his patio, glass raining down around him as his blood painted lines down his neck.

She saw Carmen. Carmen in her robe. Carmen in sky-blue silk. Carmen asking *is this okay* until Dani thought she'd come apart at the sound of it.

The restlessness she'd brought with her here was only growing, the water reminding her body of everything it wasn't supposed to feel. For a good Primera, the sense of touch was purely utilitarian, something to tell you if the plate was hot to avoid a burn, something to remind you which clothes to wear for which weather.

But Dani wasn't a good Primera anymore.

Carmen with a serpent's tail, taking off one article of clothing at a time. Carmen's breath against her neck in the tree-filled glade just before the gunshots started. Carmen's hand in hers, fingers tangled, pulses pounding against each other's . . .

Dani closed her eyes tight, the instincts born of her training demanding she shut out the images and the sensations that followed them. But Carmen was branded on the backs of Dani's eyelids like she was here in this stone-tiled stall, wet hair streaming down her back.

Before she could stop them, Dani's hands were running through her own cropped hair. Down her neck. Across her chest and down, *down* onto the skin of her belly.

There was a heat building deep within her. Deeper than her muscles or her bones or her pounding pulse. It was a primal, secret ache that she'd never allowed herself to feel before this moment.

Her fingers knew where to find the source of that feeling, and when they went wandering, Dani didn't stop them. The shame, hardwired to anything pleasurable by half a lifetime of training, sent alarm bells running through her at every pulse point. But she didn't stop. Not even with a hundred maestras' voices screaming that she was on the road to ruin.

She couldn't stop.

In only a few moments, she was lost to the sensations. The voices were gone. In only a few moments—before the water had gone lukewarm against her skin—the world had cracked open, and Dani swore she could see the stars.

Back in her room, the restlessness replaced by something fizzing and slow, Dani fell into her bed and slept without dreaming.

When she woke, it was the dark of the quietest part of the night. And as if she'd seen it in a dream she couldn't remember, Dani knew what she needed to do. In her desk was the bag of stones, the note and cards Sota had sent her at key moments. The piece of stationery her pen had bitten into as she'd forged a letter from the hospital.

From her closet, Dani took a dark scarf she'd never worn and wrapped the precious contents inside it, already mourning them. They wouldn't survive the night, but with any luck, she would. If Mateo had gotten wind of her indiscretions, if Mama Garcia was ready to strike . . .

Whoever they were, if they came for her in the morning, she wouldn't make it easy for them to prove what she'd done.

She would become a hundred shades.

She would lie until they believed.

But before she destroyed it all, it was time to get the answer she needed most. No matter the risk. Once and for all.

This time, when she reached the door, she knocked without hesitation. Carmen answered with sleep-tousled hair, her body filling her pale silk nightgown like water in a drought-thirsty riverbed. The fear in her eyes softened to something smoldering the moment she registered Dani's presence.

"Is this a dream?" she asked, her voice a little husky. "They always start like this, you know."

"You dream about me?" Dani asked, before she could stop herself.

"When I'm lucky."

For a moment, there was nothing but the space between their bodies in the doorway, and then Dani remembered.

"I need to start a fire," she blurted, even though this wasn't the way she'd planned to begin. Carmen had a habit of making disasters of all her best plans.

As if she knew it, Carmen smiled, as if somehow she'd been expecting this. "Follow me," she said, drawing her robe around her, not bothering to put on shoes.

Not knowing what possessed her to do so, Dani kicked hers off, too, and Carmen nudged them inside her door before closing it. Barefoot and triumphant at their own audacity, they raced silently through the hallways toward the kitchen.

Dani hadn't been inside the cavernous ground-floor room since their initial tour of the house, on her first day as a Garcia. She'd been impatient then, eager to get started in her new life for all the wrong reasons, desperate to put the strangeness of graduation and Sota's first appearance behind her.

Hating Carmen for a tangle of childhood insults, adolescent embarrassments . . .

And now you're alone with her, thinking about kissing her, fearing she might want you dead, Dani thought. Life was full of surprises.

Carmen looked up from rooting through the floor-to-ceiling woodpile, as if she had felt Dani's thoughts brushing against her as they passed. "What are you thinking?" she asked, her eyes liquid in the semidarkness of the kitchen.

"Just that things have changed," Dani said. "Remember the first time we came down here together?"

Carmen didn't laugh. "I'm sorry," she said.

"For what?" But it was a bigger question than she realized.

"For using you," Carmen said. "For being afraid."

"It's behind us now, right?" Dani asked, letting a little edge creep into her voice.

And there it was. The hesitation that had brought Dani here tonight, seeking answers.

"Of course," Carmen said easily, turning back to the kindling. "How big of a blaze are we talking here, anyway?"

"Big enough to burn the past?" Dani offered, and Carmen smiled.

"We might need more fuel."

Outside, the mild day had given way to a wind-tossed night. Without deciding, they walked together to the place where Dani had met the gardener who was not a gardener. The place Carmen had caught her. The place of Hermanito the caterpillar, and the first glimpse at something below the surface that neither of them had expected to find.

Sheltered from the wind and the scattered raindrops, Carmen knelt to the ground to make a tower of the larger wood pieces while Dani looked on in helpless amazement. Where she'd grown up, a fire was dead branches that hadn't yielded enough fruit, stuffed in a barrel, doused in liquor that had brewed too long. Where had Carmen learned to do this with such expert precision?

Another mystery.

Dani remembered their neighbor Old Joe, tossing in the match every summer solstice as the kids whooped and hollered and precious fresh corn sizzled on the outdoor grills. As her father slipped candies forgotten by the older kids into Dani's pockets with a wink, her modest mama waited for the cover of darkness to hold his hand.

"Are you okay?" Carmen asked, and Dani took a deep breath, her body going still.

"Are you lying to me?" she asked, her voice carrying over the wind as the flames flickered to life between them.

"What?" Carmen asked, her face too puzzled, too shocked.

"Are you lying to me?" she repeated, and then she waited, her face expressionless. A Primera, through and through.

"About what, Dani?" Carmen asked.

Too defensive, Dani thought. "The night you told me where you're from," she said. "I saw Mama Garcia leaving the house. Were you meeting with her?"

This time, the confusion seemed genuine. "What? No! I told you I had no idea she was there. What's this all about?"

The flames climbed higher between them, the larger pieces of wood catching, blackening at the edges. Carmen waited, like someone who'd been trained not to give away too much. Not like a Segunda at all.

Dani closed her eyes, for just a second, feeling the wind whip her hair across her forehead, the heat of the flames against her cheeks. Then she opened them, looking right at Carmen, feeling intimidating and fierce and brave in a way she never had before.

The day she went to see Sota, she had made a choice. Not to be the girl who held her silence despite disastrous consequences. Not to be the coldhearted Primera the Garcias had paid for, and her parents had asked her to be.

Not to be afraid.

"That night," she said, Carmen still watching her closely, too carefully. "Mama Garcia snuck out of the house alone. She tried to burn this letter. Did you write it?" Dani drew the letter out of the bag and handed it across the flames, feeling the heat bite at her wrist as Carmen took the singed scrap of paper from her.

"'Neutralize the threat'? Dani, I have no idea what this is." There was something in her tone this time. Confusion, but also relief. Carmen had a secret, yes, but this wasn't it.

"I know you're hiding something from me," Dani said. "I

need to know if this is it. Are you working with her? Are you spying on me for her?"

"*You?*" Carmen asked, her eyes darting up from the letter. "You think this letter is about *you*? But why? What reason would she possibly have to spy on you?"

The wind lifted Carmen's hair off her face, and in that moment, Dani believed her. Her mind, which had been trained to judge any situation, decipher any expression, believed Carmen's face. Her heart, a newborn thing just beginning to know itself, believed Carmen's heart.

Dani's father had always told her that secrets made her strong. Her maestras had told her restraint made her strong. But Dani knew now that to crack open what you thought you knew, to allow it to scar with truth, that was what made you truly strong.

And it was time now to be stronger than she'd ever been.

"I'm working with La Voz," Dani said, the truth taking flight, leaving her weightless. "I have been since graduation night. I've been communicating with them for weeks, passing information, working against Mateo and the family and the government."

Carmen's jaw dropped, her eyes went wide, but she didn't run.

Dani held up the bag of evidence. "This is the proof. All of it. And I'm going to burn it tonight in case Mateo or his family know anything. In case that's why he left in such a hurry today."

"Dani," said Carmen. "Why are you telling me this?"

"Because I'm tired of secrets," Dani said. "I'm tired of hiding and double talk and being a good little Primera while people die and the people who murder them get away with it. I'm telling you because . . ." Another deep breath. Confessing to treason had been less of a challenge than what was coming. "Because the feelings I have for you are real. And they're not tied to this life, or this mask, or any of these lies."

Through the flames, glowing red at the heart as the fuel burned too quickly, Carmen smiled.

"And because if you feel even a little of what I feel, and you weren't lying at that protest, or in the woods, or in the hospital . . . you might be willing to help me. Because I don't know if I can do it alone."

Carmen walked around the flames and took the bag, her fingertips brushing the backs of Dani's hands as she let it go. Carmen could run right now. Give the bag to Mama Garcia. Have Dani in a cell by midnight.

But she didn't, and trusting her felt like exactly what Dani had been missing.

"Look," Carmen said. "We have a lot to learn about each other, Dani. And I can't promise to tell you everything. Not right now. But I can promise you this." It was her turn to take a deep, unsteady breath. "This . . ." She gestured between them, to the space between their hearts. ". . . has all been true. Every word. Everything."

Dani nodded, letting the small silence grow, letting

Carmen be ready when the next words came.

"That day in the marketplace?" she continued at last. "That was the real me. All of me. The me who wanted to hold a little girl's hand behind a pyramid of platanos. The me who hid when the police passed my door and prayed to the god who abandoned the sea to keep my family safe. The me who believes the people of this country deserve better than Mateo. Better than all of this." Her eyes were shining now, fierce and honest and without a hint of shadow.

She's radiant, Dani thought, almost deliriously. *Much more than beautiful.*

"The me who can't keep her eyes off you," Carmen said, biting her lip in the firelight.

The words warmed Dani's chest better than even the fire at their feet. It was enough. It was more than enough. And the rest would come. She had faith in that.

Carmen stepped closer, her hair tossing in the wind. "Whatever happens next, with Mateo or his family or anyone else, I'm with you. You can trust me."

And then she was unfolding the scarf, pulling cards and letters and stones from within it.

"Ready?" she asked.

"Ready," said Dani, taking them from her, looking at the cards one last time.

El Rey de Espadas, proud in his blue cape, the straight line of his jaw running parallel to the glinting blade he held. A person of intellect and ambition. A person who didn't hesitate.

Next came the Siete de Bastos, the card of obligation and work. A reminder of what she'd done and the reasons she'd thought she was doing it.

Finally, the card Sota had pressed into her hand as he lay wincing from the pain of a bullet. The Cuatro de Bastos. The strength he'd loaned her, the work they'd done, together and apart.

What would they say, Dani wondered, if she laid them end to end like her mama had all those years ago? What story would they tell?

But Dani had never learned more than the meanings. She'd never spoken to the ghostly hearts that had become divine in their passing. She only knew what she could see:

That fate had made her choices for long enough.

It was time to let go of the past. Of the weak girl who had needed someone to threaten her to move her along the path to what was right.

The note Sota had written on her first day went first, followed by the cards, their glossy surfaces reflecting the flames for a moment before being consumed. Next went the paper, and its faint impression of Dani's treasonous words with it. Then the bag. The shining stones that would not burn, but would no longer hold the meanings of the days Sota had given them.

Lastly, the letter, which had not been written by Carmen's hand. The letter Mama Garcia had tried to burn. Tossing it in, Dani finished the job at last.

The leaves thrashed as the storm intensified, the flames flickering even deep within the trees. Carmen's voice joined their whispering.

"The past may comfort us," she said to the fire. *"But it cannot feed us."*

In response, the flames hissed and spat, fighting the storm, even with no chance at all that they could win. In a moment, the clouds would open, and the tiny flame would be gone.

Carmen's eyes met Dani's, and for a moment she felt like that flame. Doomed, but still desperately fighting.

Without thinking, without planning, she stepped forward and took Carmen's hands. "Carmen," she said, her voice a falling leaf, the restlessness blazing again in her bones as she reached up to trace Carmen's lower lip with her finger. "Please, can I . . . Please."

Something battled behind Carmen's otherworldly eyes for just a moment, and then she said the sweetest word Dani had ever heard:

"Yes."

Their lips met like swords sometimes do, clashing and impatient and bent on destruction, and Dani thought her heart might burst if she didn't stop, but it would surely burst if she did. So she didn't. Carmen didn't. They barely noticed when the sky finally cracked open, extinguishing the fire at their feet, though it couldn't touch the one between them.

Finally, they had to part, but they didn't go far, rain-slicked foreheads pressed together, strands of storm-tossed hair twisting around each other's as they smiled and breathed and let the world seep slowly back in.

"We need to get back," Carmen said, and Dani knew she was right. She had personally hired all thirty-four staff members. She knew better than anyone that the house never slept—not really. They couldn't risk someone seeing them.

"I know."

"But I don't want to."

"I know."

"Okay. Dani?"

"Carmen?"

"I'm going to do that again. As soon as I can."

Dani smiled. "I hope so."

Together, they walked back slowly despite the rain, taking pleasure in the closeness even though they didn't dare reach for each other again.

They weren't as fragile as a fire. They were so much more.

For a Primera, education is never finished.
    —*Medio School for Girls Handbook,* 14th edition

⊹⊱✳⊰⊹

DANI HAD BARELY BLINKED WHEN a tap on the door told her it was breakfast time again.

That could mean only one thing: Mateo had come home at last.

In the mirror—which she rarely used—Dani studied herself before going down to face him. Did she look different? Her hair was windswept, and had dried strangely against her pillow. And maybe her lips were a little swollen . . . or was that just wishful thinking?

Dangerous as it was, she found herself wanting the satisfaction of a more visible mark. How could she be sure it had been real otherwise? That she'd actually jumped in with both feet. That she'd confessed, then kissed an open flame of a girl in a rainstorm.

That she'd been kissed back.

But she had bigger things to worry about than storm-tossed kisses and newly feline smiles. Mateo was downstairs waiting for her, and she still had no idea what had been in his mysterious letter. There was every chance she was going to be interrogated about her behavior for the past few weeks, and she would have to be ready to lie better than she'd ever lied in her life.

If she couldn't, this might be the last time she walked through these hallways.

But she hadn't even reached the library when hushed voices from the guest parlor made her pause. It was Mateo, that much she knew immediately, but the other voice was unfamiliar, and it sounded angry.

"If you're going to have an affair, at least be discreet, for Sun's sake. The years between marriage and moving your Segunda into your room are long, but there are—"

"Father, please," Mateo said, and Dani held back a gasp. *Father?* "It was nothing like that."

"Mateo," said the elder Señor Garcia, his voice grave. "What else could you have been doing? Out all night without a driver? Your wives home wondering?"

Despite the surprise of the president's chief military strategist scolding her husband in her formal parlor, Dani nearly snorted. She and Carmen had done a lot of things last night, but wondering about Mateo's whereabouts had been the very least of them. . . .

"Stop, Father," said Mateo. "You'd love to believe I was doing something so easy to erase, but I was being interrogated by the police. About you."

Señor Garcia's silence was louder than his words. Dani listened closely, careful to make no noise. This was exactly the type of thing Sota had been talking about. Information no one could get unless they were inside the house. This was Dani's value to the resistance—her ticket to a life that was more than turning a blind eye to corruption and suffering.

But before she could hear Mateo's father's response, loud, efficient footsteps could be heard approaching from the entryway.

"There you are," said Señora Garcia brusquely, Carmen just behind her. "Where's Mateo?"

"He and señor are through there," Dani said, gesturing.

"And you're doing . . . what, out here all alone?" The señora's eyes were shrewd, and Dani made her shoulders slump.

"I've . . . never met the chief before," she said, hoping her false timidity would hide the rebellion shining on her skin. "I didn't want to interrupt."

"Oh, Daniela, don't be ridiculous." And with that she swept Dani and Carmen into the room, where Mateo and his father sat staring at each other like someone had died.

"Well, Mateo, you'd better have an explanation for your behavior," said his mother, narrowing her eyes like Mateo was some disobedient child who had broken an expensive vase.

"We were just getting to that," said Señor Garcia, standing to his full height. Dani looked at him for the first time, this man with all his power, who had raised such a cruel son.

He was handsome, like Mateo, with dark hair swept back from his forehead, silver streaks at the temples. His face was strong jawed and his shoulders were wide, but his eyes looked ancient, like they'd seen and done terrible things.

Inwardly, Dani shuddered.

"Actually, Father was accusing me of having an *affair*," Mateo said. "And what are *they* doing here? I'd like to discuss this privately if we have to discuss it at all."

"You give up privacy when you become a family, Mateo," said the señora. "Besides, I think your wives would like to know where their husband has been. Isn't that right, girls?"

"Absolutely," said Carmen, her eyes narrowed dangerously at Mateo. "I waited up all night for you; I was worried sick."

When Senora Garcia turned to her son, Carmen gave Dani the shadow of a smirk through her false hysteria. Dani didn't return it, too caught up in the theater of the way a Segunda was allowed to talk to her husband. It was an intimacy Primeras weren't often privy to.

"This marriage is based on trust, Mateo," Dani said somberly. "It's a partnership. And I'll be honest, I don't feel particularly respected by your behavior. So yes, I'd like an explanation as well." She felt strange reprimanding him even this much, but Señora Garcia's punishing gaze seemed to demand it, and Dani was good enough at reading power dynamics to know who was really in charge here. Clearly, Señor Garcia didn't keep *his* Primera in the dark.

"Mateo insists he wasn't with a woman," Señor Garcia said. "He was just about to explain himself."

"A *woman*," Mateo muttered. "Honestly. As if I'd waste my time on *another*—"

"Careful there," said Carmen, her eyes narrowing further still.

"Of course," Mateo said, seeming to remember his audience and rubbing the back of his neck repentantly. "I only meant to say I have far too much respect for you both to ever commit infidelity. It was a far different errand that kept me away from home last night."

Here it is, Dani thought. The confession he'd been about to make. The reason he was being interrogated. She could almost feel Alex and Sota standing on either side of her, waiting for proof of what they'd always believed about Mateo.

"You expect us to believe that?" Carmen asked, her eyes flashing dangerously. "I knew I didn't like the way you talked about that Mama Rodriguez, and you should be ashamed of yourself, *Mateo*, she's twice your age!"

Dani almost giggled. She wondered if it would be rude to send for snacks—this kind of entertainment almost demanded it.

"For Sun's sake, Carmen, calm down!" Mateo exclaimed.

"This has nothing to do with Mama Rodriguez!"

"Well then, *what?*" she asked, her glare becoming a pout. "What else could possibly keep you away from home for a whole night, mi amor?"

Dani's face was impassive as ever, but hearing Carmen address Mateo in such an intimate way had her seething again. If Carmen was going to call anyone *mi amor* . . . Dani thought, but she didn't dare finish the sentence, even in her head. Not in this company.

"If everyone could just *calm down,*" said Señor Garcia, shooting Carmen a look that raised Dani's hackles. There was something of Mateo's imposing nature in him. That feeling that he might come too close just to prove he could.

Mateo took a deep breath, facing his family with the news he'd confessed to his father alone just moments ago. "I spent the night being interrogated by the military police."

The silence returned, but this time it was tense. Mateo and his father glanced at each other, communicating something the rest of them weren't privy to. Dani memorized every moment. Every word. Every raised eyebrow. Every darting glance toward the door. It was the first time she'd ever felt like a spy first and a Primera second.

"One of the sympathizers I arrested, Jasmín Flores, is missing," Mateo continued at last.

"Who?" Señor Garcia asked, and Dani watched him in the moment afterward. Either he was a very, very good liar, or he had no idea who Jasmín was.

"That's the thing," Mateo said. "I arrested her at the Soto Primera salon and took her to the prison transport myself, but apparently she wasn't ever checked in. There's no record of her ever being dropped off."

"And what do they think you have to do with it?" Señora Garcia asked.

"I was the last person to have her in custody," Mateo admitted, grimacing in frustration. "They think I was involved in her disappearance." He paused. "Or . . . that Father was." Señor Garcia's eyes darted swiftly to his son, and even the señora's jaw dropped. But Mateo wasn't as good a liar as his father. He was performing. She could see it in the strain around his eyes, the stiffness of his shoulders. He was hiding something—she would have bet her brand-new citizenship papers on it. But what was it?

"What did you say?" asked Señor Garcia, more accusation than question. Dani tried not to look like she was reading his face when he hesitated. Señor Garcia moved closer to his son—taller than him by a few inches, he straightened up, entering Mateo's space, making him shrink back into himself. "I asked you a question." His voice was deadly low.

Dani wanted to enjoy the moment Mateo's own cruelty was turned against him, but there was nothing enjoyable about someone being frightened by a person who had power over them. Mateo had clearly learned from the best.

"I . . . I stalled them," he said, not daring to step away as his father glared down at him. "I told them I didn't know anything, and that I'd keep an eye on you to see if you were acting strangely."

"You insinuated that I had something to do with this mess? When you kno—"

"Alberto." Señora Garcia's voice was the quick closing of a curtain. He obeyed her. The room fell silent again. Dani filed this information away for further examination. Mateo would never have let her interrupt him that way. "What did they tell you to do?" Señora Garcia asked now, facing her son. Dani and Carmen might as well have been invisible.

"They want his access to normal contacts limited for the next few days while they investigate, and I've been forbidden from notifying him of the suspicion. If they find *anything* that seems even the slightest bit off, they're launching a full investigation."

"Into the department?" Señor Garcia asked sharply.

"Not only the department," Mateo replied. "The *family*, too."

Señora Garcia's reaction was immediate. Any trace of indecision or curiosity was gone, and in its place was a brisk efficiency Dani recognized as her Primera expertise taking the wheel. But whatever she was planning, she was keeping it to herself for now.

Dani glanced at Carmen, who was already looking at her, and even in the midst of all this, something urgent pulsed through her until she looked away.

"So, do we know who did it?" Carmen asked, her voice

airy and vapid. She could get away with this kind of questioning. Segundas weren't prized for their brains. But Dani knew this question was for her sake, that Carmen was keeping her promise to help her retrieve information.

"*No, we do not,*" Mateo said, clearly offended, but this time his eyes darted to the left and back, just slightly, and Dani thought the skin at his hairline looked damp despite the morning breeze coming in through the window.

The frayed edges of him were starting to show again, that cool composure crumbling in the presence of the man who had taught him to be cruel. Dani focused harder. This was when he always gave away the most valuable information.

"This is probably some trick on their part!" he said, gesturing too widely. "Those animals! They're trying to turn us against one another, and of course those crackpots in the government—"

"Mateo, that's *quite* enough," said Señora Garcia, coming out of her trance to cut off her son's rambling. His father, lost in thought, nodded in agreement.

Dani hadn't been a spy for long, but she had been a Primera student for five years and a fugitive from the law, relying on her wits alone, for a lifetime. Right now, all three versions of her would have bet almost anything that Mateo was lying. If he wasn't responsible for Jasmín's disappearance, he certainly knew who was.

But what did Señor and Señora Garcia know? Would they lie to protect their son?

"Well, I think we can agree that we'd like to avoid an investigation, hmm?" asked Señora Garcia. "Especially if we're all still interested in Mateo's trajectory toward the presidency."

"Of course we are," snapped Alberto Garcia. "But how do we avoid it?"

They tossed ideas back and forth, using family shorthand and the quick speech of people well accustomed to sharing thoughts. They ruled out asking the president to intervene and issue a pardon, then launching their own investigation to find who was responsible, and several other ideas that were cast off as quickly as they were suggested.

Somehow, they had this entire conversation without implying guilt or innocence. Dani couldn't help but be impressed. This was the way a family was supposed to function— Primera and husband working together, respecting each other. Dani had never seen it in action.

"My dear," said Señora Garcia as her son locked his jaw at the condescension. "If there's even a hint of an investigation, you go from being the poster child for law and order to being a criminal yourself before you're ever in charge of so much as a teapot. There's not a lot of room for error."

"So what would you have me do, *Mother*?" Mateo asked. "If you're so smart."

It was a testament to Señora Garcia's restraint that she didn't slap him. Dani wanted to, and she didn't even particularly like his mother.

Señor Garcia had no such restraint. He was back in Mateo's space again, his face mere inches from his son's. "You will not disrespect your mother in my presence. You got us—"

"What we'll do," Señora Garcia interrupted, speaking in precise, metallic words, "is go to the hillside vacation house for the weekend. Mateo, you will be fulfilling your promise to the police to get your father out of the way and keep an eye on him, and we'll have some time and space away to plan our next move discreetly."

Dani had to hand it to her, even if she knew Señora Garcia was keeping the details of what they'd discuss at the vacation house close to the vest. It was a good plan. Even the men didn't have a contrary word to say about it.

"Managing gossip will be the most important thing," she continued. "And the best way to do that is to go alone. Just the three of us. José and one of the kitchen girls will remain on-site if the girls need anything, but the rest of the house staff will be dismissed until our return."

Dani couldn't help but notice that she and Carmen had not been asked to attend, nor had they been asked for their opinions on the subject. Was this a normal omission? Dani had just seen the way a Primera and a husband were supposed to work together—was the entire family behind Mateo's decision to shut Dani out? Was there more than deception at play here?

Most importantly, did it have anything to do with Mama Garcia's mysterious letter?

"When do we leave?" Mateo asked, conceding at last.

Señora Garcia allowed herself the smallest satisfied smirk at having successfully wrangled her son. "Two hours ago."

"I need to pack," Mateo said, standing abruptly, leaving the room without another word, Señora Garcia on his heels.

Señor Garcia stayed behind, looking between Dani and Carmen with appraising eyes, and Dani hoped her blank expression said *I've just discovered unknown political intrigue in my new family* and not *I'm a spy trying not to forget a word until I can speak to my handler.*

"It would be such a pity," he said mildly, "if we were to discover someone close to us was responsible for leaking this regrettably false information to the military. Wouldn't it?" It was a simple statement, but the words were weighted, and something in those dark eyes told Dani it wouldn't be wise to answer.

He passed close to them as he walked out, the smell of him overpowering. Something dark. Smoke with an edge of flame. Like the liquor Mateo had poured Dani in his study that night. When he was gone, the hairs stood up along her arms.

But then Dani realized: she and Carmen were alone. And after their kiss the night before, not even Mateo's terrifying father could stop the air from turning electric between them. Dani tried to train her eyes not to drift to Carmen's lips, to her shoulders, emerging from her blue-green dress like the sun from the sea. But it was hopeless.

That image stayed with her long after she and Carmen had parted, with polite, casual goodbyes that did nothing to sate Dani's craving to be close to her. In her office, correspondence had piled up, awaiting responses that felt false on the tip of her pen.

Regretfully, we will not be able to attend. I have a previous engagement with my husband's Segunda. Señor Mateo will also be indisposed, in an unmissable appointment with a dark interrogation room. Sincerely, Señora Daniela Garcia.

It wasn't funny, but she laughed anyway. Why not? There was no one to hear her.

When it was finally time to see off the moral center of Medio, Dani returned to the front room, held up by tension alone, some of which she siphoned off as she shook Mateo's hand so hard he winced. "Best of luck, señor," she said.

"An innocent man doesn't need luck," he replied curtly, before turning without warning to kiss Carmen full on the lips. It was a longer kiss than he should have been allowed, especially when they weren't alone. The way Carmen stiffened slightly in his arms told her this was a surprise to her as well, and Dani's fear of what would happen next was lost in the rush of blood to her head.

Her hands shook of their own volition. She closed her eyes against the tide of images that rushed at her. The places a kiss like this could lead. The places they *would* necessarily lead, if Dani was still here when it was time for them to produce a child. But would Mateo really wait that long? From the theatrics happening in front of her, she was inclined to doubt it.

Dani felt as though something inside her might come apart, or that she'd be sick. She almost hoped for the latter, that she'd splatter her husband's traveling suit and the shoes that probably cost as much as her parents spent on food in a year. But the wave passed, leaving nothing but fury in its wake.

She hoped the police couldn't prove a thing. She wanted to destroy him herself.

"Be good," he said when he'd released Carmen, then at last he was gone.

"I hope I don't need to remind you of the duty you both owe to this family," said Señora Garcia when the door closed behind her son and his father. "Because I certainly won't forget it. And if you do, you won't like what happens next."

Was it Dani's imagination, or did the señora's eyes linger a little too long on her own before flicking to Carmen? They were gone before she could decide, in any case, leaving Carmen and Dani alone again.

"Hi," Carmen said, her face soft in the fading afternoon light coming through the window. She still looked shaken by Mateo's kiss, and Dani tried not to show how much it had bothered her. It was probably bad enough for Carmen without making her responsible for Dani's feelings, too.

"Hi," she said instead, taking a step closer.

"Señora? Mistress?" came a timid voice from behind them, and Dani wanted to shake whoever it belonged to for interrupting. But it was Mia, who would remain on-site with José during Mateo's absence. "So sorry to interrupt, but will you both be wanting dinner?"

Dani counted backward from five in her head, so her voice would be even when she turned. "Of course, Mia," she said. "Thank you."

When she led the way into the dining room, Carmen brushed her hand against Dani's and pouted.

In the dining room, dinner was served with its usual fanfare. A course of fruit and cheese, crisp vegetables and citrusy dipping sauces. Dani tried to focus on her plate, but the sight of Carmen eating was supremely distracting.

Mia checked in too often, and by the time the second course was brought out, Dani had abandoned her attempts to continue with her meal, focusing on keeping her composure instead as Carmen smirked.

But the meal stretched out, sangria and then tea being refilled often as Dani and Carmen struggled to find a conversation topic appropriate to be overheard. When they eventually lapsed into silence, allowing glances and smiles to speak for them, Dani's mind began to drift.

After the meal, José would return to the staff quarters, Mia to her rooms off the kitchen. The house would be all but empty. Normally, her thoughts would have been on Carmen, and on the space between their bedroom doors, but something darker had snaked its way in.

For whatever reason, Mama Garcia still hadn't acted on the suspicions she'd expressed in her secret letter. It seemed the Segunda was biding her time, letting Dani feel almost safe. But of course, she wasn't safe.

And wouldn't tonight, with the house empty and few witnesses, be the perfect night to strike? Carmen cleared her throat to get her attention across the table, but Dani's mind was suddenly a million miles away, the buzzing in her veins growing louder with every breath.

"Dani, are you okay?"

"Just thinking . . . ," Dani said, coming up against her natural hesitance to reveal too much. Trailing off. Wondering if she'd ever get used to having someone to trust.

"About the letter?" Carmen asked, her voice barely above a whisper.

Dani nodded.

"Me too," Carmen said. "Do you want . . ."

But Mia ducked back in just then, and Carmen fell silent. "Are you both finished?" she asked. "Señ . . . The *other* señora said you might retire early after such a long day. I'm happy to clear the plates now if you'd like me to."

The plates had been picked over and discarded; the drink glasses stood empty. There was no reason whatsoever for them to linger. Not one they could admit to, anyway.

Dani got reluctantly to her feet. "Yes, thank you, Mia, how thoughtful." She thought her voice had an edge, but Mia didn't seem to notice.

"Yes, of course," Carmen said. "It has been a long day."

The dining room's kitchen entrance led to the south of the house, where Carmen's rooms were located, while the double doors led to Dani's on the north side. There was also no reason for them to leave together, and Mia, ever the dutiful server, waited beside the door with her arms folded, her eyes lowered but still watching.

"Well, good night, Primera," Carmen said.

"Good night," Dani replied, not daring to look at her, her mouth lingering too long over the word.

The hallway seemed dark, empty, the house too quiet with everyone gone. Dani tried to think of some pretense that would take her to Carmen's side of the house, but even she walked back to her room alone instead, every step weighted by her desire to turn around.

Once she reached it, Dani paced, feeling exposed and restless. On the one hand, she now had information much more valuable than the dimensions of the Garcia house to pass along to La Voz, but on the other, suspicions would be heightened now that Mateo and his father were being watched.

And then there was Mama Garcia and her letter . . .

She may have been a Segunda, but she was a Garcia, too. She wouldn't act rashly, and she clearly had help. Someone within the house who knew the situation. Dani's analytical mind looked for ways to pass a message along to La Voz, but Sota had said they would be in touch, so where did that leave her?

Did she dare leave the complex to get the new information to them? Was anyone watching the house? Her mind spun in useless circles until she was dizzy, but she was no closer to finding an answer.

If she was caught doing anything remotely suspect while Mateo was being watched, it would be the end for her. There were fifteen suspected La Voz contacts missing, and the military police were clueless or looking for a scapegoat.

Had Mateo done it? And after everything she'd seen of him, did it even matter?

There were no lines the Garcias wouldn't cross to protect him from scandal. They would kill her if it meant he was never associated with a suspected sympathizer. They might be planning to do it already.

But if they were, wasn't it even more important that she get the information to them as soon as possible?

Mateo, Mama Garcia, Jasmín, La Voz . . . The threads tangled in her exhaustion, leaving nothing but a vague sense of dread in their wake. If just one of them snapped, it would all unravel.

Outside her window, the moon was low, waxing, bordering on full. The goddess in its face pulled at the tides of Dani's blood, revealing a heart that was conflicted in more ways than one.

Sleepless, she watched until the light disappeared below the sill.

Dani had just settled back into her bed when light footsteps in the hallway set her pulse to pounding, her fears springing fully formed into her mind, like they'd only been biding their time. Had someone finally come? Would it be Mama Garcia, or would she have someone else do her dirty work? Dani thought back to Mia, demure in her black uniform in the dining room.

Would her hand hold the knife steady?

If this was really it, would Dani have the strength to fight off her death, or would tonight truly be the end?

Her body shook like a leaf, heart pounding until she was sure it was audible from the hallway. She had only just begun to live her life on her own terms. She hadn't been of any use to anyone. She wasn't ready for this. She knew she should grab something heavy, hide. But all she could do was shake, frozen, in place.

The footsteps stopped at her door. The pounding in her veins reached its crescendo. And then someone knocked at the door.

All the tension left Dani's body like a crashing wave; she collapsed onto her mattress, boneless. Assassins didn't knock.

"It's me," said a slightly breathless voice from outside, proving her point. "Can I come in?"

The emotional swing from impending doom to heart-pounding romantic jitters was almost too much for Dani's already frayed nerves. "Come in," she said weakly, lying back down before sitting up, then lying back down again.

"It's too quiet in the house," Carmen said, a nightgowned silhouette in the doorway, her voice barely more than a whisper. Dani hoped the darkness would conceal the trembling in her fingers. "Plus, I thought you might be torturing yourself over that letter. Do you mind if I stay in here tonight?"

"Yes," Dani said, hoping her breathlessness sounded like something besides ebbing terror. "I mean . . . no. I mean, of course I don't mind." She was grateful for the way the night hid the heat in her cheeks. Should she scoot over? Did Carmen want to lie beside her in this narrow bed?

The heart-pounding feeling didn't recede. Dani was nervous, and not in a butterflies-and-fireworks way. She had never let herself consider what lay down the path from their frantic rainstorm kiss the night before, and if she was being truthful, she didn't think she was ready to. Not yet.

But while her mind was racing, Carmen was settling into the lounge chair beneath her window, covering herself in the blanket she'd trailed across the floor from her own room. Dani thanked the gods in the walls, in the cushions of her chair, even the ones that lived in her accelerated, nervous heartbeat.

The sound of Carmen's body shifting were strangely intimate, and Dani couldn't cool the heat that spread through her belly, seeking more fuel to set fire to.

Finally, all was quiet.

"Are you okay?" Carmen asked into the starlit darkness.

"Yes," Dani replied. "Just thinking."

"Worried about Mama Garcia?"

"More worried about La Voz . . . ," Dani said, the words still resisting the trust she was placing in Carmen. For some reason uttering them made her more conscious of the space between their bodies. Of the quiet in the house and the dare her presence seemed to have issued, even though she didn't move closer.

"Maybe they'll all go to prison," Carmen said, so casually that Dani laughed, a short, shocked thing that lingered. "I don't know, is that a bad thing to hope for?"

"I wish it was that easy," Dani said, though she didn't. Not really. She wanted to be the one to take down Mateo. Circumstance would never be enough. "The system will protect them, like it always does."

"It doesn't seem fair," Carmen said, her voice soft.

"It's not," Dani said, and she felt the truth of it in her bones. "That's why we fight."

"How?"

"We get to La Voz. We talk to the people who can make him pay when the government just wants to protect him."

"Where do we find them?"

"I don't know," Dani admitted, frustrated. "I've met them in the marketplace a few times, but they said they'd find me when it was time . . ."

"So we wait?"

Dani took her time answering, weighing Sota's instructions with the beating of her heart, the urgent pounding of her pulse that said it would be foolish to delay. Were these her instincts? Was this the reason La Voz had wanted her? And if so, wouldn't she be foolish to discount them?

"They said to lie low," she said, unable to keep the uncertainty out of her voice. "Regain the Garcias' trust. But all I want to do is climb out that window right now and go find them. Tell them about Mateo fleeing the complex on his parents' orders."

"So what are we waiting for?" Carmen asked, her words heavy with the thrill of adventure. For a moment, Dani saw it, too, the two of them sneaking out into the night, making their way to the capital on a secret mission.

"It's risky . . . ," she said. "For all I know they have eyes on Mateo already. And if Mama discovers we're gone, it'll just solidify her suspicions and put me in more danger." She looked at Carmen, a small smile lifting her lips. "Put *us* in more danger," she amended.

"Don't worry about me," Carmen said. "I live for trouble."

"I got that impression, yeah." They chuckled softly, their laughter making music together in the charged space between them. But underneath the laughter there was something stirring in Dani. Something that made her want to take more risks than this one.

"Either way, it wouldn't be smart to go at night, right?" Carmen said, the suggestive tone in her voice mirroring Dani's restlessness.

"Definitely not. I barely know where to find them in the daytime."

"So tonight we just . . ."

She trailed off, and Dani felt the need to be close to her twining with the new bravery her role in the resistance had given her. The Primera mask, which had been cracking and splintering for days, fell away for the first time since she'd put it on, and Dani got up from her bed, her feet knowing where to go as her heart pounded at every pulse point.

A stolen kiss was one thing. There was an absolute cut-off point. But tonight, with José and Mia the only people in the house, and the night stretching out until morning before them, there would be no one to tell them when to stop. How could a thought be so thrilling and so terrifying at once?

Tomorrow, there would be plans to make, and loyalties to discover, and a corrupt government to compromise. But tonight, there was Dani, and there was Carmen, and there was time.

As a Primera, you must be decisive. A moment of hesitation can spell disaster. Assess the situation, make your choice, and follow through.

—*Medio School for Girls Handbook,* 14th edition

⊹⟩✳⟨⊹

THIS WAS NO MIDNIGHT EVIDENCE burning. No rushed trip into the marketplace trees. This was an empty room, and the staff dismissed for the evening, and Carmen reclined on a lounge chair waiting for her.

This was Dani's wanting, for once, getting the best of her fear.

When she kissed Carmen this time, there was no clashing of teeth. No rolling thunder. No threat of rain. When she kissed Carmen this time, it was the sun breaking through the clouds, and Dani could see everything for miles.

"Wow," Carmen whispered when they pulled apart.

"Wow," Dani agreed.

They giggled then, and Dani took fistfuls of Carmen's hair and pulled her gently back until their lips met again, and again, and again.

Dani had worried and wondered so often what came after kissing, but there had been no need. Kissing was a kingdom all its own, with a million secret places to be explored. There was no telling what tomorrow would bring. What threats would be leveled, what secrets would be explored. Either of them could be dead by morning, or arrested. Fleeing across the border to escape treason charges and assassins.

Her feelings for Carmen were so much bigger than one night, but if tonight was all they had, Dani was determined to make it count.

What could have been hours later, they lay beside each other on the lounge, breath slowing down, lips tender and used and smiling.

Between them, Carmen traced lazy shapes with her index finger on Dani's palm. "So, what's next?" she asked, and Dani felt her languid muscles tense.

What did Carmen expect? She was a Segunda, of course; maybe kissing wasn't enough. Dani tried not to balk at the thought of clothing coming off, of touching someone else the way she'd barely touched herself, but the idea of it loomed like something dark ahead of her, pulling at her even as it warned her away. She wasn't ready. Not yet.

"Hey," said Carmen, tugging at one of Dani's curls, pulling her back down to the ground. "You okay? I just want to be able to talk to you about resistance stuff, you know? We're in this together and—"

"Oh!" Dani barked, interrupting in her relief. "Yeah! Right! Resistance stuff!"

Carmen looked utterly puzzled, then her eyes went round as coins. "Oh, did you think . . . ? Because I didn't mean . . . No. We don't have to . . ."

Dani couldn't help it; she started giggling. And then she couldn't stop. And then Carmen joined her, both of them laughing until their sides were sore and everything was quiet.

In that quiet, Carmen reached over again and took Dani's hand. "Look," she said, drawing Dani's eyes to her face, her lips . . .

"Don't worry about that, okay? If we want to . . . when we're ready . . . we'll talk about it. But for now, I just want to do this until I get dizzy."

The halting, stuttering sentence, designed to ease Dani's fear, did nothing but ignite the feeling that they were on borrowed time. What if there was never a later? What if they never got the chance to be ready?

Carmen, oblivious to her thoughts, leaned in, keeping their fingers intertwined as she bumped noses with Dani, pulling back a bit, a question in her eyes.

Dani answered it by closing the space, her fear gone, nothing but the desire to make the most of every moment driving her. By the time they pulled apart again, the dark velvet of the sky was lightening, and neither of them could ignore basic human necessities anymore.

"Why can't your lips also have nutrients?" Carmen wailed. "I'm starving!"

"I mean, they do, but you'd have to eat them," Dani said logically.

"And what a waste that would be," Carmen smirked, getting to her feet and letting her nightgown fall in folds around her thighs. "Stay here?" she asked when Dani stood up, too. "I'll bring something back. I don't know if we can keep the air from catching on fire between us right now, and that would be kind of suspicious, don't you think?"

When Carmen left, Dani walked into her bathroom and splashed water on her flushed face, taking in her reflection and all the ways it had changed since last night. She didn't look like a Primera anymore. She looked like a girl who knew the taste of lips and tongues. A girl who had wondered what was next.

She closed her eyes and breathed deeply, once, twice, trying to forget the world outside this room. Mama Garcia, who might still want Dani dead. Jasmín, who was somewhere worse than prison. La Voz, in the dark without the information Dani had gathered. The whole of the outer island, where people were starving and sick and dying while she bloomed.

Suddenly, the room seemed airless. How dare she find joy when there was so much suffering in the world? When she was the cause of more than a little of it?

"Back!" Carmen cried from her bedroom, but Dani couldn't move. "Dani? Are you . . ." When she caught sight of Dani's reflection, she paused. "What's wrong?"

"I'm sorry," Dani said, trying to smile. Trying to recapture a little of the dreaminess that had carried them to sunrise together. "It just feels . . . wrong, somehow. To be so happy when everything is so . . ."

"Awful?" Carmen asked, and inexplicably, she was smiling.

Carmen crossed the room, coming up behind Dani and wrapping her arms around her waist, settling her chin in the curve of Dani's shoulder. In the mirror, they complemented each other. Their skin melting from the deep brown of Dani's to the golden hue of Carmen's. Even Dani's face looked softer.

"The bad stuff will be there," Carmen said, kissing the side of Dani's neck. "If we want to fight it, we have to find joy where we can. We have to find beauty. We have to take our moments to be happy. Because the joy is what keeps us strong and reminds us we have something to fight for."

Dani turned to face her. "How did you get so smart?" she asked, and Carmen answered by kissing her again, on the lips this time. Something lingering and slow that carried them back into the bedroom, where there was fruit, and tea, and a hundred more kinds of kisses.

While they ate, Carmen asked questions, and Dani found she could answer them honestly. Her favorite thing about home, the thing she missed most about her family, her favorite place in the world. Dani turned the tables before long, and while Carmen told her about growing up in Mar de Sal, Dani watched her eyes drift, her face open up.

She missed home as much as Dani did.

"My family is gigantic," Carmen said, when she asked. "A million cousins, sisters, aunts and uncles that are like parents. We were a huge, rowdy bunch, always on some adventure or another."

"And you were the ringleader?" Dani asked, twisting a strand of Carmen's hair around her finger, wishing every day could be this endless.

"Is it so obvious?" Carmen asked, her smile a little sad. "I was one of the youngest, but I was smart and sneaky, and I could always get the adults to believe whatever story we cooked up about where we'd been."

"That makes sense," Dani said, though the idea that Carmen had always been so good at lying caught like a thorn in her thumb.

"Does it?" Carmen mused. "I've always considered myself an open book."

"All the best lies have some truth in them," Dani said, the whirlpool of reality starting to pull at her feet, dragging her out of their perfect night and into a morning where no one could be trusted. Where disaster was always looming.

"There's this light when there's a storm coming in off the ocean," Carmen said, and Dani could tell she was trying to pull her out of the darkness. "It's like everything beneath the clouds is glowing from within."

"I remember," Dani said, giving in. "It felt dangerous and beautiful, all at once."

"Kind of like you," Carmen said.

"Kind of like *you*." They kissed again then, and Dani realized that the girl pushing her backward, laying her head against Dani's chest, had a power she'd never given anyone.

To expose her.

To break her.

Dani had never allowed anyone that close before. But Carmen had slipped in and taken her place in Dani's heart like the world's gentlest thief.

Maybe this was trust, she thought, her thoughts growing hazy as Carmen's fingers traced circles on her arms, her stomach, as the warm weight of them relaxed into the rug. Giving someone the power to ruin you, betting your life on the belief that they wouldn't.

"We're out of tea," Dani said as the sky turned rosy beyond the windows. "Be right back." Carmen let her go, even though it was clear she needed more than tea. The night had been magical—something she never thought she'd be allowed to have—but with the dawn came decisions, and Dani needed space to make them.

She'd almost made it to the kitchen when she heard voices, and her breath caught in her throat as she retreated back into the early morning shadows, hoping against hope that it was just Mia and José discussing the deliveries from the market. But something in the hair prickling on the back of her neck told her it wasn't.

As she waited, Dani's breathing came slower, each inhale shorter as fear wound its way into her stomach and lungs. By the time the footsteps came, her heart was almost loud enough to drown them out. But not quite.

The first thing she felt was a sense of déjà vu. Flattened against a wall in shadows, listening to heavy footsteps in the hall. The same footsteps, she could be almost sure, that had broken her and Carmen apart the night of Jasmín's arrest. The ones that had disappeared toward the south end of the house.

But tonight, she was barely ten yards from the kitchen, and she had a feeling she was about to find out who they belonged to.

"I told you, we can't talk about this here," came a voice in a hissing whisper. A man's voice. But where was it coming from?

". . . And I told *you* to tell me where you're sneaking back from at dawn!"

When the woman's voice joined in, Dani realized the door to the patio had been left open, and outside it, two people were arguing.

"I'm on an errand for the little señor, as you know," came the reply. "I've been asked not to divulge the nature of it."

José, Dani realized, when the larger of the two silhouettes moved into the light. So it had been him, the night of the Primera salon? And who would he dare to talk to in such an insolent manner?

He outranked Mia, but what would *they* have to quarrel about before sunrise?

And then the second silhouette stepped forward, and Dani had never wished so much that her grizzled driver was having an altercation with the kitchen girl.

"As your employer," came the unmistakably haughty voice of Mama Garcia, making Dani's blood run cold, "I demand you tell me what you're doing. In detail."

Dani shivered as the shadowed Segunda stepped closer to José. Was this who she had been meeting the night of the salon? When her husband and Primera were out of the house and her son was making a high-profile arrest?

"I know all about that awful little Primera Flores," Mama continued, an edge in her voice. "I know he's planning to move her, and that the police are watching our every step. If you think I'm going to allow both of you to walk into a trap because he can't neutralize a threat when he's instructed to, you are sadly mistaken."

The shock sent buzzing waves even through Dani's fear. The phrase, almost straight from the letter she'd found in the fire, burned her like a brand. No wonder Mama Garcia had never made a move against her. Dani had never been the threat she meant.

It had been Jasmín all along, and here was the proof that

Mateo had been the one who made her disappear. But to where? And what did he want with the sympathizers anyway? What was so sinister it couldn't be done within the walls of Medio's notorious prison? Every answer led to a thousand more questions.

"I have my orders, Pilar," José replied, and Dani almost gasped. It was against every rule of society for house staff to address a family member by their first name. It simply wasn't done. But Pilar Garcia didn't shout, nor did she slap José.

She stepped closer to him.

Suddenly, Dani realized exactly how much danger Jasmín Flores was really in.

"You and I will go together, tonight, and save this family from destroying its future," she said in a voice more seductive than commanding. "My son does not outrank me."

This time, José stepped closer, an action that—as far as Dani knew—was punishable by whipping in most households.

"In my heart, he does not," he said. "But . . ."

Whatever José had been about to say, it was swallowed by Mama Garcia as she claimed his mouth in a passionate kiss. One that clearly wasn't a first between the two.

Dani clapped her hands over her mouth, her mind racing. She wanted to feel relieved that the threat against her had never been real. Mama Garcia didn't suspect who she really was. But right now, she was too consumed with what was at stake.

Mateo had Jasmín. That Dani knew for sure. It stood to reason he had the rest of the prisoners, too, and was testing out some unproven methods of interrogation on them out from under the government's eye. But with the heat coming down and Jasmín's disappearance noted, he was going to move her. Tomorrow.

Dani's head spun as she realized: Mama Garcia was willing to murder Jasmín rather than allow Mateo to pay for his crimes. The only thing standing in the way was José. And in the battle for his loyalty, the twined silhouettes against the door painted a grim picture.

Tea long forgotten, Dani turned and fled to her room, bare feet soundless on the tile. She was going to tell Carmen everything, plot their next move, but when she opened the door, the other girl was sound asleep across her bed.

If there had been any doubt about what needed to be done, it was gone. She needed to get to La Voz as soon as possible if there was any chance of saving Jasmín's life. But did she dare endanger Carmen, too? It would be so easy to leave now, be the lone wolf she had always been, turn her back on the trust that had barely taken root between them. . . .

Carmen stirred, sniffing in her sleep and turning over before burrowing back into the pillows. Dani watched her, frozen, until she went still.

There was no clear answer. No path ahead with guaranteed success, or even survival. For either of them.

Dani sighed too loudly and Carmen stirred again. This

time, Dani felt hope rather than fear. If Carmen woke up, they'd both be in danger, but she wouldn't have to face it alone.

"Dani?" Carmen asked, patting the bed beside her.

"Hey, I'm here," Dani said, moving closer, not even the panic in her chest enough to prevent a small kindling of flame beside it.

"What time is it? I fell asleep. . . ."

Dani weighed her options one more time. She could tell Carmen to go back to sleep—she was still halfway under. It would be so much easier that way. But Dani wasn't a lone wolf anymore. She had faith. In the girl next to her. In the power they had claimed together.

"Wake up, mi amor," she said, kissing Carmen's cheek. "Everything has changed."

When a Primera's intellect fails her, when her restraint isn't enough, she has one final weapon: her determination.
—*Medio School for Girls Handbook,* 14th edition

⊹⊱✳⊰⊹

THE SUN ROSE IN EARNEST as Dani and Carmen made their way down the road, sticking to the shadows, not relaxing until they were in sight of the gate leading into the capital.

"You know we're about to break about a dozen laws and even more social codes, right?" Dani asked, looking at Carmen somberly as the morning's first rays illuminated her face, painting gold streaks in the dark of her hair.

"I know," she said.

"You know we could get arrested? Or found out? Or . . ."

"Tortured? Killed?" Carmen asked, something steely in her eyes. "Yes, Dani, I know."

"So why are you coming with me?"

A familiar-seeming shadow flitted for a moment across her eyes, too quick for Dani to truly be sure it was there. Then Carmen smiled her usual smile, and the swooping feeling in Dani's stomach made her forget everything else.

"Dani, I knew who I was when I was nine years old. I knew I could talk adults into or out of anything. I knew who I wanted to be and who I wanted to love. I never, ever expected to meet someone like you. To *feel* the way I feel about you. Even if this wasn't what I thought was right, there's nothing I wouldn't do for you, don't you see?"

In that moment, Dani thought she could see right through Carmen's amber eyes, right into the goddess who lived in her soul.

She didn't ask again why Carmen was coming with her. She didn't need to.

This early in the morning, the complex was nearly deserted, and the checkpoints weren't for people going out— only coming in. Since returning wasn't something they could take for granted right now, Dani put it out of her mind.

They made good time to the marketplace, which was still coming to sleepy life around them. In Medio, almost nothing was done until after a leisurely breakfast, but despite the ease of moving through the uninhabited city, Dani wished the rest

322

of the capital's citizens would hurry over their tortillas. She and Carmen were too easy to spot without a crowd to blend into.

"So, what's the actual plan, though?" Carmen asked as they skulked in still-dark aisles with wax cloth over the produce.

"There's a place where I've met them a couple of times," she mumbled, just in case someone was listening. "I'm hoping if we go there, someone will be nearby, that they'll be willing to hear me out."

"*That's* your plan?" Carmen asked. "I thought there was like a rendezvous point or something. You know, something a little more concrete?"

"Do *you* want to come up with a plan then, genius?" Dani asked, but her voice was teasing, and she stepped closer.

"I couldn't possibly hope to compare," Carmen said, her smile blooming in answer.

After a furtive glance around the empty stalls, Dani was about to step recklessly into Carmen's arms—how could she help it?—but a voice from behind stopped her cold.

"Oh my goodness, Daniela Garcia?!" It was a sugary-sweet voice, the kind she'd come to expect over wine and appetizers and thinly veiled gossip. But not here.

She turned slowly, ready to lie with everything in her, but the owner of the voice was much closer than she'd thought, and she found herself pressed against a wall with a forearm at her throat before she could identify a face.

"What are you doing here?" her attacker growled. "We specifically told you to stay put."

Alex, Dani thought, relieved and terrified at once.

"I . . . ," she croaked, nails scrabbling at flesh that might as well have been iron.

The pressure lessened, but not by much.

"I have . . . information," Dani spluttered. "I came to find you." Her heart raced when Alex's eyes narrowed and she showed no signs of stepping away.

"Let her go," came Carmen's low, steady voice from behind Dani, and Alex's predator eyes snapped up before widening in shock.

"You?" she asked, clearly confused, finally letting Dani go in her distraction.

She turned just in time to see Carmen shake her head frantically, purposefully.

In an instant, the wolf-eyed girl's demeanor changed entirely. "What are you doing here?" she asked again, her eyes back on Dani like Carmen's head-shake had rendered her invisible.

Dani wanted to ask a hundred questions about their strange interaction, but the murmurs of the gathering marketplace crowd were a ticking clock, and she hadn't come all this way to run out of time.

"Thirty seconds, new girl."

"I know I was supposed to lie low, and I'm sorry," Dani began at once, words tumbling out faster than she could choose them. "You know Mateo was planning on moving Jasmín tomorrow night, but last night I overheard his father's Segunda talking to our driver . . ."

Dani spilled the whole story as quickly as she could, and though her thirty seconds passed less than halfway through, Alex did not interrupt her. She told her about Mama Garcia's letter, apologizing for not telling them about it sooner, explaining that she'd believed the threat was for her, that she thought she could handle it on her own. She left out the part about questioning Carmen's loyalty. Protecting her, even now.

Nearly finished, she conveyed the elder Segunda's unexpected ruthlessness, her not-so-veiled hints about her deadly plans for Jasmín Flores, the illicit kiss between her and José. Alex's eyes darted between Dani and Carmen and the mouth of the aisle, but once or twice they widened, and Dani knew this was new information.

"Look," Dani said when she had reached the end. "I know Jasmín isn't a priority for La Voz. She spoke to her señora. She put us all at risk. But I still don't think it's right to let her die."

"What?" Alex asked, clearly confused again. "Salt and sea, of *course* we're gonna help her! What kind of monsters do you think we are?"

Dani raised an eyebrow.

"Okay, nice job, new kid. You cracked the case. Let the grown-ups handle it from here."

"Wait a minute," Dani said. "We risked everything coming down here. I did everything you asked of me. Now you want me to just *run home* like some scared little girl? I want to help get Jasmín back! I want to be useful!"

Alex's eyes flashed. "You don't get to make those kinds of choices. You go where we need you. You do what you're told. That's it."

"Wow, you know, you sound exactly like my husband right now," Dani said, taking a step toward Alex, surprised at her own boldness.

"Don't push your luck," Alex replied, not backing down. "Not today. I would *love* to show you just how unprepared you are to tangle with me, but right now you need to get out of here as quickly as possible, okay? You need to trust me."

"It's kind of hard to trust you when you're not *telling* me anything," Dani said, still furious.

"Look," Alex said, the anger on her face making way for concern. "I can't get into it. Just . . . The marketplace might not be a completely safe place today, okay?"

"What does that mean?" Carmen asked sharply, but Alex ignored her.

"Walk east out of this section, then north until you get to the restroom meeting place, then west toward the hospital.

You can regroup there and head back to the government complex. Do it now, and don't dawdle, do you understand?"

"Alex, *what* is going on in the marketplace today?" Carmen asked, stepping closer, her arms crossed.

"There's no time," she said. And to Dani: "We'll be in touch."

Before either of them could protest, she had disappeared into the shadows.

"Come on," Carmen said, tugging at her wrist, heading east with a sense of urgency that made Dani's heart speed up.

When they reached the center of the marketplace, the crowd was thicker. No one here seemed aware of any danger, but something prickled at the back of Dani's neck.

There was a sudden influx of bodies. She whirled around, narrowly avoiding a cart piled high with melons, a squat, wide-shouldered man calling out prices into the muggy air. By the time she righted herself, she had lost Carmen.

She searched for a few minutes, growing more helpless as the crowd filled in around her, knowing she couldn't shout her name without drawing too much attention to herself.

They had been heading back to the house, Dani reassured herself. If she wasn't at the bathroom or the hospital, Dani would find her at home, wouldn't she? This was just a simple case of losing each other in a crowd . . . nothing more. Despite everything they had shared, last night and this morning, Dani couldn't quite believe herself. Something had changed.

But what?

She said you could trust her, she told herself sternly. *She wouldn't lie to you.*

Unfortunately, Dani had bigger problems than Carmen's trustworthiness. She'd gotten turned around in the aisle looking for her, and with the crowd pressing in, she was no longer sure which direction they'd been heading.

Dani was jostled by running children, large men with no concept of how much space they should reasonably occupy, and women with trays offering samples of fruit and wine. Her chest began to feel tight.

East, west, north, she told herself.

Or was it north, west, east?

And did it even matter, if she couldn't remember where she'd started?

Dani closed her eyes, taking a deep breath, trying to settle her thoughts and come up with a plan. Her maestras had always warned her that lust would distract her, and here was the proof.

She was breaking thirty laws, at least. She was always moments away from being discovered as an active agent of La Voz. She had recently been informed by a known outer-island rebel that this marketplace was not safe.

But the only thing concerning Daniela Vargas—wife of Mateo Garcia, star Primera of the Medio School for Girls and beyond—was whether the girl she'd just lost track of was as trustworthy as she'd thought when she'd kissed her for a whole stolen night and half the morning.

Just when Dani decided to ask for the nearest restroom and hope it was their meeting place, evacuation sirens split the air, further complicating absolutely everything.

The reaction was immediate. Everyone near Dani either froze, screamed, or ran futilely into a wall of other panicking people. As one of the smallest bodies in the crush, any sense of direction Dani had established was immediately lost. The only option was to find a less crowded aisle and wait out the exodus.

Pressed in among bolts of fabric and jugs of sangria, Dani clutched herself around the ribs and breathed deeply, trying to shake off the feeling of being at the mercy of the punishing crowd. The sirens were shrill, overpowering everything. What had Alex meant, exactly, by her parting words?

The marketplace may not be a completely safe place today. . . .

When the sirens cut off midscream, the silence was more ominous than the sound. It had only been a few minutes, but the aisles had emptied significantly, and with one more deep breath, Dani left the sanctuary of her abandoned stall and began to cautiously search for the way out.

There was no hope of returning to Alex's prescribed route. This deep in the cool labyrinth of rows and stall fronts, Dani couldn't even see the outside light. She'd just have to pick a direction and keep going, until she could get out of the market and reorient toward the hospital.

Aside from a few stragglers, the way ahead was clear, and

Dani took turn after turn at random until finally, the light of the late-morning sun was visible through a flap in the canvas tent. She hurried toward it with a growing sense of urgency.

Though the air in the market had been fresh enough, the first thing Dani did when she pushed out into the open was gulp down several large breaths, the sense of confinement gradually loosening its grip on her lungs.

When she was breathing normally at last, she looked up and took stock of her surroundings. One thing was for sure: she was nowhere near the hospital. Or the La Voz meeting place. Or anywhere she remotely recognized.

She leaned against a pillar to catch her breath, looking out on a large plaza—the kind where street performances took place. A small knot of people huddled at its center, and beyond was a wall of shifting, nervous spectators. Dani wanted to move closer, but something warned her back.

The prickling feeling returned, this time over her whole body, goose bumps springing up in its wake. She needed to get out of here. But then people began singing, and she couldn't turn away.

Tucked behind the tent flap, invisible to all, Dani watched in a trance as the members of the group on the plaza began to fan out in slow, deliberate steps.

In head-to-toe, close-fitting black, they contrasted sharply with the crumbling stones of their surroundings and the rainbow of colors worn by their audience. They couldn't have stated more proudly that they didn't belong.

The formation became a dance, enhanced by painted masks obscuring the performers' faces. They came into Dani's eyeline one by one. A wolf. A jungle cat. A fox. A butterfly. Then the dance shifted again, and all she could see was their backs. Midnight black. A statement.

Beyond, sounds came from the crowd; they undulated in pointless waves. Behind them, Dani realized for the first time, was a line of still more figures in black, linking arms to block their exit. Whatever was about to unfold, they wanted a captive audience. Literally.

After a few dreamlike moments, the forms went still. A tall figure—there was no doubt this was the leader—emerged from the center wearing a vulture's mask so true to life it caused Dani's heart to skip a beat.

A predator. A scavenger.

A survivor.

For the first time, Dani wondered if she had made the wrong choice. If she should have run in the other direction. If she should now. But in the moment, the fear that had driven her was silent. She couldn't look away.

The song continued, louder now, and Dani's heart reached out to meet the notes—even though the words were a mystery to her. They were defiant. Joyful. The rhythm spread slowly like honey, the song half protest and half worship. It demanded reverence for the very act of living.

Still as a statue, caught up in the magic of it, Dani had the strange desire to weep.

The formation spun to surround their leader, synchronized, every step part of a larger plan. Torches appeared from nowhere, and the masked figures extended them inward. In the vulture's mask, the leader held up a metal cone, hammered thin with patient hands until the light caught its every dip and divot.

Between his fingertips was a single lit match, and when it touched the head of the first torch, he began to speak.

"You have all heard the lies spread by the Median government," he said, the cone amplifying his voice. The people behind him, held captive by the wall of black-clad protesters, went strangely still. "You've seen the headlines. Calling us criminals. Violent. Accusing us of the intention to destroy all civilization."

He lit the second torch.

"But our demonstrations thus far have been peaceful. We only wanted you to pause. To think. We wanted to spread awareness and show you our humanity."

The flames of the third torch danced in the eyes of a fox's mask.

"But now we have been blamed for crude violence we did not commit. Framed for a riot that allowed them to kill and imprison our families and friends. Today we will show you what it looks like when we are pushed beyond the peace we love."

Half the torches were alive, a punishing rhythm beginning as the masked protesters beat them against the stones of the square again and again.

"We ask for one thing, and one thing only: to have what is ours by right returned. We have little love for violence, but even less for watching our elders and children starve, all while you demonize us for the deceitful actions of your own military."

There was only one more torch to be lit. His own.

"That," he said as it caught, "will not be tolerated."

A chill ran down Dani's spine, something tugging at her subconscious, something urgent and half formed.

"Viva!" he called.

"Viva!" the rest answered, raising their torches until the air was alive with their crackling.

The flame bearers fanned out, and the chill in Dani's bones began to grow roots. Wings.

The warning.

The speech.

The song.

The evacuation sirens.

The screaming.

They were going to burn the marketplace.

Dani's heart leapt into her throat, hammering twice as loudly to make up for the moments she hadn't been afraid. Her Primera mind pushed forward through the haze, analyzing each possible decision before she could arrive at it.

The air behind her filled with the acrid smell of things that should not burn.

And in front of her, still, was that wall of linked arms. In order to pass through them, she'd have to declare herself a sympathizer, loud enough for anyone near her to hear.

While the masked performers entered the marketplace with determined strides, torches held out before them, the Vulture remained in the center of the square, his own torch thrust high into the air, as if daring someone to try to stop them.

Dani knew she should run, but there was nowhere to go. Nowhere that didn't require a payment too costly to consider.

Behind her, someone screamed. The single, desperate sound fractured and multiplied. The air was full of smoke and pain, but everything inside Dani was cold. She'd thought the aisles were long empty by now.

Carmen. What if Carmen hadn't gotten out in time?

Startled into motion by the thought, Dani turned from her hiding place and plunged back into the twisting labyrinth, careful this time to remember where she'd come from. She didn't dare cry out, lest she attract the attention of one of the masked torch bearers, but she scanned the empty stalls with stinging eyes until the thickening smoke began to choke her.

Tears streaming down her face, her head swimming, her throat raw, Dani retraced her steps to the tent flap and gulped down air for the second time that day. She'd go back, she told herself, she'd go back as soon as her head stopped spinning. . . .

But behind her, the smoke had swallowed everything, and her heart sank.

Going back, said her highly analytical mind, wouldn't save Carmen. It would only get Dani killed. She would just have to trust that she had made it out. That she was waiting for her at the hospital, or at home. There was no other option now.

Besides, Dani had more immediate problems. Behind the smoke came the twisting flames, the screams echoing off the burning stalls.

It's not Carmen, Dani told herself. *It can't be Carmen.*

Not after everything they'd already survived.

Sweat poured from Dani's skin as the heat behind her grew to a blaze. The air itself seemed combustible, and she knew her body would be little more than kindling. Above her, an ominous groaning sound sent her heart racing again, almost musical even as it promised destruction.

With no more warning, Dani's peripheral vision was nothing but light and heat and smoke. The tent she'd been hiding behind had caught fire, and she was out of time, with an impossible decision staring her down.

Would she burn to keep her secret?

She had the sense that La Voz would expect her to. That any one of them would, in her place, and for a moment she felt full of a nameless determination. She would prove herself worthy of the commitment she'd made, even if the proof was her own life.

Then the low heat behind her focused into a point of blinding pain against her upper arm, a pain that built and built as Dani spun, trying to keep her movements from attracting attention, aware at last that her sleeve had been burning, and the fabric was now melting into her skin.

When the fabric was gone and the flames made contact with her arm, there were no more thoughts of secrets. Of protecting her family, or her cause. Of dying for it. The pain burrowed into her flesh and bones, blades and burning, stripping away every pretense.

Dani forgot herself, moving forward to escape the flames, beating at the fire that was just out of reach with all the strength she could muster, screaming again and again until the marketplace finally coughed her up and spat her at the Vulture's feet.

The figure watched, mask expressionless, as she rolled on the stone stage, trying desperately to put out the fire that had taken over her every thought and feeling. When the flames finally died, the fabric of her expensive dress had become one with her skin, and when she tugged at it her vision went black in spots, coming back slowly to reveal an inferno where she had just been standing.

The eyes behind the Vulture's mask were swallowed in shadow, but Dani locked onto them anyway, pleading with her gaze if she couldn't with her scream- and smoke-ravaged throat.

Please, she tried to say with her eyes alone. *Don't kill me.*

As if in answer, the Vulture's arms darted up, encircling her like steel bars. From a boot came a short knife, which was held to her throat as she raised her hands in surrender.

Dani didn't know the faces in the crowd. She didn't know the Vulture's hard eyes. She didn't know how far her voice would carry on the smoke-tainted wind. All she knew was that she didn't want to die. She wasn't *willing* to die. Not today.

"My name is Daniela Garcia," she said, barely more than a whisper.

"And?" The voice was cold.

"You can't kill me."

The Vulture laughed, one short, sharp blast. "And why not?"

The flames were still raging, but the screaming had stopped. The people inside didn't have anything left to scream with.

"Because I'm one of you," Dani said, and the words were bitter in her mouth. They tasted like regret for every life lost today, and the weight of responsibility nearly choked her. Did she even want to be a member of La Voz anymore? If this was what they were capable of?

But the burn seared into her skin, reminding her of what she'd be if she wasn't La Voz.

A pile of ashes. A body without blood or a name or a voice.

"I'm a spy for the resistance," she said. "For Sota."

His eyes didn't change. The people behind them didn't react.

It was as if Dani hadn't said a word.

But she could feel it inside. The weight of the words she'd spoken. So much more real than when she'd made her commitment in the soft, safe light of Sota's infirmary as the sun set.

The knife pressed harder against her throat, kissing her skin until it broke. A trickle of blood dripped down into the neckline of Dani's dress, but it was nothing next to the burning.

Just when she'd run out of time, when one more increase in pressure would open her throat, the Vulture pulled the knife away.

"Fly, little bird."

Dani flew.

Across the empty plaza, into the throng of people who had resumed their futile pushing and shoving. Her arm didn't know the flames had gone out, and the pain of it bored much deeper than her skin, traveling from her bloodstream until every inch of her felt fevered, the heat focused on her arm, the rest of her going clammy and cold.

Sobs, unbidden, bubbled up in Dani's throat, and she choked on them, their sound lost in the chaos surrounding her.

She only needed to get to the wall of protesters. They would know to let her through, wouldn't they? The Vulture had sent them some kind of signal. . . .

Screams echoed through Dani's tender skull, memory or reality or both. Before her, the crowd would not give way. A hysterical sort of strength possessed her for a moment, and she scratched and tore and bit at everything in her path, forging a way forward, refusing to quit.

If she quit, she would never see Carmen again.

She wouldn't live to see if her sacrifice had saved Jasmín.

To see Mateo and his twisted family brought to their knees.

The bodies pressed closer, and the humid air left Dani gasping, too short to reach the clean air above the shoulders of the desperate crowd. She jumped as high as she could again and again, trying to scrabble over backs, to take one gulp of air untainted by bodies and sweat.

From the shoulder of a large man, she was thrown to the ground.

Carmen. She would never see Carmen again if she didn't get up. She had to get up.

Sheer force of will brought Dani to her feet once more, but the dizziness was worse now, and her teeth were chattering with fever.

Bodies. Pain. Screams. Were they the screams of the crowd around her or the echoes of the people in the marketplace? Her vision swam. She no longer knew what was real.

Fly, little bird.

Dani pushed harder, she gritted her teeth. She fought. But in the end, she fell.

Among a Primera's deadliest weapons are facts and the truth.
—*Medio School for Girls Handbook*, 14th edition

⊢⟩✳⟨⊣

THE FIRST THING DANI SMELLED when she woke was smoke, and for a moment she thrashed her limbs, gasping around the scream still lodged in her throat.

"Shh," said a low, hypnotic voice in her ear. "It's alright. You're alright."

Strong but gentle hands pressed her shoulders back against a mattress. She stopped struggling when she realized they were holding, not restraining.

Every gasp tore through her throat, even the air corrosive.

"You're in the hospital, Dani," said the voice. "You're okay."

The room came into sharper focus. Eggshell walls, a generic wool blanket, the sound of calculated hurry in the distance.

Hospital, the voice had said, and Dani had the good sense to look for its source.

Above her hovered a figure, soot-stained around the eyes, his mouth half worried, half smirking. His foxlike features gave him away.

"S—" she began, but he pressed a finger to her lips.

"Not here," Sota said. "I can only stay a moment."

The door was closed, Dani noted. The window was open.

Panic shot through her chest as her awareness deepened. "Carmen," she rasped. It sounded more like a wordless groan, but Sota's mischievous smile told her he'd understood.

"She's okay," he said. "Hasn't left your side for hours; I had to wait until the doctor called her out to slip in. I'm sure she'll be back any minute."

Relief flooded Dani, making her limbs heavy, killing her pain if only for a moment. Carmen had made it out. She hadn't been burned. But all those other people . . .

"Gotta admit, I didn't see that one coming," Sota muttered, and Dani smiled with cracked lips before another spike of panic overtook her.

"Jasmín," she said, her voice stronger this time. "She—"

"Save your voice," Sota interrupted. "Alex passed along the info in time. Consider it taken care of."

"Taken care of?" Dani croaked, wanting to be sure. "You can't . . ."

"Listen," Sota said, grinning sheepishly as he rubbed the back of his neck. "That's part of why I'm here. Since you were so instrumental in saving her life tonight, I feel like you deserve to know." He took another deep breath as Dani waited, too tired to be impatient. "Jasmín . . . is one of us," he said at last.

Dani let her accusatory eyebrows do the talking for her this time.

"She's a double agent. She was arrested intentionally after we planted the info with you that she'd double-crossed us. We made up the blackmail to find out whether we could trust you when it came to giving up an old friend, and to reinforce the consequences if you decided to talk. It was . . . the most risk-free way to test your loyalty."

"Risk-free for who?" Dani asked, wincing again at the pain, but her mind was recalling the night Jasmín had been arrested. The look of determination on her face when Mateo had knocked at the door. Her perfect certainty, even then, that what she was about to do was right.

The certainty Dani hadn't understood until now.

"We knew prisoners were disappearing," Sota continued, his voice hushed, eyes darting often to the still-closed door. "We assumed she'd be taken to the same place, find out exactly what was being done there. That she could send word to us and we could send someone to get her out. But if it weren't for you, she'd have been killed tonight, and we would have lost any information she could have told us about the rest."

Dani relaxed her brow a little, nodding, wincing. At least some good had come of this horrific afternoon. Or was it evening?

"So what now?" Dani asked, her voice growing smoother with use. "Is my cover blown? Do I come with you back to La Voz . . . headquarters or something?" Her heart squeezed at the thought. Little as she could imagine going back home to Mateo and pretending none of this had happened, the idea of leaving Carmen was worse.

The worry line between Sota's eyebrows was back. "That's the other thing I'm here to talk to you about," Sota said. "We need you to go back. To the Garcias'. So far no one knows why you're here or what happened—although *please* let us know next time you suspect someone does, hmm?"

Dani nodded absently. Mama Garcia was, for once, the least of her worries.

"If you can get back in time," he said gently, "we think you can control the story. Tell them what you want them to know. Keep your cover."

Her mind went blank. Numb with pain, exhaustion, and fear. Go back. Continue to lie for her life and the lives of others, knowing every moment she was one step closer to being arrested or tortured or killed.

She thought again of the screams in the marketplace and closed her eyes, stopping all but a single tear from falling.

"We set off the evacuation sirens ourselves," Sota said

quietly, reading her face correctly. "We wanted everyone to get out safely. No one was supposed to get hurt."

"But they did," Dani whispered. "They were screaming, and . . ."

"I know," said Sota, and when she opened her eyes there were tears on his face, too. "We feel those losses. We honor them. We avoid them when we can. But stopping isn't an option. Not when we're losing so much ourselves."

"I thought we were just trying to raise awareness . . . ," Dani said, though the words sounded naive even to her.

"That was the . . . optimistic route," Sota replied. "We hoped once the Median government saw who we were and what we wanted, they would understand. But things changed when they framed us for those explosions. We're looking at more drastic measures. Tonight was just the first step."

Dani didn't want to understand, but she did. She didn't want to be the kind of person who could justify violence, but after all she had seen—after all she had *done*—how could she not?

"Change isn't easy, Dani," Sota said. "Freedom has a price. People who want easy and pretty stay in their cages."

"I don't want to stay in my cage," Dani said, her voice still smoke-edged and strange in her throat.

Sota smiled ruefully. "That lock was broken a long time ago."

And despite her sadness, Dani was glad. She knew now that she'd rather be free. Even when it hurt. "I'll go back," she said, determination in her voice. "To Mateo's. Whatever it takes."

Sota bowed his head. "Thank you," he said, then he raised a palm. This time, Dani knew what to do. When she pressed her own against it, it felt like a promise.

Footsteps in the hall had Sota halfway to the window before anything else could be said. But before he hoisted himself out into the night, Sota turned to her with a strange look on his face.

"Whatever happens next," he said, "remember that you changed for you. Not for me. Not for La Voz. Not for anyone but you."

"What—" Dani began, but the doorknob turned, and he was gone before Dani could turn around.

"Oh, thank the diosa you're alright!" Carmen said, nudging the door closed behind her and running to Dani's side. She seemed to want nothing more than to throw herself into Dani's arms, but between the bruises and the burns, there was barely a safe inch of skin for her to attach to.

For a moment, Dani was glad of the distance. Despite everything that had happened since, she hadn't forgotten the strange feeling of distrust that had sprung up when she and Carmen had been separated. She couldn't explain why, but she was on guard, and the feeling only intensified when she looked into Carmen's eyes.

Carmen stood beside the bed, wringing her hands, until Dani finally took pity on her, reaching out and gingerly squeezing one of them in her own. The contact warmed her, suspicion edging aside to make way for relief. They were both here, alive and whole and mostly well. The rest they would figure out when they got home.

"I was so worried you didn't get out," Dani said, her voice heavy with tears she wouldn't let herself shed.

"*You* were worried!" Carmen said, her eyebrows disappearing into her hairline. "I was at the hospital five minutes after I lost track of you, waiting in the courtyard out back. I didn't want to leave in case you showed up, but I was so scared when you didn't. I didn't even know there had been a demonstration until people started showing up with burns." She said this in a rush, like she'd just been holding the words in her mouth since the moment she'd heard Dani was hurt. "Where does it hurt, querida?"

Dani grunted, knowing laughter would only cause more pain. "Everywhere?" she said.

Carmen glanced at the door for a moment before turning back, reaching out, letting her finger slide ever so lightly down Dani's unmarred cheek. "I thought I lost you," she said.

Even in a hospital bed, with her cover story and her life hanging in the balance, with every inch of her skin burned or bruised or tender, Dani felt a familiar heat in her chest. It was so absurd she almost laughed.

"How can you do this to me, even here?" she asked aloud, and Carmen smirked.

The moment stretched and swelled, and Dani would have kissed her if she could have moved. But she couldn't, and so it passed. Carmen glanced at the clock and turned back to Dani, guilt etched in every line of her face.

"I know it hurts," she said. "But they say nothing's broken. . . ."

"We have to go, don't we?"

Carmen bit her lip. "It's just . . . most of the Garcias are still gone, but we don't know for how long. If we make it home before he does, your cover stays intact."

"Kind of hard to hide all this," Dani said, gesturing to her battered body.

"You've hidden worse for longer than it'll take to heal," Carmen said, and the feeling was back. The prickling at the back of her mind that told Dani something was off.

"Help me up," she said anyway. "I can do it."

"Are you sure?" Carmen asked, and Dani laughed without humor.

"It's not like I have much of a choice."

The first few steps were agony, but Carmen kept an arm on her waist as she walked laps around the room, feeling the burn stretch and pull as she moved, feeling the thousand individual aches that made up her body. After a few minutes, she could hobble unassisted.

"Ready?" Dani asked through gritted teeth.

Carmen nodded, but her eyes were somewhere else. As

they walked through the hospital's hallways toward the street where they could hire a car, the prickling feeling intensified. The feeling that Carmen was keeping something from her. That her trust, so hard to come by, had been misplaced.

"You okay?" Carmen asked, but before Dani could answer a car pulled up to the curb. Carmen stepped toward it a little too quickly. "Government complex?" she asked, already pulling the back door open. The driver must have assented, because the next thing she knew Dani was being helped into the back seat, her thoughts swirling as Carmen closed the door and climbed in the other side.

"Garcia residence," Dani said, almost relieved when the driver put up the partition.

Carmen didn't seem to share the sentiment. She didn't meet Dani's eyes, shifting back and forth on her seat.

The gods only knew what was waiting for them at home. If Dani wanted the truth, it was now or never. But the minutes stretched on, the city uncharacteristically muted out the windows. Fear had cast a strange spell over the capital tonight, and Dani felt like it was inside her, too.

They were pulling onto the dark, windy road leading to the complex gate when Dani found the words at last. What good would an accusation do, when she really only wanted to know one thing?

Her eyes were soft when she turned to Carmen.

"Sota came to see me in the hospital," she said softly.

Carmen didn't look at her, but she nodded once, tersely. Dani took a deep breath.

"He asked me to go back to the house, keep things up for a little while since my cover is still intact, see what else I can find out, but it won't be forever."

"I know," Carmen said, her voice resigned as if she'd had years and not seconds to process this. But Dani went on. She didn't have time to stop and wonder.

"Carmen . . . ," she said, pausing until Carmen met her eyes at last. The little jolt in her stomach told her she was doing the right thing. That no matter how scared she was, it was okay to trust her. That Carmen could be good, even if she had secrets. That they both could. "I don't want this to end."

There. She'd said it. And like a miracle, Carmen smiled, reaching for her hand across the seat and tangling their fingers under the cover of darkness. "I don't, either," she said.

"Can we be careful?" Dani asked. "Figure it out?" She was impatient now; she didn't wait for an answer before plowing forward, caution to the wind. "And when it's time for me to go . . . will you come with me?"

Carmen turned the rest of the way toward her, drawing her leg up under her on the seat. Her face was joyful, her smile twice as wide until that all-too-familiar shadow passed over it again. "I want to," she said. "Dani, of course I want to. But . . ." Now it was Carmen's turn to take a steadying breath.

"There's something I have to tell you first."

The car wound up the mountain, climbing higher toward the center of the island, leaving Dani's stomach behind as it went. The look on Carmen's face said this wasn't a casual admission.

"Of course," Dani said, trying to keep the panic out of her voice. "Anything."

Carmen nodded, her face determined, then faltered and chewed at her lip. Dani waited as patiently as she could, as each second crawled by and each mile raced.

"Look," she said at last. "I haven't been completely honest with you. But I want to be."

Another endless pause, but Carmen didn't let go of her hand, and Dani took it as a good sign.

"It started before I even went to school," she began again, haltingly. "You have to know that. It was before I even knew you existed. And by the time there was an us to consider, it was just . . . it was too late to change anything."

Carmen turned to look out the window again, worrying her lip so hard Dani was afraid she'd draw blood. But this time, she didn't continue. Instead, her eyes widened in shock. "Salt and sea," she said, and Dani followed her gaze, not sure how many more surprises she could take tonight.

"Is that Mateo's car?"

Dani's heart was racing for a much different reason now. Carmen's aborted confession forgotten for the moment, she looked past her and up the hill. There was no mistaking the sleek car, even at a distance, even in the dark. Mateo prided himself on having the only one in the complex, after all.

She didn't panic when she saw José at the wheel, but then she saw who was beside him.

Mama Garcia.

And just like that, Dani knew: They had Jasmín. La Voz hadn't gotten to them in time.

✦✦✦

THE CARS WERE GOING TO pass each other in just a few minutes. Dani drew blank after blank. There was no way for her to get to them, get to Jasmín. She had done all she could, and it hadn't been enough.

Beside her, Carmen's eyes were wide with nerves, but her jaw was tight, determined. She looked just like Jasmín had looked moments before her arrest.

What had she been about to say?

"Dani, look," Carmen whispered, pointing, drawing her out of her thoughts.

At first, Dani saw nothing but the car and the dark road, but as the seconds passed, a shadow distinguished itself from the rest. Slim, low, darker than the tree-lined road behind it.

"Is that a motorcycle?" Dani asked.

Carmen didn't need to answer. The next moment the bike pulled right up behind Mateo's car, and it didn't stop. Dani gasped as it nudged the back of the car with its front wheel, swerving on impact but correcting and returning to position.

"They're trying to push them off the road," Dani whispered into her hands, still over her mouth in shock. Was this what Sota had meant when he'd said they were *handling* the Jasmín situation?

Another nudge, this time just behind the rear tire, sent the car perilously close to the rock face the road hugged on the left side.

The next time, the rider's aim was true. José clipped the wall, sending the car swerving wildly into the middle of the road. Dani thought he'd make it, but he overcorrected then, slamming into the wall with an ominous crunching sound she could hear even from the insulated back seat. Dust billowed in the glare of a single functioning headlight, and it was the last thing Dani noticed before the hired driver swerved, too, avoiding the spraying gravel and the ruined car blocking the road ahead.

Carmen and Dani pitched sideways, landing in a painful tangle of limbs that had Dani's burns and bruises screaming again. She bit back a cry of pain as Carmen scrambled to relieve the pressure on her arm, avoiding her worried gaze, the secret she hadn't had time to tell sitting awkwardly between them even now.

Out the window, the billowing dust had swallowed the motorcycle.

Dani swore just as the driver lowered the partition.

"Something going on up ahead," he said, already slowing down, pulling off to the opposite side of the road. "No matter what happens, you two stay in this car, understand? This looks like a resistance attack."

Dani didn't bother to tell him it wasn't an attack.

It was a rescue.

The driver staggered toward the smoking car, drawing a gun as he drew closer. Dani shifted restlessly in her seat, wanting to do something to help, not having enough information to act. Could she even walk? And where was Jasmín?

Beside her, Carmen pushed herself into the window. They watched arm to arm as the dust began to clear and the motorcycle came into view for the first time since the crash.

A slim, hooded figure was leaping off the bike, darting toward the wreck. No one could see it, but from this side of the hired car's headlights, Dani's view was clear. Was this La Voz? she wondered. Come to rescue Jasmín?

Could she take the chance that it wasn't?

"I have to go," she said, more to herself than Carmen. "I have to make sure she's safe."

She reached for the door handle, but Carmen's hand closed over hers, her grip surprisingly strong. "You can't," she said quietly.

"Carmen, I know it's dangerous, but I can't let anything happen to Jasmín! I promised Sota . . ."

"Jasmín is fine," she said, her voice still eerily calm, like she was reading from an instructional booklet and not guessing in the aftermath of a car crash.

"You can't possibly know that!" Dani said, wrenching her hand away, not even feeling the pain as her anger flared.

At the back end of Mateo's car, unseen by the armed driver, the slender silhouette was fiddling with something. The trunk sprang open. Dani tried to push past Carmen but again met with resistance.

"What are you *doing?*" she asked. "Let me go!" There was no time to wonder about Carmen's secret, about the reason she was currently holding Dani hostage when she had claimed to be on her side.

"I can't," Carmen said again, the shadow back in her eyes. "You have to trust me, okay?"

From the trunk of the car, the figure drew a body, limp and bound.

Jasmín, Dani thought, relief and terror beating beside each other in her chest. Still, Carmen kept the door blocked.

Three things happened in quick succession:

Dani lunged for the opposite door.

Carmen went after her, pressing her painfully against it.

And a gunshot rang out in the street.

Dani managed to get the door open at last, leaping from the car, turning around just in time to see the hired driver on the ground, lifeless, a pool of blood spreading under him. The silhouette, now encumbered by Jasmín's unconscious body, staggered toward the motorcycle.

"Hey!" Dani screamed. "Stop!"

The screeching noise of metal on metal drowned her out. The motorcycle revved to life as José and Mama Gacia stumbled from the smoking car, dazed and blinking in the headlight beam.

Dani was furious at the sight of the elder Segunda, and this time she let her rage take over, burning in her veins. This woman had been ready to murder a young Primera just to keep her privileged lifestyle intact. Just to see her son in a position of power he hadn't earned and didn't deserve.

Before Carmen could object again, Dani was running. She didn't know what she'd do when she reached Mama Garcia, but she knew she needed to get to her, and fast.

The older woman's eyes widened in shock when she saw Dani, whose rage must have reached a fever pitch, because a high, thin whining began to sound in her ears.

She was almost there. Every muscle was screaming, but she wouldn't let that monster get away. Even if Jasmín was safe, what about the next person who got in Mateo's way? And the next? It had to end. Tonight.

The whining reached an almost unbearable frequency. From behind Mama Garcia, José was shouting something wildly, waving his arms. But Dani couldn't hear him.

She was almost there.

Just before she could reach Mama Garcia and put a stop to this, Carmen slammed into her from behind, knocking the wind out of her. She didn't say a word as she scooped Dani up into her arms and flat-out ran back to the car.

The whining was deafening now. Above them, the air seemed to grow thinner, the stars too bright. Carmen threw her painfully to the ground behind the hired car, barely covering Dani's ears with her hands before the darkness exploded all around them.

Dani thrashed against Carmen, her screams lost in the sonic boom of Mateo's car being rent to pieces against the rock face. Flames licked the sky. Carmen didn't let go. Eventually, they collapsed on the street, breathing heavily, the ringing in their ears the only thing reminding them they were alive. And though she didn't understand anything, though there were more secrets than truths between them, Dani clung to Carmen with every singed, bruised, wounded part of her and sobbed.

It had been minutes.

It had been an hour.

It had been a hundred years.

Dani didn't know anymore. She only knew that the moment she stood up, the moment Carmen let go, she would have to face what had just happened, and she wasn't ready.

But as usual, La Voz didn't care if she was ready.

"Hey," said a gruff voice from above them. "Get up."

Dani opened her swollen eyes a crack to see a black-clad

figure standing above them. Carmen loosened her arms automatically. Together, slowly, they got to their feet.

Beside the hired car was the motorcycle, unharmed, Jasmín, unconscious but still alive, curled up in a small cargo trailer behind it. In front of them was Alex, her mask dangling from one ear.

And she was drawing a gun from her waistband.

Instinctively, Dani stepped in front of Carmen. "It's okay," she said. "She's with me; she knows everything. We can trust her."

"Dani," Carmen said, and her voice was pained. "It's okay, I . . ."

But before she could finish, Alex pointed the gun. Right at Dani's temple.

Her mind went blank. She looked from the unconscious Jasmín to Alex's cold, lifeless eyes over the barrel of her gun, and finally to Carmen, who looked like she'd rather be anywhere else.

Carmen, who didn't look surprised or afraid.

"Alex," she said now, in a low, warning voice. "Put the gun down."

And then, at last, Dani knew. The reason her suspicion had flickered to life in the marketplace. Carmen had called Alex by name then, too. But Dani had never mentioned her name. She was sure of it.

"How . . . ," Dani began, but she trailed off at the look on Alex's face. The pleading on Carmen's. Her life was in the balance here. Was she going to die? Without ever knowing who Carmen really was? Without ever understanding why?

"Alex!" Carmen repeated, sharper this time.

The silver-eyed girl looked at her at last, but she didn't drop the pistol. "You know what you told me," she said to Carmen. "If she's a liability, she has to go. She just saw *everything*."

"She's not," Carmen said, pleading. "I know what I said, okay? But things have changed. You have to trust me."

Dani's ears were still ringing. Every part of her hurt, somewhere under the shock. She felt invisible. Like she could scream at the top of her lungs and not interrupt whatever was playing out before her.

"The only thing that's *changed*," Alex said, looking between them with skepticism in every line of her face, "is that now you want to get under that prissy skirt of hers. I'm not risking the entire mission to be your wingman, Santos."

This is a dream, Dani thought, her mind floating up above the trees where it was safe. This was a dream where Carmen and Alex knew each other, and they were debating over whether she lived or died in front of the dead bodies of José and Mama Garcia.

This is a dream, this is a dream, this is a dream.

"Can someone . . . ," she said in a small voice, "please tell me what's going on?"

Carmen looked at Alex, and her eyes were begging. It scared Dani more than anything else she'd seen tonight. The deference. The obvious familiarity.

"You have twenty seconds," Alex said, backing away. But she still didn't lower the gun.

"This is what I was trying to tell you in the car," Carmen said in a rush, taking Dani's limp, unresponsive hands in hers. "About how it started before I knew you. Dani, I'm . . . a member of La Voz. I have been since before I even started school."

Dani didn't reply, but she didn't pull her hands away, and for a second she hated herself for it.

"I'm the one who let the protesters in before graduation," Carmen whispered. "I was supposed to get placed with you, watch you, see if you flipped after Sota approached you. I'm so sorry, Dani, I wanted to tell you a hundred—"

"What did you tell her?" Dani asked, nodding at Alex, her voice flat and hollow.

"It was before, I swear," Carmen said, tears gathering in the corners of her eyes. "I stopped reporting once you and I . . ."

"What did you tell her?"

Carmen's shoulders slumped. "I told them the first week that I didn't think you had what it took. That you seemed conflicted. That I didn't think we'd be able to win you over."

Dani's heart turned to solid, freezing stone in the humid night.

"But I was wrong," she said, turning back to Alex. "She's one of us. Please, Alex, you have to trust me. If you don't, we lose the closest spy we've had in *years*. We need her. We can trust her. I swear . . ." She paused here, gathering her strength. "I swear on the tree."

The words, nonsensical as they were to Dani, seemed to have an effect on Alex. She charged forward, pressing the cold metal of the pistol into Dani's temple, no mercy in her face.

"Alex!" Carmen shrieked, the tears finally falling. "Please!"

Alex roared in frustration, and Dani was sure this was it. The last moment of her life. Her knees went weak, but she stayed standing. She looked at the stars. The gods there would welcome her.

But when the gun fired, there was no pain. Alex had turned and fired it into the burning car instead. Three times. Four. Emptying the magazine before turning back to Dani.

"You better be worth it," she said. And then, to Carmen: "Let's go."

But Carmen ran to Dani, throwing her arms around her, trying to pull her close. There was a part of Dani, even now, that wanted to melt into her. But she had changed herself for Carmen. Given her the kind of trust she'd never given anyone. She had maybe even loved her. And Carmen had let her, even though she'd known all along that it was a lie.

Dani had never known her at all.

"You lied to me," she said, surprised at how cold her voice could sound when every part of her was on fire.

"We lied to each other, querida," Carmen said, trying to

reach out and touch Dani's face.

Dani turned her head. "So, was this how you were supposed to *win me over*?" she asked. "The poor, loveless Primera."

Alex scoffed audibly from the other side of the car, throwing her leg over the bike. "I said let's *go*!"

"Dani, *no*," Carmen said, ignoring Alex. "You have to believe me. I never expected to fall for you. I wasn't supposed to. That's why I haven't checked in for weeks. I didn't know how to tell them. . . ."

"If you're not on this bike in thirty seconds, this is all for nothing, Santos."

"Give me a minute!" Carmen yelled, frustrated. "I have to explain plan A!"

"What does she mean?" Dani asked, hating the sinking feeling in her stomach. For a girl who had once thrived on control, she had never felt so helpless. "Thirty seconds until what? What's plan A?"

Tears were now streaming freely down Carmen's face, but Dani's eyes were dry.

"I have to go back with them," she said, her voice heavy with guilt. "I take the fall for tipping off the police to Mateo's plan with the missing sympathizers, but by then I'm gone. Protected. It takes the suspicion off you and pushes you two closer together. So he'll trust you. You can find out what they're planning next. Dani, I'm so, so sorry, I never wanted—"

"What was plan B?" Dani interrupted, her voice metal and ice.

Carmen trailed off, looking at the ground.

"I'm not cut out for the job, and you shoot me right here? Is that it?"

She didn't reply, and it was all the answer Dani needed. She had wondered for weeks whether Carmen would be responsible for her death, but this was a configuration of players she had never even imagined.

"NOW, Santos!" Alex revved the bike again, louder this time.

"Dani, I'm so sorry, please. Know that I never wanted to hurt you. Everything I felt for you . . . feel for you, is real."

But she was backing away.

"You have to get back to the house. Tell them everything you saw. Tell them it was me, and you were knocked out in the blast, and you woke up alone."

"Carmen," Dani said, though she hadn't given herself permission. Absurdly, through all her anger, there were tears leaving streaks in the soot on her face. "Wait."

"Sola will be in touch soon with new instructions," Carmen choked out, one leg already over the bike, her hands hooking around Alex's waist to stabilize her.

This, somehow, felt like the worst betrayal.

"We'll get you out of there soon," she said, backlit and ethereal in the motorcycle's single headlight, her skirt whipping in the exhaust from its tailpipe. "Trust me. Please trust me. We'll see each other again."

And then she was putting on the helmet Alex handed her,

and the growl of the engine was too loud to hear over, and Dani could do nothing but watch as the two of them disappeared in a haze of red light and smoke.

The wreckage of the car was everywhere, and destroyed among it was everything Dani had known for certain ten minutes before. If there had been bodies, they were hidden, or weren't recognizable as bodies anymore.

Mama Garcia and José were dead.

An innocent man, whose only crime had been picking up the wrong passengers in his car for hire, was dead.

The cause Dani had believed in, had sacrificed everything for, had been willing to put a bullet in her head without a second's hesitation.

Every bone in her body was sore and aching; fever radiated from her burn through the rest of her, unchecked.

Carmen was gone. Carmen was someone else. Someone Dani had never known.

And still, if she wanted to survive, the only thing to do was to put one foot in front of the other. To make it home, to whatever was waiting for her there.

Dani took the first step up the mountain. Strong enough to take the pain and shape whatever came next, just as she'd always done.

Alone, but alive.

Broken, but free.

Acknowledgments

✝✝✱✝✝

This road to publishing this book has been a long one, paved with pep talks and tears, tacos and wine and excited shrieks. If I have shared even one of those things with you, I thank you from the bottom of my heart. A (not-remotely-exhaustive) list:

To my agent and friend, Jim McCarthy. You believed in this book, and in me, before even the beginning, and you have stood by me and with me so many, many times since. I will never stop being grateful to you.

Claudia Gabel, Stephanie Guerdan, copy editor Jessica White, and the incredible team at Katherine Tegen Books. You saw a spark in this story and helped me fan it into a flame. Thank you for your support, your expert eyes, and your patience with my infinite (seriously, *infinite*) questions.

To my magical cover artist, Cristina Pagnoncelli, who brought the book to life with her vision. It took my breath away from the first sketch, and I'm so proud that it's the first thing people see when they pick up this story.

To my family. Blood and chosen.

My writing comadres, who have blown me away with their empathy, their wisdom, their talent, and their superpowers. You are all magic, and this book and I would be nowhere without you. Nic Stone, for being the first person to read this book and see something worth working for. Meagan Rivera, for early reads and candles and crushes and everything in between. Michelle Ruiz Keil, for tarot and philosophy and endless phone yarning into the small hours. For reminding me to be proud. Nina Moreno, for seeing my heart. For the being the moon and magia del mar and chisme for days.

The Chicas Malas! Lily Anderson, my fierce mama bear, who lets me get away with being petty, but never with making myself small. Anna-Marie McLemore, my sister in fever dreams and fairy tales and all the places they meet. Candice. Amanda. Montgomery. For everything. My sunflower. My best friend. You already know.

To Sam, who gave me the best thing in my life. Who taught me in a million ways (some intentional, some not) to tune out the noise and trust the work—trust myself.

My grandparents, for believing that I was as tall as the stars I reached for. My mama, Dyanne, for weathering my sorrows and triumphs, for believing I could do it before I did. My dads: Bill—for grounding me, for being my shelter in the storm, and Jeff—for teaching me all my favorite ten-dollar words, for showing me how a book fit in my little hands.

My brothers: Brenden, for reminding me to find joy even when it's elusive. Brad, for seeing the kind of world I want to live in. Dominic, for my soundtracks, for getting it, even when I don't.

My sisters: Auburn, who treats my dreams like they're already realities, who always knows what to say. Jade, my first friend, who's never afraid to dig deeper, who taught me to be fierce even when you're trembling.

And last, but never least: to my daughter. For giving me a reason to reach. For reminding me why I'm here. For teaching me more in these short years than I'll be able to teach you in a lifetime. I love you, querida. Forever and ever and . . .

Read the scorching finale.

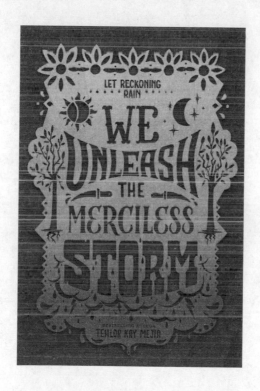

‑I⁊✴⊰I‑

It is said that only two living souls saw the Salt God leave the earth for the last time.

At the edge of the island, where sand met sea, what had once been a glorious and peaceful land lay in ruins. The neatly painted homes with their abundant gardens were destroyed, the white sand pockmarked with craters that children played in and old women clucked their tongues at.

It had all come to nothing, they said, this last stand by their once-benevolent god. In the end, the Sun God had taken what he wanted and cast the Salt God and his chosen people into shameful shadow—all for the love of a fickle woman.

But still, when the Sun God banished his brother, the outer island believed. That he would set right the wrongs his rage-filled heart had visited on their land. That he would leave them with peace and dignity, to watch over them from the skies. That they would have a chance to say goodbye to his mortal form as he climbed the ladder to the heavens.

They were wrong.

A vulture, picking apart the carcass of a fish as night gave way to morning, watched as the divine man who had been the outer island's protector walked barefoot from his village. Fury was etched in the lines of his face.

As he marched down the beach, it is said his brother's banishment burned on his skin like a brand, embers falling to make glittering glass beads of the sand where they landed. A crow, attracted by the shine, followed behind, gathering the beads up to weave into her nest, her eyes curious as the god's strides became longer.

Sea spray trailed from him like smoke as the flesh and bone that held his mortal body together loosened and unhinged, revealing the pure light of the god-being within.

Jealous of the crow's bounty, the vulture approached, oblivious to the transformation happening before him. But just as he beat his massive wings at the slender crow, it is said that the Salt God's eyes—terrible and awesome as they took their divine form—turned on them like a lighthouse's lantern, freezing the two scavengers in place.

In those eyes, the birds saw all that had passed in the world, and all that would come to be. With that knowledge, they rose up, a man and a girl, naked and unashamed in the god's divine presence.

Eyes drawn by the transformation, the god bent down, taking the beads from the girl's hands, the last of his mortal form still curling away from him like paper set aflame. In his own glowing hands, he made of them a silver ring, set with a stone of turquoise.

Handing the ring to the man, it is said that the god looked him once more in the eye, and in it he saw the boy's soul. His true nature.

'El Buitre y La Cuerva,' he called to him in the gods tongue. The spirits within them came forth, meeting the god's spirit of pure light as at last his human form was abandoned forever. 'You will care for them,' said the air where the god had only just stood. 'They are yours now.'

In the water where he disappeared, a glow remained, fading slowly as the sun rose. Attracted by the light, other animals came to drink from it, and as they did, they, too, stood up, men and women, boys and girls.

El Buitre held the ring aloft. 'We will protect the people,' he said, the first words in his human tongue.

The glow disappeared from the shore, the god's last farewell.

'We will protect the people,' the rest replied.

'We will be their voice,' La Cuerva said, her long black hair blowing in the breeze.

'We will be their voice,' the rest repeated.

And so it was . . .

—*The Legend of La Voz, A People's Oral History*

From this moment, I pledge my life to the service of La Voz. I will hold no other person or organization in higher esteem. I will accept no responsibilities or roles that conflict with the mission of rebellion.

—*La Voz Membership Pledge*

╼╆➤✳✦╾╆

CARMEN SANTOS HAD IMAGINED HER homecoming a thousand times.

During sleepless nights, unnerved by the quiet of the government complex, she'd lain with her eyes closed, picturing it in detail so vivid her heart squeezed with longing for the salted earth. The ghostly beauty of the barren trees. The colors and sounds and smells of home.

In some of her fantasies, she returned victorious, someone's blood (usually Mateo's) on her hands. In some, she stole away in the dead of night and slipped in like a shadow, sliding back into her old role as easily as she slid into silk dresses and heavy silver rings.

But she'd never imagined it this way. In the dark hour before the sun painted the horizon pink and gold. Exhausted, dehydrated, delirious from fear and travel and hunger. Fleeing the scene of a botched fire in the capital's biggest marketplace after a rescue attempt gone wrong.

She'd never imagined herself hunted, broken by the choices she'd made, clinging to Alex's tattered shirt with the last of her strength as the dirt bike sputtered over the invisible boundary line.

When it stopped, Carmen slid off the bike onto the hard ground, her muscles finally giving up the fight, tiny rocks pressing into her face like knives. The earth beneath her cheek smelled like metal. Or was that sweat? Blood? Her thoughts swam; her chest felt tight.

"Get up," said a voice. Alex's. Images swam in front of Carmen, her ears ringing from the explosion, from the drone of the engine over countless miles.

She couldn't get up.

"Santos, *get up.*"

Why? Carmen wondered as more bodies crowded around Alex's. There was shock in their expressions. Suspicion in their tight lips and the whispered words Carmen couldn't make out.

"There were three of them behind us a mile back." Alex

was on her feet again, turned away from Carmen, though her voice carried. "I thought we lost them, but . . ."

"What's the matter with her?"

The words penetrated the haze around Carmen like nothing had since she'd fallen. Maybe since before then, when she'd left Dani on the side of the road. This voice was sharp but weighty. A voice that had lived beneath Carmen's ribs for as long as she could remember. A voice that told her she was really back.

Every muscle screamed as she pushed herself up off the ground. The rocks falling away from her cheek now bit into her palms, drawing blood. But Carmen was no stranger to blood.

She could feel him moving toward her, even through the darkness, even through the sting of sweat and dirt that made her squint to make him out. She turned toward him like a flower to the sun.

"Cuervita," he said, closer now. "Is it really you?"

In the harsh light of the torch he carried, the Vulture looked older. The fine lines beneath his eyes reached for the corners of his mouth. There was a little more white in his eyebrows, and in the bushy tangle of the hair he refused to trim.

As he stepped closer, Carmen realized he was as tall as she remembered from childhood—though she had grown taller, too. He still had that hunter's grace that age could not rob him of; it was present in the way he held his shoulders, the way his clothes hung, the way the light played off scars and knotted muscle.

Even here, with her vision swimming and everything inside her splintering to pieces, Carmen remembered: this was a man worth believing in. A man worth following. A man worth everything she had done and more.

"El Buitre," she said, not bothering to hide her sudden tears. "I'm back."

His gaze softened as he took her in, and Carmen imagined how she must look to him. Defeated, the remains of her silk Segunda costume hanging from her in filthy ribbons, barely able to face him.

Behind him, two men helped Alex lift Jasmín's lifeless body from the motorcycle's trailer, and Carmen braced herself against a wave of emotion as it all came flooding back. Jasmín, unconscious and vulnerable; Alex, masked, armed, ruthless as ever.

Carmen, caught between two worlds, tackling Dani to the ground as the explosion rent the air around them, turning everything they'd known to shrapnel on the roadside.

Dani, the truth dawning like a new day on her face.

Dani, Alex's gun pointed at her temple.

Dani, looking at Carmen like she'd never seen her before. Never laughed with her. Never kissed her dizzy.

The pain in her chest was searing, worse than any amateur explosive attached to the engine of a sedan. Worse than anything else she'd ever felt, and Carmen was no stranger to pain, either.

"I'm back," she said again, more to herself than El Buitre.

But something of her memories—and the things they had begun to unravel in her chest—must have shown, because El Buitre's eyes narrowed, his gaze calculating now where it had been welcoming a split second ago.

Reaching forward, he took Carmen's chin between his finger and thumb, looking at her as if he could read her thoughts. Her motivations. Despite everything, Carmen forced her thoughts to quiet, her emotions to calm. For a moment, she had felt like his daughter. But she was a soldier first and foremost. It was what he had raised her to be. And soldiers were obedient. Soldiers didn't let their commitment slip. Not even for a moment.

"Back?" he asked, his voice quiet, inaudible to the growing crowd pretending not to listen. "I suppose that remains to be seen."

Carmen's heart dropped into her stomach, the haze of pain and exhaustion clearing as cold terror took its place. El Buitre's gaze, still searching, said she'd been away too long, living among the enemy. It said he'd heard tales of her exploits.

It said he didn't trust her more than any other outsider, and he didn't intend to start until she proved herself to him. To all of them.

A gunshot split the night, and Carmen (who had once been so steady under pressure) dropped to her knees at the sound, the memory of the explosion too recent, her heart beating a jackrabbit's rhythm in her chest.

Return shots, and El Buitre shouting as the border patrol agents who'd followed them from the wall entered the camp, guns blazing, torchlight flickering on their shining helmets and boots as the camp prepared to fight back against the intruders.

From the ground, Carmen tried to quiet her heartbeat. How many times had she been woken in the night to gunfire and shouting? She was a soldier, not some weak-kneed girl in need of rescuing. If she was going to prove she was really home, she'd have to start here. Now.

Your home is under attack, she told herself, rising on shaking legs.

But as she called out for a weapon, steeling herself, she knew: this was no longer her home. Her home was a thousand miles away, beating in the body of a girl she might never see again.

And if anyone found out her loyalty was divided, she'd be dead.

The officers were outnumbered, unprepared for what they would encounter in the eerie light of La Voz's nomadic hideout. Taking it in for the first time, Carmen saw they'd chosen this location well. A grove of long-dead trees, their trunks bleached white with the salt in the ground, hid the rebels as the border officers stumbled between them, firing wildly at plant and person alike, hitting neither.

With a weighty, bladed staff in her hand, Carmen's pulse began to slow. She had never been the most aggressive fighter, but she'd trained with weapons since childhood, and every member of La Voz was expected to fight. Despite her Segunda training, and her years of using more subtle weapons to achieve her goals, she still remembered the feeling of a heartbeat at the end of her blade.

Following the sound of shuffling footsteps, Carmen caught the light of a nearby torch off one of the officers' polished buttons and moved silently in his direction, the bladed end of the staff in front of her.

He never saw her coming.

She was behind him, her staff between his shoulder blades, ready to strike when the wind shifted, and something squeezed tight in her chest. The smell of the burning torch. The fire. Dani across the flames confessing everything, telling her she wanted more than just almost-kisses and lies.

What would she think of this Carmen? The one ruthless enough to leave her behind. The one ready to kill a man just because she had been trained to. Could Dani ever love someone like that? And did it matter? Could Carmen change? Or was it already too late . . .

Her moment of hesitation cost her. Sensing her presence, the officer turned, and Carmen froze. It was kill or be killed now. The girl she had been, the one Dani had wanted, wasn't strong enough to survive here.

And still, Carmen hesitated—even when his eyes met hers, even when he drew his gun level with her chest. Her heartbeat was too loud in her ears, the grove going blurry in her peripheral vision.

Had she come all this way just to die because she didn't know who she was?

When the officer crumpled to the ground before her, Carmen felt a moment's relief. Maybe this wasn't her moment after all. But when her rescuer stepped forward, gray mane glinting in the torchlight, she knew the bullet would have been safer.

El Buitre hauled the dazed officer to his feet, never breaking eye contact with Carmen. He had looked at her tenderly first, like a daughter. And then with confusion, like a stranger. But the story his expression now told was one Carmen had learned by heart.

One that was much more dangerous than any bumbling officer with a shiny new pistol.

He had seen her waver. Seen her doubt. And that made her a traitor.

Carmen had only been eight the first time she saw a La Voz agent accused of treason, but she'd never forget his hearing around the table, or his punishment.

Exile. Total excommunication from La Voz and all their resources.

The accused man had wept when El Buitre handed down the verdict, the sound wild and terrible, and Carmen had understood. It seemed like a mercy, letting him live, but excommunication was just another kind of death sentence. The only thing more dangerous than being a La Voz agent on this island was being a *former* La Voz agent.

And that man had been *captured* by border patrol. Cracked under interrogation. Passed along information that was functionally useless by the time they got ahold of it.

If El Buitre thought Carmen had actively conspired with a highly placed operative within the government complex? Given her classified information that would go straight to Mateo and his father? Jeopardized active plans?

She'd be lucky if excommunication was the worst they had in store for her.

But there was more than just distrust in the Vulture's eyes tonight. As Carmen held his gaze, she saw something new, too. Something like mania. Something with an edge of uncertainty to it. A hint of fear.

The marketplace fire had been sloppy work, lazy. Carmen had thought so even before it led to the end of her residence at the Garcias'. But was there more to it than just poor planning? What had been going on in La Voz since she'd left?

She wasn't the same girl she'd been, but maybe this place had changed, too.

"Drop that, and come with me," he said to Carmen, and she obeyed. In order to discover what he was hiding, she'd have to survive the night.

El Buitre pushed the officer roughly toward the crowd beginning to form, Carmen following behind him. The other officer had been killed by someone with a steadier hand than Carmen's, his body laid out at the center of the circle, seeping blood into the thirsty ground. Beside him, two men were building a fire, already glowing faintly against the predawn darkness.

"Tie this one up," the Vulture said, pushing the second officer into the center of the circle, where he looked at his partner and went ghostly pale.

Alex made quick work of the ropes. Jasmín was nowhere to be seen. The ghosts of their long ride to the outer island were with Carmen as she stayed close to El Buitre, not restrained, but aware she was far from trustworthy in his eyes.

She awaited her sentence. Had he seen enough to excommunicate her? To lock her up? To kill her? Growing up in the nomadic resistance camp, she'd seen worse punishments for lesser crimes. To survive here, you had to hold loyalty sacred.

Had Carmen betrayed them?

Her heart, still aching for Dani, still wondering where she was and whether she was safe, made a pretty compelling case. But how much of that had El Buitre seen?

He turned to her, the crowd still growing as the commotion woke the camp.

"Carmencita," he said. "Come here."

The flames were flickering, the officer was struggling against his bonds, and the eyes of La Voz were on her as she faced him, her warring loyalties snapping behind her like a flag in the wind. How could she hide her feelings when she didn't understand them?

A sizzling, fiercely feminist fantasy duology

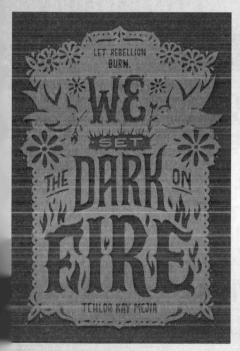

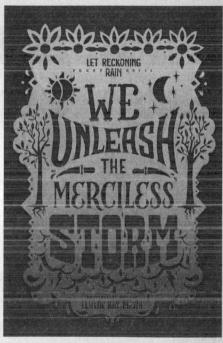

"Mejia pens a compelling, gripping story that mirrors real world issues of immigration and equality."
—BuzzFeed

JOIN THE

Epic Reads
COMMUNITY

THE ULTIMATE YA DESTINATION

◀ **DISCOVER** ▶
your next favorite read

◀ **MEET** ▶
new authors to love

◀ **WIN** ▶
free books

◀ **SHARE** ▶
infographics, playlists, quizzes, and more

◀ **WATCH** ▶
the latest videos

www.epicreads.com